Whispers From Beyond

A Publication by
Dark Holme Publishing
Edited by Kerry Holmes
Cover Creation by Elissa Hess

First Edition

Paperback ISBN 978-1-0686164-2-6
Hardback ISBN 978-1-0686164-0-2

www.darkholmepublishing.uk

Titles Available by Dark Holme Publishing

Ethereal Nightmares Trilogy

Ethereal Nightmares: An Anthology of Twisted Tales – Book One

Ethereal Nightmares: The Second Sleep – Book Two

Ethereal Nightmares: The Final Awakening – Book Three

Dark Descent: Whispers From Beyond

2025 Anthology

Contents

A Year in the Dark

Welcome to the Descent.

This anthology marks one full year of *Dark Descent* — the monthly horror webzine from Dark Holme Publishing, created to showcase unsettling, emotionally resonant fiction from voices often overlooked by traditional publishing.
What began as a quiet experiment has grown into something far more powerful: a space where horror is raw, human, and unpolished — where microfiction cuts deep and lingers long after the final line.

Dark Descent: Whispers from Beyond gathers a year's worth of horror stories from the webzine, collected in one haunting volume. Inside, you'll find Reader's Choice winners, editor-selected standouts, picture prompt highlights, and microfiction chosen for its ability to crawl under your skin and stay there.

For many of the authors within, this is their first time in print — a milestone we're proud to honour. For others, it's another chapter in an ongoing journey into the dark. Each story was chosen for the way it unsettles, provokes, and refuses to be forgotten.

This book isn't just a collection — it's a record of what we've built: twelve months of community, craft, and creative courage. A shared descent into horror that's only just beginning.
Thank you for reading. Thank you for supporting independent horror.

And most of all — thank you for descending with us.

— Dark Holme Publishing

Spring Never Comes

(June's Winner)

Alex Hunter

They came when the spring did not.

Everyone knew something was wrong.

Spring in England is the same as most places – a time of rebirth. Something that had never been recorded in nature was birthed that year.

The seasons had changed–it was gradual, the human race simmering like frogs on the hob. Autumn had slipped into winter unnoticed; people welcomed the new year without a coat.

Winter bled into spring, but nothing changed, not least the temperature. We didn't pay much attention, the world went on, oil burned, wars raged. We knew nothing. Or we pretended not to.

They knew.

I was at school, for the last time, I'm sure. Tuned out during biology. Or, maybe, it was trig. As I say, I'd tuned out.

What I *do* remember is a girl up front, staring at her phone and giving an audible gasp. I didn't know her name. She put her hand up, only to be ignored.

By the end of the period, the news was everywhere, global. Some were afraid, many thought it some kind of joke.

They had come from the cracks in the ground, from dark, forgotten places. Some walked, others flew. All destroyed.

I remember seeing one for the first time. It was on that same day. It was dusk, and the world was soundtracked by screams. I'd never heard screaming before, not in real life.

I was walking with my buddy, fast. We were trying to get home, alarmed by the reports, by the unnatural dusk and by the people running by.

Cars. There were cars everywhere. Gridlock as people tried to escape the city, fumes belching, choking, people shouting and fighting.

One of Them came from the trees.

Its eyes were yellow, its skin pale. A walker, not a flyer. Vast.

The cars were paper underneath its clawed hooves. Teeth ripped through human flesh and bones. The world was blood. One of Them took my friend, his fluids hitting my face like the rains that hadn't come.

I ran.

Now I hide, I wait. They are here. Our time is done.

MB Wolfe

Swollen with contents unknown, the potato sack lies on a bed of brittle grass bleached by the Louisiana sun. It wasn't there yesterday, and I haven't seen anyone alive for weeks. *So, who the hell dropped it,* I wonder? Sitting astride my horse, I cast a wary glance in every direction: across the dying meadow, along the dried-up creek, then toward the thick pine forest beyond. Nothing. Still alone but safe…for now.

I swipe at the sweat along my brow and slide from the saddle, only confident on the ground with my weapon in hand. Sharpened at its edge and made of iron, the fireplace shovel has been both constant companion and saving grace since everything went to shit. Unconventional? Sure. But, in a world where ammo is hard to come by, anything that can keep you alive is just as good. Gripping it, I edge forward.

I kneel beside the mystery bag; my heart wild as it throws itself against my rib cage. Drawing in a deep breath, I extend one hand forward. *Best case scenario*, I think, *food dropped by someone on the run. Worst case?* An image flashes through my mind: heads severed from their undead hosts, milky white eyes gaping up at me, their gore-stained teeth grinding and gnashing. I've seen it before--not the most welcome surprise. Clenching my jaw, I push the thought aside. Whatever is in it, I have to know. Seizing a corner of the sack, I yank it upwards and spill its contents beneath the summer sky.

Tumbling out comes a baby doll tightly swaddled in stained cloth. *A doll? No…* I watch it shudder to life, squirming against its bindings but never crying out. *A baby! But how did it end up here?* My mind sifts through the possibilities, but the sudden realization that I'm sharing space with another human cuts through the noise. *Now I'm not alone anymore*. The corners of my mouth twitch upwards. *I'm not alone.*

I go to reach for the tiny form wriggling before me, but something stops me. *Something isn't right.* My short-lived smile dies. The baby is pallid blue. Blue like a fresh bruise. Blue like mould scabbed across week-old bread. Blue like the flesh-eaters. My breath catches. *Maybe it's only been born,* I tell myself. *They can look like this after birth, can't they?*

Its eyes begin to flutter. The moment of truth constricts around me, unwanted and suffocating. Looming over the infant, I set the tip of my shovel just inches from its throat. My heart frenzied; my hands steady. I wait. Watching as it undulates beneath its cloth, fighting to free itself. Waiting to see if when it opens its eyes if they are human.

Michael Errol Swaim

I was nervous when I got closer to town. I hate going because I hate people. They get on my nerves. Hopefully, I won't run into any idiots today. Surely, I can get to the store, go in, and get out with no incidents. I focused on the roundabout ahead and the blue Ford Ranger in front of me. The driver stopped at the yield sign.

"It's not a stop sign!" I yelled, honking my horn.

The driver, a man wearing his ball cap backward, looked into his rearview mirror. When he saw me looking, he reached his left hand out the window and flipped me off. I gripped my steering wheel tight, trying to calm my nerves. I wanted to slam my car into his. Finally, he went.

I followed him through the circle, and we took the second exit on the other side. Great, I hope he isn't going where I am going. I could see the store ahead on the left. He was driving so slowly that it was irritating. When we got close, he didn't signal, so I assumed he was driving on, but he turned into the parking lot.

"Use your signal moron!" I yelled.

I sighed. I hope I didn't get in line behind this idiot, I wanted to bash his face in.

I exited my car and went in, the doors opening for me as I passed. I walked in and went for the aisle with the coffee stuff. I grabbed a box of Columbian medium roast pods and a box of French vanilla cappuccino. I turned to leave and crashed right into the guy who drove the Ranger and dropped my pods.

"Sorry," I said through gritted teeth, even though it wasn't my fault.

I bent down to pick up the pods, and he walked by.

“Watch where you are going, asshole!” He said.

I stood up and stared at him as he walked away. This guy was pushing all my buttons. I decided to be the better man. On the way to the front, I got a litre of sparkling water before heading to the checkout. I got a Black Cherry.

When I neared the checkout, he suddenly cut in front of me.

“I’m next,” I said.

“Not anymore,” He replied.

I had had enough. I balled up my fist, dropped my coffee pods, and tapped the guy on the shoulder. When he turned around, I swung my fist as hard as I could at his nose. I heard a loud crack, and blood spurted out. He stepped back, and I hit him in the abdomen, so he doubled over. Finally, I grabbed a handful of his hair and smashed his head into the counter before he could react. His teeth hit the corner, and some of them broke. He slumped to the floor.

I smiled. I felt a lot better.

Ten Years

Diana Parrilla

Luke burst in the door at the sound of Delila's scream, his eyes locked on the ruined gown.

"What happened, babe?" he asked.

She stammered, "I knocked over the bottle of calligraphy ink. And on top of that, you now see the dress before the wedding. That's a really bad omen."

"Don't believe in those superstitions, darling. Tell me honestly — is it really the dress that upsets you, or the thought of us getting married?"

"It's almost been a decade since my husband passed away. Sometimes, I feel as if I'm betraying his memory."

"Don't blame yourself. He would want you to be happy. Or aren't you happy?"

"So much so, that I feel happier than I ever was with him. When he died, I felt like I died with him, and now, almost ten years later, I meet you and…"

"And there's nothing wrong with that. We've already postponed the wedding until after September 20th. If waiting until the full ten years have passed brings you comfort, then so be it."

Luke went to his place; their apartment would be ready after the wedding. At nightfall, something wicked broke in upon Delila's peace. A hideous, coal-black ogre with a chameleon's head emerged into the moonlight; below the waist, his body was missing, and his upper half was affixed to a floating hoop. Delila cowered back, and the thing grasped at her soiled gown, its corrosive spittle eating away the taut, velvety fabric.

"You won't be needing this," the ogre hissed, its guttural voice piercing her ears. Delila lurched to get her dress, only for the monster's caustic saliva to scald her skin. Writhing in pain, she passed out, convulsing. When she awoke a few hours later, the aseptic hospital room greeted her. There, the ogre reappeared, this time with its lower body present and linked to a second floating ring.

"Your husband made a final wish when I took him. He wanted you to join him in death, believing you couldn't bear his loss. But since it wasn't your time yet, we granted him a maximum waiting period—ten years, and that is September 20th. Now, it's your turn to make a wish."

As the ogre removed her breathing tube, Delila struggled for air. With her face growing red with anger, she muttered, "Let my late husband suffer the same torment he's inflicting on me, even in hell, for denying me happiness without him."

The ogre brandished a gleaming scythe as it reattached the endotracheal tube. Delila's blurred vision started to recover, and she caught a glimpse of the blade plunging into Luke's sleeping form next to her.

"But you know what? He changed his mind and ended up wishing to be reinserted into a human body in order to marry you once again. We also applied the ten-year period to that wish." The ogre cackled as Luke, or rather Delila's late husband, bled out, his organs spilling onto the inhospitable floor with a gooey splattering sound.

Be Careful What You Ask For, As It May Just Come True

Diana Parrilla

Coraline sat at a window table in a café but was repulsed when she found a half-empty coffee cup left by a previous patron. She motioned to the waiter, who replied, "I'll take it away immediately, my apologies," as he attended to other tables in the crowded restaurant.

Meanwhile, her gaze fell on the cup, which was not fully white but contained graffiti-style writing that read, "Drink and wish for anything, and it shall be granted." Coraline didn't believe in such things, but what did she have to lose by giving it a shot? She took a sip of the coffee, finding it extremely bitter, and at that moment, the letters began to transform. "Make your first wish."

Coraline laughed, figuring it must be one of those novelty cups, but decided to play along. "I want a handsome, muscular boyfriend," she murmured.

The letters changed again: "He's waiting for you at home." Intrigued, Coraline headed home, only to find a man bleeding on her living room floor, whose muscles and tendons were exposed, glistening grotesquely as his skin had been gruesomely peeled away in large, jagged strips. He screamed in excruciating agony, his face devoid of skin gradually turning into a ghoulish waterfall bloodstream. "No, that's not what I meant!" she shouted, turning to the cup, which now displayed a 60-second countdown timer. "Make your second wish."

Horrified, Coraline wished for something else. "I don't know, I want a big house!" Suddenly, the ceiling of her own terraced house seemed gigantic, as did the furniture. She understood why when she saw herself in the mirror—she had shrunk to the size of the cup, just tall enough to read the message that now appeared: "You have 30 seconds to make your third wish."

Coraline screamed, her cries mingling with the dying mans on her blood-soaked carpet. "Make me grow again!" she begged, wishing to regain her size, and so she did. But not only that, she continued to grow. The mirror now reflected her creased face, like a wrinkled raisin, and her hands trembled violently, making it impossible for her to push her grey locks away from her face. She must be at least 95 years old.

Coraline grew increasingly nervous, and her old, tired heart started beating heavily and precariously until it stopped completely. A man then entered through the door, seeing the two corpses lying on the blood-red floor of Coraline's house, and searched until he found the cup, which now read: "Take me back to the bar."

The waiter at the bar didn't move for a few moments, and the letters changed once more: "You wished to stop being a simple waiter with a boring job, and this is pretty entertaining, if you ask me. But you know how it works: misfortune either happens to you or whoever holds the cup. Your choice."

Dejectedly, the waiter made his way back to the café.

Lost or found

Diana Parrilla

Vance was driving home from work one evening, just like any other, though deep down he knew this day was different—it was the anniversary of his son Azrael's death, who had passed away mere hours after being born. It was a date he couldn't forget June 25th, 5 years ago.

As he drove through one of the tunnels that would lead him to the county road straight to his home, the usual darkness seemed more profound, until even the LED lights on the road disappeared. Suddenly, he found himself standing, hands still in position on a transparent steering wheel, now in a living room—his own. There, he saw his wife, Talia. Her hairstyle was different—blonder than her usual light brown—and her face was a picture of shock.

"Who are you and why are you impersonating my deceased husband? How did you get in?" she said, grabbing her phone, likely dialling the police.

"Deceased?" Vance stammered.

"My husband Vance died the day after I told him I was pregnant," she said, looking down. "And in a terrible way he was kidnapped by a group of madmen experimenting with head transplants on humans."

Vance couldn't process anything before seeing a child running through the dining room, grabbing onto his mother's leg as if seeking a hiding place.

"Azrael, go to your room, there's an intruder in the house, and don't come out!" Talia told the 4-year-old child.

"Wait, did you say Azrael?" Vance started pondering. Was he in another dimension, one where his deceased son was alive, but he was the one who had died? In both realities, they had never met, but now he had the chance. "Talia, please, it's me, Vance. At least let me embrace our son."

Talia hesitated but seemed to recognize the real Vance in his eyes. "Azrael, stay here for a moment."

Vance reached out the child's hand, looking into his eyes, but as he did, he saw a blinding, hellish light, and suddenly found himself facing the headlights of a truck coming in the opposite direction. With a miraculous swerve of the steering wheel, he managed to dodge it and steered his car straight in the tunnel.

Sweating, he returned home, where his wife awaited him. "Honey, you look dreadful," she said with concern. "Come here, this will cheer you up. I have incredible news. I'm pregnant! Yes, we've finally made it. I didn't want to tell you before as a precaution, but now it's safe. It's a boy, and he's healthy. We'll name him Azrael, everything will be fine this time, you'll see."

Vance's eyes landed on a bottle of hair dye on the entrance hall table. "Oh, that. You know, the grey hairs are getting more noticeable, and I thought blonde hair would hide them better. What's wrong, honey?"

Vance swallowed hard.

Chills

Plamen M. Gerzilov

Chills ran down her spine and she shivered. It was probably for the fifth time this month and it was still the beginning. It all started with the death of her husband half a year ago and only worsened when their three kids disappeared without a trace, just like that, they simply vanished.

She was all alone in a large two-story house, which until recently was filled with laughter, quarrels, noises and music. It was terribly depressing now, but she was holding on. Only the quiet moans of her husband's ghost, which seemed to emanate from the walls, floor and ceiling, and the creaking of the wooden floor from his footsteps broke the silence.

I will not give up! I know what you want, but it won't happen! At least not while I'm alive... she told herself.

With every cold touch of the spirit, she could feel it trying to possess her, and more and more she believed that there was some demon living in the house besides her dead husband. The only thing she had left was her wits, and she was determined to keep it that way.

Let me make the damn salad! She was nervously trying to cut the cucumber, which, for some reason, had become as hard as a rock. She picked up the cutter and slammed it down on the wooden board with quick, accurate movements. Her whole face spattered in blood as she was slicing the small hand, the skin of which was stuck to the cabinet under the sink and the floor, cut into narrow strips. And the screams of the child sprawled on the cutting board, loud as they were, never reached her ears...

Dark Pool

Bard Lyre

At the edge of the woods, a secluded pool lay.

Locals called it - with a hitch to their voices, which was never quite hidden - the 'dark pool'. They warned of its eerie allure whilst never explaining why.

Ever the sceptic, after just a few days in town, Ethan ventured out through the trees, eager to see the legend for himself.

It took him until dust to reach the clearing. The surface of the water was unnaturally still, its surface like a polished stone. He found himself, almost unwillingly, kneeling to stare into the pool's depths.

His reflection wavered, shadows rising around him as the light faded.

Gradually, as it always did, the water altered consistency. Depthless black replacing the reflection, revealing a shrieking abyss. Faces began to emerge, pale and contorted, eyes wide in terror.

Ethan's heart raced, but, of course, he couldn't look away. As the faces grew clearer, the agony became more pronounced.

Whispered voices filled his mind, pleading, accusing.

Then, shapes twisted beneath the surface—monstrous, formless beings. Their existence defied reason and stole the sense from all who saw them. In response, Ethan's own reflection twisted, merging seamlessly with the tormented souls.

At the very last, he tried to move, to flee, to escape, but those ancient, invisible forces held him fast.

The water rippled.

Cold, spectral hands reached out, grasping, pulling. Ethan's scream echoed through the trees as he was dragged beneath.

And then, as it always did, the dark pool stilled, its surface once again a perfect mirror, reflecting nothing but the encroaching darkness.

Visitors thereafter found only silence.

But, of course, what else would have been expected?

Snow in June

Kerry Holmes

The mist rolled in not far behind. How strange to have snow in June. An eerie reddish and purple glow illuminates the world outside, whilst a throbbing vibration fills the air. Big fat snowflakes fill the steely grey sky. The streets are void of any signs of life. Why aren't children rushing out with squeals of delight to build snowmen and pound their friends with snowballs?

I am afraid!

Before the newscaster in her black and white stripey suit blinks out of existence, she assures us we aren't to worry. 'Just a freak weather storm,' she says.

The sound of humming static now fills the air. Even though the last broadcast is hours ago, I don't dare turn it off for fear she might return.

My arms burn from yesterday's sun!

The ground is now covered with the stuff, stuff that doesn't look like snow anymore. The hazy yellow tint omitting from the blanketed landscape reminds me of driving down a darkened motorway, the glowing embers of the cats' eyes beckoning me whenever I veer off course.

The thickening mist devours my hedge, as a dark cloak falls upon my street, casting the rows of neat little houses with their perfect little lawns into the abyss.

I am alone, the world is silent!

Walking silently to my bedroom, I seek refuge in my bed, pulling the covers over my head, I feel like a child again, terrified of the monsters under my bed. A flood of memories of my dad rises to the surface, and I choke back the tears. I want so badly to feel his strong arms around me now, just one last time. Even if his prickly hairs tickled my nose and made me sneeze.

My eyes feel heavy. I allow them to close, only for a second, I tell myself, yes, only for a second.

Instantly my dreams are filled with the image of a dark, looming creature with blood-red eyes and rows upon rows of needle-sharp teeth. My path is obstructed by the foreboding landscape, filled with yellow-tinged mountain ranges and a blackened sun from which no light can escape. It is a world of death. Only nightmares can thrive here. I am running! The thing is close behind me; my heart is beating wildly, and crunching under my feet is the snow that's not really snow. With every step I take sinking me deeper into the "stuff". I hear rasping behind me, feel the fetid breath on my neck...

My eyes fly open, droplets of sweat drip off my nose and trickle down my back.

I hear it!

There is no mistaking that creak in the floorboard!

It is here!

Tom Sterling

It's two AM. I'm wide awake.
Last night drank coffee way too late.
Don't feel like reading or watching TV.
Too tired for Netflix to entertain me.
I leave the lights off and walk downstairs,
then go to the kitchen, grab one of the chairs,
and sit by the window and stare outside,
waiting to come off this caffeine ride.

The glass feels cool against my head
but I still can't quite go back to bed.
My eyes adjust and I start to see
that the neighbourhood's empty except for me.
The moon is out, October sky.
The night is crisp, the air is dry.
The colours have all faded away.
A world in shades of black and gray.
A light breeze rocks the trees around
and leaves are drifting to the ground
where they dance and swirl around the trees
and whisper softly in the breeze.

Unseen, I watch the peaceful show.
My eyes get heavy, then droop low
when movement catches me off guard

as a large fox trots across my yard.
He moves with confidence and ease
stopping and sniffing and marking trees.
He pauses briefly and gives my window a stare.
I hold my breath and pretend I'm not there.
Then the fox wanders off again
across the road toward an old storm drain.
His ears flatten as he crouches down
and approaches the drain hunched low to the ground.
His fur begins to stand on edge
and I hear him growl as he nears the ledge.

Unseen, I stare out into the night.
And struggle to see in the pale moonlight.
What is the fox hunting? What's in that drain?
Then I get my answer. I've gone insane!

Unseen, I jump up from my chair
as two thin, white arms snake out of there
and grab the fox around the neck
and then begin to pull him back.

Unseen, a scream builds in my brain
as two more arms come from that drain
and grab the back legs of that fox
and drag them to that darkened box.

Unseen, tears fill my burning eyes
as the fox howls out his desperate cries.
He bites and scratches turns and twists
but can't escape those iron fists.

Unseen, I sink down to the floor
as the fox is dragged through that dark door.

His howls turn into hopeless moans.
Then silence, and I'm all alone.

Unseen, I wipe tears from my face
and crawl up from my hiding place.
Then sadness turns to madness as
I hear a scratching at the glass.
I jump back falling over my chair
and turn toward the window, where
smeared in blood upon the screen
were these three words

You were seen.

Transference

Lars Vermeulen

"Sudden-onset chronic pain syndrome, extreme case my doctors diagnosed me. "Therapy options exhausted". They seem content to have finally found their labels.

They have, however, done nothing to ease the inescapable agony that has left my body bedridden. Every fibre of my being burns and screams at every moment of my miserable existence. I'd beg for them to put me out of my misery. But there is one thing that keeps me going.

I think I've figured out how she did it.

***

I am at the farmer's market. I stoop to deposit a candy wrapper in a wastebasket, and an older lady in a wheelchair next to it makes eye contact with me. She looks terribly sick. I give her a friendly smile. She does not return it.

Instead, she closes her eyes and lets out a long, ragged breath.

I stagger back - my body instinctively repelled. Her foul-smelling breath seems to surround me. To this day I am at a loss for words to describe the smell - like what I imagine Death himself would reek of.

She looks somehow better now, except for her eyes - they contain a depthless sorrow. For me? I've no time to consider it, as I feel the warm tendrils of her breath curling into my nose, slowly but relentlessly drifting into my throat, making it increasingly harder to breathe.

***

That's the last thing I remember before waking up in the hospital in excruciating pain, now 11 months ago. Despite the legions of doctor's efforts, the illness has not relented since she forced it upon me, and it has become my entire world. Its invasion leaves me unable to think most times, but there have been moments - when my chemical cocktail of painkillers is just right - where I've had time to explore my new state of being.

I have learned much in those stolen moments, by trial and many more punishing errors than I care to recall. I still don't know exactly how it works, and I cannot get rid of the pain, but if I concentrate hard enough - I can *steer* it.

In the months since this discovery, I have been practising painstakingly on how to flow the pain into certain body parts and coax it out of others. All of last week I worked to direct most of the poisonous fog out of my brain, so I could think. This morning, I've reached my decision. I've spent today concentrating every last foul-smelling bit of this mysterious illness into my mouth and throat. It is all but choking me. But I've only got a little time to go.

In a few minutes the night nurse will come check on me.

In the Moments before Death

Kelly Matsuura

Priti had lived in Okinawa long enough to know that very few fae people stayed there. Even during peak travel season, she only encountered the odd one here and there, mostly Japanese demons, shapeshifters or other yokai from the bigger islands, with only the occasional international fae guest. None of her own kind though.

She had run a busy Indian restaurant in Naha with her husband for two decades, and for the most part was happy. But Sharad had died several months ago, and Priti now found herself unsure what to do. Stay in Japan alone, or return to Mumbai?

Lonely, she had started going out hunting at night. Habits she had long ago learned to control, now took over with surprising speed. Night after night, she cornered men in alleys, propositioned them in hotel lobbies, and lured them away from one izakaya after another.

These were all human men who succumbed to her charms, her curves, without being under compulsion. None had any idea what she was until it was too late. Even then, in the moments right before death, they didn't know the name to call her.

Until one night…

"Churail!" A Thai businessman accused.

She was holding him by the neck with one strong hand, the other, with diamond-like claws poised to strike. She froze at that one, powerful word. Churail. A vampire of the bhoot. She couldn't escape it.

Her eyes dropped to her backward-turned feet. She no longer bothered to hide them when she was alone with a man—what difference did it make when they were going to die?

In the split-second that she glanced down, he lunged and wrestled her to the ground.

Surprisingly, he still had strength, though she had already broken a few ribs and scratched him deeply just prior to her final strike.

"You will not best me!" She managed to flip him over and sit astride him, once again in control.

Before he could recover, she slashed his throat viciously with both hands, the sharpened claws shredding his skin and veins like paper. His warm blood covered her entirely, soaking through her dress, but she revelled in the chaos. She drank deeply from his raw veins and licked every drop of nourishment from her soiled hands.

All the years she was married, she had stayed home at night. Stayed in control. Even if Sharad had gone away on business for a night or two, she had held herself in check, surviving only on animal blood.

Now, she had no reason to fight her true nature.

P.D. Williams

The young girl screams. Her high-pitched cries assault my ears, making me grimace. I want to speak to her, calm her, let her know I mean no harm. But I can't seem to form the words, much less release them. Her small face is unfamiliar to me. I watch her, hoping for recognition on her part or mine. But she only gapes at me, round-mouthed and trembling; harsh wails rush from her slender throat like a song of terror.

A masculine voice travels from another room. "Katie?"

At least, I think that's what he calls her; the walls and distance make it indistinct.

"What's going on in there?" he asks.

In between deep pants, the child yells, "Daddy, come quick!"

"Katie, go back to sleep," he says. "Remember, bad dreams can't hurt you."

Is that what he thinks is going on in his daughter's shadowy room? He should check, but then, that would ruin everything.

She continues staring at me, her gaze so intense that it penetrates my form. Her wide, wet eyes are broad with a horror that can only be generated by terrible things seen and unseen. She rolls her delicate hands into tiny fists. She doesn't move—does she dare?

I swivel my head, taking in the full view of the room. The dolls and stuffed animals that adorn this dark space seem familiar to me somehow. Disjointed thoughts coalesce into opaque memories. But memories of what? I will the scattered images to come together like pieces of a puzzle, but they resist.

The girl—is Katie her name? —looks as if she's trying to make sense of me. I do the same for her. She reminds me of someone. But whom? A thought enters my head.

Another little girl slept in this room, but no longer. Where did she go? What was her name? The answer hovers in the ether.

Katie raises her head from her pillow. The images are sharpening, each visceral picture lining up in sequence to tell the story.

A woman is packing up toys and clothes . . . she leaves with a child . . . someone remains . . . deep despair . . . a pop of noise . . . then lightness.

Oh, my! Bella! That was her name! That was my little girl's name! The child here now is not Bella. But where did she go? Please. Where's my Bella?

The girl screams again.

I hear shuffling in another room, a creak of bedsprings. This time, a woman calls out. Unlike the man's voice, this one is patient, warm with love. "Baby, is it the same dream?"

"Yes," says the frightened child. "It's the man floating on my ceiling."

Banquet

Khala Grace

A cool breeze grazes my cheek as I walk through the forest. Where the hell did they go? I wonder. Splitting up is a terrible idea. For some reason, my group disbanded at the campsite. They didn't even care to extinguish last night's fire.

Memories surface. Everyone else celebrated graduation with cheap booze and a radio. I thought we're here for an escape! My complaint stung. No one cared about the starry sky. Clayton's question came unexpectedly: when are you going to make like your namesake and start taking chances? I've known him since we were kids. Honestly, that was the most clever thing he said.

Out of breath, I take a break. True, I'm livid but I can't deny that I'm worried.

"What really happened?" I ask.

A moment passes and I continue my search. Despite the forest's beauty, I feel anxious. How can anyone be calm when nothing seems right? An intrusive thought hits. What if a bear got them? I can see Steph and Ashleigh fighting the furry fiend with rocks. Even Lucas would struggle as dependent on his inhaler as he is.

"A bear wouldn't pick a fight with nine people," I mumble. "Right?"

I must be reasonable. There's power in numbers. Optimism emerges with a halt. If that's the case, then I'm in deep... My words cut short as I stumble on something big.

"Dominic's pack!" My voice shakes. I bend to investigate. "Is...That..."

Frantically, I sprint away. Shit's getting serious! My stomach lurches. Maybe I'm wrong. I want to be. Besides, I can't judge much on a quick glance. No matter what I saw, I can't backtrack.

"They need me." I huff.

Suddenly, the trail changes. I slip down a hill. My arms flail overhead. All thoughts seem lost when...

Thunk!

Campfire crackles as drums beat to a primal tune. How long was I out? My head blares. I readjust the broken spectacles on my face.

"What's going on?" I panic.

My vision blurs. I hear talking but can't make out the words. Someone's hand pushes a plate into my chest.

"Eat," they insist.

I listen to the ache in my gut. I grab a warm piece of meat. I nibble on the morsel. Dry and stringy. Still, a craving pulses through me and I dig into the rest. The singing heightens while I'm given a glass of thick liquid to drink. I happily devour my meal.

Suddenly, my eyes twitch and burn. I scream as I throw my glasses on the ground. To my surprise, I can see clearer than before! The strangers around me cheer as others seem to be healed by the feast. My heart cheers and I join in their commotion. However, when the host gives me a second plate, I notice something on their person.

"Ling's necklace!" I scream.

A rush of disgust singes my veins. Then, while enticed by the smiling faces around me, I change my mind. Perhaps, this is my time to start taking chances.

Eight Tips for Enjoying a Safe and Fulfilling Vacation Despite the Leak in Reactor Three

Steve Loiaconi

Thank you for taking your annual federally mandated two-week vacation here. Your itinerary has been downloaded to your device. Please review these reminders to ensure you can relax to the full extent required by law without exposing yourself or your loved ones to radioactive material:

1. All rides will begin promptly as scheduled. Any absences will be investigated.
2. Meals have been rationed based on your weight and dietary needs. Do not exchange sustenance pills with other guests.
3. Under no circumstances should you engage with costumed performers. They are, technically speaking, no longer human, and will interpret eye contact as a sign of aggression.
4. Keep your containment helmet with you at all times. If a cloud of yellow smoke approaches, cover all orifices immediately. The smoke is only toxic if you inhale it.
5. If you are exposed, notify the medical team right away. Once the transformation begins, they cannot help you.

6. Keep in mind that you signed a comprehensive non-disclosure agreement, as well as an extensive liability waiver.
7. Please visit the gift shop before departure. Souvenirs have been selected for you.
8. Smile. This is still the most magical place on earth.

We recognize that you have no choice in your vacation destination, but we would like to believe if you did, you would have chosen us. Thank you for doing your part to maximize profits and bolster economic activity in central Florida. Your loyalty to the Corporation is appreciated.

Have a hot dog day!

The Highway Code

Doug Jacquier

Keith had just poured another glass of cabernet sauvignon when a white SUV towing a gleaming white caravan pulled up some fifty metres away. A man in his sixties with a belly ponderously overhanging his shorts emerged, puffing noisily, and shouted to Keith 'Great spot you have here'. He was followed shortly after by a woman of a similar age, who intoned gaily 'You look like you could do with some company. You never know who's out on the road and there's safety in numbers.'

Keith looked at them coldly and said 'There's no numbers here except for me and Arfer. How do you know I'm not an axe murderer and that Arfer doesn't live off the leftovers?' The man said 'Come on, mate, you're scaring the missus. There's no need for that sort of talk.'

Keith said 'Sorry, when you live alone you tend to forget that not everyone shares your sense of humour. And you forget the unwritten highway code of kindness to strangers. My apologies.'

The man visibly relaxed and said 'That's OK. By the way, I'm Jack and this is my better half, Carol.'

'Keith.'

Carol said 'Well, I'll get drinks organised while you ask Keith about the hitching thing.'

'Alright, alright,' Jack said, 'I've only just met the man.' As Carol left, Jack said 'Women, ay?'

'What's the problem?'

'Ar, can't seem to tighten up the coupling properly and every now and then it pops up and down. Got chains of course so it won't come loose but Carol freaks out every time we hit a bump.'

‘I’ll just get my tools’ Keith said and returned with a long grease-stained kit bag.

Jack bent over the caravan coupling and, as he turned to Keith to point out the issue, he had just a split second to see the axe descend. Carol emerged smiling from the caravan with a tray of food and some wine glasses, cheerily calling ‘Drinkies time’ before seeing Jack hunched over the coupling.

Dropping the tray, she ran to Jack and began screaming at Keith ‘What have you done?’ Keith said ‘Just what I’m about to do to you. I mean. Fair’s fair.’ He swung the axe as he explained ‘Can’t have a loose coupling.’

‘Well, Arfer. It’s going to be a freezing cold desert night, so I think it’ll be alright if we dress them in the morning.’ Keith and Arfer returned to the campfire.

Keith picked up his well-worn leather-bound journal, pumped up his lamp and said ‘Arfer, what do you think of this passage?’ Keith read the passage in his sonorous voice. When he’d finished, Arfer revealed nothing. Keith said ‘You’re right, it needs work. Time for bed.’

He doused his campfire, turned off the lamp, burrowed into his swag and, as he drifted off to sleep, he noticed the moonlight glinting off his axe and heard Arfer laughing in his sleep.

The Darkness Within

Tonny Kyule

I trudged through the thick, oppressive darkness, my footsteps crunching on the gravel path. The inky blackness enveloped me, seeping into my bones and constricting my chest. I could barely see a foot in front of me, the shadows swallowing any glimmer of light. Up ahead, a looming shape materialized out of the gloom - an ominous, crumbling manor, its windows gaping like hollow, soulless eyes. A chill ran down my spine as I approached the foreboding structure. The air felt charged, heavy with an unseen energy.

As I pushed open the creaking door and stepped inside, the darkness seemed to close in around me, thick and suffocating. The interior was shrouded in shadow, shapes and corners vanishing into the inky blackness. I could barely make out the contours of ancient, decaying furniture. My footsteps echoed through the cavernous hall, the sound bouncing off the walls. It felt as if the very house was watching me, studying my every move with a predatory gaze. The hairs on the back of my neck prickled, and I had the unsettling sensation of being followed, of unseen eyes boring into my back.

Deeper into the manor I ventured, drawn by a magnetic pull, a force that seemed to both terrify and allure me. The shadows grew thicker, darker, until I was consumed by their inky embrace. It was as if the darkness had a sentience of its own, a malevolent intelligence that sought to envelop and devour me.

I stumbled through the gloom, my hands reaching out to guide me. Suddenly, my fingers brushed against something cold and smooth - a polished surface, like glass or mirror. Intrigued, I ran my hands along it, tracing its contours. As my eyes adjusted, I made out the faint outline of an antique mirror, its surface reflecting only the surrounding blackness.

Without warning, the mirror began to shimmer and ripple, as if stirred by some unseen force. I watched, transfixed, as a figure materialized within the glass - a shadowy, humanoid form, its features obscured by the darkness. A chill ran down my spine as it seemed to beckon me, its movements fluid and hypnotic.

"Who are you?" I whispered, my voice barely audible in the oppressive silence. The figure did not respond, but I sensed a malevolent intelligence behind its movements, a power that both terrified and enthralled me. Drawn by an irresistible compulsion, I reached out to touch the mirror's surface, my fingertips grazing the cool, glassy material.

In that instant, the shadows surged forth, enveloping me in their inky embrace. I felt a searing pain, as if my very soul was being torn asunder, and a sensation of falling, of being pulled into the abyss. The last thing I saw was the shadowy figure's sinister grin, its eyes glinting with dark power, before the darkness consumed me entirely.

Weight of shadows

Bard Lyre

Evelyn sat on the edge of her narrow bed, a single candle on the nightstand barely piercing the gloom. Shadows pooled in every corner, thick and oppressive as tar.

The walls of her room inched closer around her with every breath.

The silence was a living thing wrapping talons around her throat. She clutched the threadbare blanket, her knuckles white, eyes fixed on the window where the night outside remained impenetrable.

Then, inevitably, it began.

Tap. Tap. Tap.

Soft, almost polite. Each sound slicing through the silence like a blade. Her heart pounded in her chest; each beat an attempt to push back the weight of her fear. The tapping continued, steady, unrelenting.

She wanted to move, to flee, but her body couldn't obey. The room breathed with her, the shadows shifting and tightening, a noose of darkness.

Tap. Tap. Tap.

With effort, Evelyn dragged herself into standing. Her legs wobbled, unable to support her. She took a halting step toward the window, drawn by the same dreadful compulsion. The darkness outside smeared itself against the glass, dense and malevolent.

Her hand trembled as she reached for the curtain, sucking against the heavy air as she pulled the curtain aside.

The window revealed nothing but her own pale reflection.

The glass was cold, almost burning in its chill, and a small, ghostly handprint slowly appeared on its surface.

Evelyn’s breath hitched, and the air shattered into shards in her lungs. She stumbled back; her footfalls silenced by the weight of shadows. The room closed in around her, the walls bending inwards.

She sank to the floor, the shadows pressing down, constricting her movements. The tapping grew louder, resonating within her skull.

Tap. Tap. Tap.

She squeezed her eyes shut, her breath shallow, every gasp a struggle.

The candle flickered and died, plunging her into darkness. She felt it then, the presence in the room, the unseen watcher. The air grew colder, the shadows heavier, wrapping around her like a shroud. She could feel the weight of it on her chest, relentless.

Hours passed in a torment of fear and anticipation, the darkness swallowing her hold. Each breath was a fight, the air thick and stale.

Tap. Tap. Tap.

The sound was inside her now, dominating her mind.

As dawn's weak fingers crept through the window, the shadows retreated slightly, but the weight remained. She forced herself up, every movement a struggle against the lingering horror. The day would bring a temporary reprieve, but she knew the night would return.

The tapping would return. And the shadows, ever patient, would close in once again.

Magenta's Chair

(August's Winner)

James Hancock

The heavens rumbled as dark clouds rolled across evening skies. Distant flickers of white warned of the storm to come, and the five village elders agreed to waste no time in making their decision. Meeting in the old barn at the edge of the village, they addressed Magenta's fate. In the half-light of an oil lantern, they talked with haste and found a convenient answer.

Magenta was a girl of great beauty and innocent charm, blessed with empathy and understanding for all. Keeping to herself, she walked the willow woods, preferring the company of animals and the simple offerings of nature. She understood beast and wildflower far more than man, and although born of the village, her soul was that of Fay. She dreamed of the day when fawn and fairy would take her before the Earth Mother, and she would join them in their lands. But her dreams and prayers were never answered.

Over the years, Magenta learned from plants, seeds and roots. She discovered things which helped those in need with all manner of ailments, and her brews and poultices cured man and beast. Thankful of her talents, the villagers took more and more notice of Magenta, and men considered the woman she had become. Her beauty brought increasing fascination, leading to uncontrollable desire. Men wanted to bed her, and women became jealous.

However, Magenta showed no interest in the men's advances.

Rejected, their thoughts turned sour, her abilities were questioned, and Magenta's name was whispered through accusing lips in the home and on the workers' fields. They branded her 'Witch'.

Magenta's kindness had helped many when needed, but that wasn't enough for lustful men and resentful women. The village would be a simpler place if her name no longer fell from the tongue and her face no longer captivated the eye.

In the old barn, on that stormy night, innocence was disregarded and deeds quickly forgotten. The elders made their decision.

They found Magenta at the bend in the brook and took her without a struggle to the old barn, where she was thrown upon a table, bound, stretched, and whipped bloody.

As the storm closed in, the villagers hurried a tight noose around Magenta's neck and lynched her upon a mighty oak tree.

The crowd watched as Magenta's spirit left her body, finally taken to the lands of Fay. And as she died, a bolt of lightning leapt from the heavens, setting the old barn ablaze and burning it to ruin. A sign for the simple folk. This dark act would not be forgiven.

Years later, villagers felled the hanging tree and crafted a beautiful rocking chair from it. Beautiful and deadly. Nature's daughter had been punished for no wrongdoing, and the Earth Mother hadn't forgotten it. Witch or not, a curse was born on that hanging night, and as the villagers would soon discover, came alive upon the chair's making. Any who sat upon it would be struck dead before the year was done.

Desolation of the Wendigo

Caleb James K.

It walked between the scorched tree trunks and smouldering brush. Acrid smoke permeated throughout the skeletal remains of the forest. The firefighters couldn't stop the blaze. After days of burning, *it* was the only thing left. The Wendigo. A spirit with no other place to go.

Miles and miles, acres and acres of desolation stretched long and far before the Wendigo. For its whole existence—as long as the forest itself, some say—the Wendigo has roamed the land in search of fresh victims. Its greed for flesh is insatiable. Yet now, amidst the ruins of its home, the Wendigo is for the first time at a loss.

There will be no more hapless humans lost in the dense forest. Nor will there be any animals that the Wendigo can mimic to lure humans into its realm. For the first time since the before times, the Wendigo must go without feeding. But for how long?

Through the charred dead forest, it marched in deathly silence until it reached the top of the great overlook. Now, with only a sea of fiery death before it, reality set in. The Wendigo, unable to leave the boneyard it once called home, is destined to spend many human lifetimes alone and starving; forced to roam the desolate wild until life can grow anew; until the humans and animal's return.

When that day comes it will be ready. It will feast on the weary and devour the flesh of the lost. The Wendigo, luring its victims once more into the great forest. But for now, it can only wait and watch. Seethe and lament. The wait will be long. The Wendigo will grow restless and more vengeful.

Death is the mercy afforded to its victims, but the Wendigo only knows hunger. It will starve but not die. It will feel pain but not succumb. These agonies it will hold onto until the day the spirit can feast again.

As it ruminates on its fate, a sound stirs something deep within the malevolent spirit. From the peak of desolation, the Wendigo hears faraway voices. Faint and innocent. Through acres of ash, it sees a couple. They hold cameras and document the destruction. Fools. Flesh. That's all they are.

The Wendigo moves as the wind pushes toward the couple. It breathes death through an already dead world. It cries as a bird cries.

"Did you hear that?" the young man says.

"Sounded like a bird," the young woman says. "Let's go check it out."

Darkness

A.J. Brown

Jay wakes to darkness. His head is foggy, his body tired and weak. He goes to wipe his eyes with one hand, but it bumps into something solid inches above him. He thinks of bunk beds at summer camp and how much he hated the ceiling being so close to his body. Being the smallest and youngest of the brothers, he always got placed on the top bunk. Though he never did, he hated the very idea he could fall from the top bunk in the middle of the night.

His elbows touch walls on either side of him. His hands go no further than two or three inches above him. He lifts his head and bumps his forehead. The fogginess rushes away, his eyes wide and unseeing in the dark that surrounds him. His heart speeds up. Sweat beads along his face. He tries to roll onto his side but can't.

Fear swells in his chest, his mind speeds up, pushing all but one thought away.

"Help!" he yells, then hits what he now believes is the top to a pine box, a homemade casket. "Help!" His voice sounds hollow and weak. He pushes up with both hands, using every bit of strength he could muster. Maybe if he pushes hard enough the top will come off. It's not likely, he thinks. Still, he tries. Still, he screams for help. Still, he is surrounded by an almost suffocating darkness.

Above him comes a heavy thud, then the sound of something dragging across the floor for a second. Then he hears it again, and a third time. He strains to hear, his eyes squinted as if that can help. Someone is there, shuffling above him. He doesn't realize he is holding his breath until he goes to speak, and he has to release it and take another.

"Hey. Help me. Please, help me. I'm ... I'm ..."

His eyes grow wide when he hears the muffled laughter followed by footsteps fading away, the owner of the shuffling feet leaving.

“No!” He screams. “No. Don’t leave me here.”

More laughter is followed by another muffled sound, a door closing.

He thinks of summer camp, how much he hated the bunk beds, how afraid he had been to fall from the top bunk. This ... this is worse.

Alan P. Marks

"C'mon, turnip, kick," Sally prays, for maybe the hundredth time or so. She ain't exactly been keeping track. The prayer is only a whisper, though. She doesn't dare make any noise.

She runs her hands over her enormous beachball of a belly, tryin' to perk up the little guy (or girl—Sally'll be happy either way), careful not to bother the ugly black bruise near her bellybutton. Must've happened when she fell sprinting upstairs, or maybe scramblin' up the ladder into the cramped, sweaty little crawlspace of an attic where she's been stuck the past two days. No food. No water. Only the far corner for a potty.

No one for company 'cept the turnip and it's been too quiet for too long and that's scaring the hell out of Sally.

"Hey . . . wake up in there," she whispers for the hundred and first time. Give or take.

The turnip's all she's got left. Daddy's been dead more 'n a week now—and looked every minute of it when Sally heard the crash of the front door breaking in, and come runnin' to find him on the couch on top of momma, face buried in her throat, rippin' and tearin' like a hound on a piece o' raw steak—one of momma's legs stickin' out from between his, givin' a little twitch ev'ry time he took another bite.

So, now momma's gone, too.

At this point, Sally'd even be happy to see the turnip's daddy, not that she expects to ever again. She ain't seen a hair on Bobby Corkum's useless head since she first told him she caught pregnant.

Likely dead now too. *And good riddance,* she thinks, but don't really mean it.

Of course, momma's prob'ly up and about again downstairs. With daddy. That's how it works, the fella on the news said. He didn't ever use the z-word, exactly, but Sally's seen enough movies to know what's what. To know what it means when they come back.

"Any time, turnip," she whispers, thinkin' it's also maybe time to crack open the trapdoor into the upstairs hall again, to see if the coast is clear. Been clear all the other times, but she ain't ever had the nerve to go back down.

Sally lets out a yelp when she sees her momma's milky, dead eyes looking back up at her from the hallway, and the trapdoor slams back shut as she falls over hard onto her backside, pain from her bruised belly shooting through her.

She cries out louder, then, not from the hurt but because the turnip finally wakes back up at last—thank you God—and gives Sally a good hard kick. And another. And another. Hurts fierce, like maybe somethin' important tore inside her—is still tearing—but Sally don't care. She's not alone anymore.

"Hush now, Turnip." Sally whispers, cradling her wriggling belly. "Rest easy."

A trickle of blood seeps from her bellybutton, drips between her trembling fingers.

"Everything's gonna be okay."

The Carpenter's Store

Milan Kovačević

When Evelyn entered the small furniture shop, the bell above the door chimed softly. The place had an old-world charm, filled with rich wooden pieces and ornate fixtures. She'd walked past it countless times, but today, an inexplicable pull guided her through its doors.

The shop was quiet, almost too quiet, the kind that makes you instinctively lower your voice. She walked through the dusty showroom, running her fingers along the smooth surfaces of the tables and chairs. Each item appeared expertly made, radiating a deep sense of long-gone times.

"Can I help you, ma'am?"

The voice startled her. She turned to see an elderly man behind the counter, his loose face framed by thinning white hair.

"Just killing time," Evelyn replied, forcing a polite smile.

He nodded, but his eyes never left her. "Let me know if you need anything. I'll be in the back."

She watched him shuffle through a door behind the counter. Alone, Evelyn ventured deeper, her footsteps barely heard on the polished floor. The shop's layout grew increasingly bizarre, with endless rooms adorned with intricate carvings. The stale air grew heavier, and the silence more profound, as if the shop was observing her every move. She sensed the walls shifting, subtly warping the space around her. Frowning, she turned to retrace her steps, but something was amiss. The entrance had vanished, the back door was gone, and the fitments had formed twisting, unfamiliar passageways. Panic gripped her as she raced through the maze, each room blending into the next with no windows or exits, only an endless labyrinth of furniture.

"Hello?" she called out, her voice trembling. "Sir?"

Evelyn's heart raced, her mind grappling with the impossibility of it all. The scent of varnish and dust filled her nostrils. The familiar path had disappeared, and each step led to further confusion.

In one of the countless rooms, she paused to catch her breath and saw it: a familiar dresser with a small scratch. It can't be, she thought. It was her childhood locker. Though different, she knew it was the same one where she was hiding from the wicked man. Her once safe place. Then came a trenchant knock; from inside of it. Desperation took over as she sprinted through the store, knocking over chairs and tables. “Please, someone, help me!”

The cabinets closed in, the walls narrowing. Trapped in a place that shouldn’t exist, Evelyn saw an old, withered hand emerging from the locker. You are dead. The decaying hand reached out but fell short. With one last burst of energy, she crashed through one of the doorways and found herself back at the counter.

The old man was there, standing behind it as if he'd never left. “I see you've found what you were looking for,” he said, his voice low and knowing. She fell silent and could only watch as the walls closed in and there was nothing but darkness.

The inside of the old locker was as comforting as ever.

James Hancock

Huddle around the hearth and heed the warning. Remember these words before they are lost to the winds and the age of humanity ceases. The gods are cruel, and we are mere toys for their amusement. The Ylyd, as old as the earth, wind and sea, was gifted man to give it purpose. A wicked thing cannot be without a victim on which to prey. The Ylyd is the first of infinite demons, and those who know its tale are few and fading.

Beast of shadow, the Ylyd were children born of night and day, forever waiting in the half-light of evening gloom. Cold and still, they hid in plain sight among the disregarded shapes our mortal eyes ignored. Waiting for their time to strike and claim lives as they leave the earthly realm. Do not go into the beyond unprepared, without the light of open eyes, for the way is blocked by the beast who feeds upon your soul. And they are many.

As tired eyes of the dying close and a final breath is released, the Ylyd emerges to collect it within the deep black bowl of eternal screams. When the death whispers of a thousand souls are stolen, the Ylyd drinks its fill and begins the transformation from shadow to flesh: with pale skin, darkest eyes, and a fierce hunger, it walks as one of us. Addicted to the taste of death, it thirsts after the life force of mortals, and no matter how much its cup fills, the Ylyd is never satisfied.

Listen and remember. Tell your children and their children. Evil hides among us, and it is ever-growing. When the last of us has been consumed, and the Ylyd can feed no more, night has triumphed over day, and the world will become darkness eternal.

An Inspector Calls

Malcolm Timperley

"Mrs Wilson?"

"Er, yes, can I help you?"

"I'm Detective Inspector Harris. It's about your son Colin."

"Well, you can't talk to him, he'll be asleep by now."

"Actually, I'd like to have a few words with yourself, if I may, I've already spoken to Colin. I think you'll find that he isn't in his bedroom; we spoke in an interview room at the station in the presence of Ms Makinde, the duty social worker."

"What? I've warned him about being out after dark. It's those trouble causers from the council estate. What have they done to him?"

"It's alright, nothing terrible's happened to him. He's simply helping us with our enquiries, that's all. So, you were unaware that he'd left the house."

"Yes, we've always been very strict about him not going out after teatime. So, after dinner he plays for a while then goes to bed; he's very good you know."

"Plays? By himself I take it?"

"Well, with his dolls."

"Dolls? Don't take this the wrong way Mrs Wilson, but isn't that more of a girl's thing?"

"Dr Maudsley said it was all right; it'd help Colin learn to manage his emotions. Something to do with feeling safer when you're in control of things."

"Hmm. Well, I suppose a doll's easy enough to control."

"Yes, he has lots of them, about thirty or so. He spends hours arranging them."

“Arranging them?”

“Yes, they’ve got to be just so, he’s very particular about it. A month ago the au pair tidied them all away and he was furious; I’ve never seen him so angry. We haven’t seen the poor girl since, you know.”

“Right. Would you mind if I take a look at his room? It might tie up a few loose ends as it were.”

“Well, if you must, it’s through here. There, you can see for yourself. But please, don’t touch anything.”

“Don’t worry, I just want to look, I never touch anything, I leave that to forensics. Well, I see what you mean about arranging them. Very precise, I must say. Does he always separate the white dolls from the black ones?”

“Oh yes, he’s meticulous about that.”

“And the black ones… they’re always like this? Sort of… well… taken apart.”

“Yes, I don’t know what he does with the hands. Or the eyelids.”

“Or the heads?”

“Oh, they’re on that shelf over there. I think they’re that way up to catch the candle wax.”

“I see. Now, Mrs Wilson, I must ask you to leave everything untouched. My colleagues will be along later for a closer look. But first I really must call that social worker.”

“But you haven’t said what all this is about.”

“In due course, Mrs Wilson, in due course.”

“Well, I want to see if my son’s all right. He’ll be very stressed; I don’t know if he’ll be able to cope.”

“Oh, I’m sure Colin can look after himself, Mrs Wilson. He is thirty-two years old, after all…”

Raven

James Hancock

You walk the night streets, a neon dream of seedy bars and piss-soaked tarmac. Only gutter filth belongs in this part of town. The lice who huddle together and find comfort in a friend's ruin. Lost and forgotten. Poisoned by bad decisions and a cruel slap from life's wickedness. But you want to be here. You want to walk the sticky corridors of Club Paradise; a name so far from the truth it forces a chuckle as you tap knuckles against her door. She answers immediately. Expecting you. Dressed for the occasion in black lace lingerie and squeaky leather boots. She whispers for you to enter and pushes the door closed behind you.

The room is thick shadow and vanilla incense. Under the pleasant smell hides the sweat of a thousand visitors. Raven, that's her name. Long dark hair and pearl white skin you want to bite. But mustn't. It's against the rules. You kiss her neck gently as she unclips your belt. You were told she's worth every penny. When downtown, go see Raven. She's the queen of the night who'll make you forget dreary, broken mornings.

She clicks a key in the door and tells you to unbutton your shirt. Commands it. And you obey. She watches; her face lit by the moonlight from partially open curtains. Clouds part as the sky looms in to brave a glance, and streetlamps bend, dismissing shadows and showing Raven's full beauty. She flicks back her hair and tongues ruby red lips as you toss your shirt onto the bed, awaiting her next instruction.

Heels clack on polished floorboards as she walks around you, stroking long fingernails across your cheek. She asks if you've taken anything. You tell her about two shots of Jack you supped in a cheap bar, and she smiles. A smile so white. Teeth so perfect. So straight. So important for her way of life. Of unlife.

In a flash, she is standing in front of you with hands wrapped around your biceps, pinning your arms to your sides. You struggle but fail, and in an instant realise the full extent of Raven's smile. Her bloodshot eyes burn into you as the room dims once again. The night turns its gaze away, and you are about to scream when she bites. Cold needles puncture, and hot blood pumps. She growls like a wild beast, her embrace forcing you to remain on your feet as she feeds. You want to fall. To cry. To shout for help or beg her to stop. But this is Raven's sweet addiction, and nothing will stop her fix. She drinks deep, cries out with satisfaction, and lets you drop in a heap at her feet. Wiping a red smear across her face, she takes a moment to regain composure.

Fading words echo in your mind: Go see Raven. She's the queen of the night who'll make you forget.

The blood stops flowing, and Raven brings down her boot with a head-splitting crack.

The Meal

Mishan Denna

"Do you like your meal?"

The question forced me to take a pause, I looked at my plate for a long while before I gave Emily my attention. It had been my first time eating at her place, going in I expected us to order take-out, but found out she had spent the entire day cooking us a meal. I hadn't even known she could cook. As I ate the meal in front of me, I found I couldn't stop myself, I kept taking bite after bite of the dish, I had been in awe of her talent.

"It's wonderful," I said, as I used the napkin to wipe the corners of my butter and herb encrusted mouth. Once clean, I looked over to her once more and felt my heart skip a beat. The look on her face, her smile, I felt every hair on the back of my neck stand on end.

I wanted to ask what it was, but the way Emily looked at me kept the words stuck in my throat. It was as if my mind was trying to tell me that I knew the answer before I could get the question out of my mouth. My eyes wandered around the dining area in which we were sat. It looked like any other thirty-something year old's apartment, like out of a magazine. I looked towards her kitchen and could feel my heart start to pound in my chest.

Her cat was perched at the kitchen sink's edge, it licked and pawed at something in the sink. As the cat continued, I could see the orange tabby struggle to pull its tongue away from whatever was in the sink. I couldn't be certain due to the distance, but it looked like human hair. *Human hair.* I looked back at Emily, whose gaze grew darker as she kept her eyes fixed on me. Had she expected me to elaborate on what I liked about the meal?

Was I meant to be *her* meal? I looked at my plate and tried to find my voice again.

"What type of meat is this?" I asked her, as I tried to ignore the pounding of my heart inside my chest. She took a drink of the wine I had brought, and set the glass on the table, she placed her hands on either side of her plate and said plainly, and to the point.

"I think you know."

My thoughts were scattered. *Do I run? Do I get through the meal and never see her again?* So much ran through my head at one time. I looked down at my nearly empty plate, as I tried to figure out my next move. To this day, I cannot explain what happened at that moment, but I looked back up at Emily and asked with a soft smile.

"May I have some more?"

DW Milton

The light came through the fractured window. Colours. All the shades of red; from the fairest rose to the deepest scarlet. Light of a particular spectrum in all its hues and guises, painting the warm wood floor below.

The man sat staring, attempting to remember.

Was blood always this slippery when drenching the floor? Did the coagulated clumps get in the way? Does the cooling heat pulse as it dies, too?

It frustrated him that he could not recall. Then again, in his frenzy he didn't not stop to learn the answers.

As he looked at the window, fractured into so many pieces on purpose, he realized how much it reflected his own mind and his own psyche; intact on the outside but perforated into a million pieces on the inside.

***

He sighed, drawn back to the reality of the then still oozing body on the floor. She was the fleeting glimpse of unimaginable beauty, lost. Where had he met her? What did he know of her?

The trivial details eluded him. The window needed to be fed, dyed and coloured. Every day, bombarded with sunlight, bleaching, leeching its colour its delicate beauty fading. It needed fresh blood to remain beautiful.

When did it first speak to him?

Again, he could not recall.

Was it not the body and the blood that brought salvation and redemption?

Only this stained window in the far corner of the church had revealed its needs and as the priest in residence, he must obey.

It Only Happens Once

Pamela K. Kinney

"Want a unique experience?" The feminine voice curled into his ear as a sweet, seductive odour drifted to his nostrils. "Something that only happens once?"

Joe paused in his drunken struggle to walk down the sidewalk from the bar he'd just left and turned. A tall woman dressed in a tight mini dress and stiletto heels leaned a hip against a lamp pole rising from the cement sidewalk like a steel tree. Her long, red hair gleamed in the soft glow of the lamp's light. Even in his inebriated state, he could see how attractive she was.

He asked, "What do you have in mind?"

A chuckle escaped her mouth, and the sound drew his eyes to her red, moist lips. A flick of the tip of her tongue slipped out, its caress across the flesh making the colour even shinier. "It's something I know for sure that you never done before. Makes you a virgin of sorts."

Joe shook his head and resumed wobbling down the sidewalk. Even if he wanted to accept the prostitute's invitation, he doubted he'd be able to get it up. Not in his condition.

The woman must have followed him, determined not to let a 'John' and his money get away, as her hand curled over his left shoulder, the grip tightening.

"Come on," her voice purred into his ear as if telling him a secret, "I'll make it unforgettable. You'll never have something like this ever again. I promise."

He turned around and looked into her eyes. There appeared something off about them. Maybe it might be prudent for him to say no and leave. A flowery scent infused into his nostrils, and he felt more befuddled than he already was. He shook his head, looked at her again. Suddenly, she seemed hot. Beautiful. Unbelievably, he hardened. *Guess I'm wrong, I can still get it up.*

The woman smiled and took his hand. "This way, handsome."

She led him down a dark alley. They stopped beneath a sickly yellow light losing a battle against the darkness.

Joe said, "I want you to know I've done every sexual position you can imagine."

"Oh, this isn't about sex, but I'm about to do a trick." Her smile widened unnaturally into a cavern of shark teeth as she pressed against him.

The prostitute vanished, replaced by a monstrous creature. Before Joe could scream or struggle, she brought his face to hers for a parody of a kiss and bit his lips off.

***

The creature consumed the man, taking time to savour every piece of him. She even licked up the blood splashed all over the ground and its flesh. Something about the terror humans felt when they understood her true self added a unique flavour nothing else on this planet had.

When the monster costumed herself once more as the human woman, she patted her bulging belly. "I hope you enjoyed the experience of being my meal. I did."

The Boy Under the Bridge

Terry Campbell

I have a friend who lives under the bridge that crosses the creek down the street from my house. I call him Jack. I don't know his real name. He doesn't talk. My momma used to say kids like that were "deaf-mutes". You can see my house from the bridge. I go there sometimes.

I used to come to the bridge a lot, especially during summer when there was no school. I would catch tadpoles and crawdads, and sometimes, big long-legged birds would land and walk in the water looking for minnows.

But one day, a bully climbed down into the creek. He called me names and pushed me around, and he beat me up pretty good. I was bleeding and screaming for my mom, but our house was too far away for her to hear me. I stopped going to the creek for a while, afraid that the bully would show up and hurt me again.

But I decided it was safe to go down there. That's when I met Jack. He doesn't talk, but he listens real good. I tell him all about when I went to school, and what happened on Gilligan's Island the day before. I think he likes my stories, because he never leaves. He's always there, so I think he lives under the bridge.

One day, I was telling Jack about the episode where Gilligan thought he was going to die after the bug bit him. Have you seen that one? Then I heard a noise. Someone was coming down the sides of the hill and into the creek. I told Jack to be quiet. I was scared it was the bully.

But it was only a lady. She looked under the bridge and saw me, and she screamed and turned to run. I don't know why. I guess she thought I wasn't supposed to be there and went to tell on me, because a little while later, there were police cars and an ambulance.

I was scared, and I think Jack was scared, too. I stayed with him, though. I wasn't going to leave my friend alone.

The policemen and some men in white coats walked under the bridge. They didn't say anything to me, but they took Jack away. I keep hoping he'll come back someday, but he hasn't.

But I wait under the bridge for him. I talk to myself now, because there's no one else to talk to. Momma doesn't watch Gilligan anymore.

Did you see that one? Gilligan doesn't die, but the bug does. It's funny. It's my favourite one.

I wish I could watch Gilligan again. I wish Jack would come back. I miss my friend.

I wish I had someone to talk to.

The Hollow

Thomas E. Stone

For years, Nathan had fought to keep the darkness at bay. First, it was subtle—a small nagging voice questioning his every decision, sowing doubt where there should be certainty. Over time, the voice grew louder. It wasn't just self-doubt anymore. It was a gnawing pit within his chest that craved something he couldn't name.

Sat alone in his dim apartment, windows shut tight to block out the world. His phone rang occasionally, friends checking in, he never answered. They didn't understand. How could they? Out there, everything seemed bright, functional, normal. But inside Nathan, it was crumbling. He could feel it—the gradual erosion of his mind, the sense that something dark was creeping in, laying claim to the fragments of his soul.

Nathan had always tried to fight it. He had gone through the motions, attending therapy, talking to God, or ultimately turning to the bottle. But it remained—persistent, patient. The more he resisted, the more it seeped into his thoughts, becoming an unwelcome companion.

One evening, as the rain battered against the window, the darkness finally took shape. While staring at the mirror, searching his own eyes for a glimpse of the man he used to be. The reflection that stared back was not his own. The face was twisted and hollowed, the eyes were the worst of it. They were vacant, cold, as if nothing human remained beneath.

Panic surged through him, quickly giving way to something darker. There was a strange fascination in seeing himself this way, like a detached observer watching someone else's life unravel. And then, the voice that had plagued him for so long spoke again, only now it wasn't a whisper.

"Why do you fight? You know what you are."

Nathan staggered back, his heart racing. Blinking, shaking his head, but the reflection didn't change. The twisted face leaned closer, grinning with grim amusement. The voice, deep and cold, filled his mind again.

"You crave it, don't you? The release. The power. You were never meant to be like them."

The words slithered through him, and for the first time, Nathan didn't resist. Part of him understood, recognized the truth in the voice. He had always felt different—separate from the world around him. The darkness had always been there, lurking beneath the surface, waiting for his embrace.

Nathan stared at the figure in the mirror, his breath steadying. The fear that had gripped him moments before melted away, replaced by something else, acceptance.

"This is what you are," the voice said again, now almost soothing.

And Nathan, without hesitation, reached out, pressing his hand against the cold glass. The reflection smiled as their fingers touched. In that moment, something shifted. The boundary between Nathan and the darkness blurred. He wasn't just looking at the hollow reflection anymore—he *was* the reflection.

The phone rang again, but this time Nathan didn't even notice. The world outside had become irrelevant. The darkness had finally won.

Depredadora

S. C. Mills

Alicia sits cross-legged on the yurt's hardwood floor; her feet numb from a nightlong vigil in this circle of aging hippies. The shaman taps at a hand pan, accompanied by waffling flutes and fuzzy, choked drums through a cheap speaker. Daisy-chained golden Amancay flowers crown his head. A stained jar filled with dark liquid sits before him, emitting a sickly rotten-molasses smell. Depredadora—Peru's newest chemical-spiritual guide.

The shaman will abstain, but everyone else will drink at sunrise. *Any minute now.* Alicia can just spy the outlines of treetops through the yurt's lattice walls, their black fingers clawing a greying sky. Depredadora's supposed to grant visions of ancient gods, make you one with nature. *Whatever. As long as it gets me high.*

The hand pan mercifully halts, leaving only the tinny wail of the background music. A headache pounds behind her eyes, worsened by the neighbouring man's overpowering yet ineffective patchouli deodorant. He fishes out a handful of mint leaves from an NPR-branded tote bag. "A chaser," he whispers.

The shaman paces the circle, offering the chunky purplish potion to each tired new ager. At last, his dirt-caked feet, edges yellowed with calluses, halt before Alicia.

She throws the plant medicine back, eager to ascend—or descend—to any plane it commands. It tastes like the sweet slime on expired kale, decaying in the crisper. Her stomach curdles but doesn't rebel.

Agonized screams cut above the low-fi flutes.

Across the room, a man's skin cracks and peels off in curling pale strips—papery birchbark, exposing bone and moving sinew.

A wailing woman grips his shredded arm, her fingers becoming grasping tendrils and choking vines.

Panic twines around Alicia's chest and squeezes. *Can't be hallucinating already*. But she must be—she *must*.

"Depredadora and her meal." The shaman cackles, his eyes empty, knots in a hollowed-out Andean oak. "Which is which now?"

"The plants are screaming!" Half-chewed mint leaves tumble from patchouli-man's mouth. "We're hurting them!" He digs his fingers into and around his ears. Sap-like blood, sticky and translucent, oozes from his jagged nails.

Alicia recoils, gagging, trying to retch. *Too late.* Searing pain shoots along her spine and scours down her arms, lifting welts that harden to hooked thorns. She writhes on the floorboards, thrashing, ripping off hunks of her own skin. High-pitched screams—no, *chittering*—rises above the music. From her own mouth, from others, from the forest, even from the mint. Inhuman, yet familiar. Like it's always been there, everywhere, whispering below hearing.

"No respect," the shaman scoffs. His rough fingers grip Alicia's jaw, forcing her to look east.

The sun lifts above the horizon—a burnt-orange ember, the end of a cigarette. She stares, captivated. Her retinas smoulder; her skin *hungers*.

Alicia crawls toward it. She tumbles over the edge of the yurt to the forest floor. Blessed wet dirt, her home, soothes her flesh and silences her mind. Her chittering fades. Blisters swell and pop with final ecstatic release as her roots sprout and burrow into the earth.

The Ancient

Hidayat Adams

It emerged from deep under the desert sand, during the darkest part of the night – a blacker blemish against the absence of light. It was shapeless, but its consciousness – as ancient as the very foundations of the world itself – knew it would soon coalesce into its true form. It was patient. It had been created to be patient, to bide its unholy time. And its hour had finally come.

Far to the south of where the malevolent presence had crawled out from under the dunes, in the small oasis of Baraa, Raeesa felt its presence as surely as if a heavy shawl had been wrapped tightly around her face to smother her. Shuddering, she sat up in her bed, listened intently to the regular night noises of the near-silent town. The priestess' heart thundered painfully against her chest. Lowering her aching legs carefully to the floor, Raeesa rose to walk over to the sole window that faced the stark beauty of the stretching sand dunes, ghost-lit by a pale crescent high up in the firmament.

"It is among us. The Beast has awoken," Raeesa whispered in fear. Her eighty-six-year-old body trembled; her usually keen mind having suddenly lost its acumen. The old woman felt lost, adrift, unable to think coherently.

A barely felt and even less heard thump, like an echo lost among mountainous valleys, brought the woman instantly out of her stupor. Raeesa's eyes widened in alarm; her nostrils flared in terror. Throwing on a heavy kaftan to combat the night air, Raeesa hurried out of her small adobe house.

Its hour has come. We are all doomed if we fail to awaken its nemesis, Raeesa thought as she made a beeline for the tribal chambers.

Marhoub. That was its name, the Beast mused as it materialised near the home of its summoner, who was also the one who had released all restraints from the demon. It revelled in its new freedom; the power this earthly body gave it. Its massive form towered over the houses huddled together in the town. With a smirk of dominion, Marhoub stalked towards the clearly marked house. It bore a pentacle with the six-point form of the Seal of Solomon upon its flat roof. The symbol was a blazing invitation for Marhoub to enter unhindered.

The Beast obliged.

The human summoner, an emaciated crone with eyes darker than the deepest pits of hell, grinned wickedly when Marhoub appeared in front of her, its enormous form absorbing all the light, plunging the house into darkness.

"Glorious Marhoub! Your Era of Dread has finally dawned!" the witch cackled, prostrating herself, extending her arms out in front of her, palms up, her filthy, long nails crooked and cracked.

In a voice that sounded like boulders grating together, Marhoub declared, "And yours has ended," before the demon mercilessly squashed the woman.

Raeesa heard the blast of wicked laughter coming from the centre of the town. She feared that she was too late to save the world.

Scythed From the Same Cloth

Scott M. Brents

As of October 31, 2024, I became the last player.

Danny Edwards held the penultimate position. I was with him when he passed on Halloween.

* * *

Coach King was magnificently hung over in 1972 as he revealed the name of our soccer team. A bourbon-soaked cigar hung below the walrus mustache. He could have been a Cajun chef explaining how to prepare crawfish étouffée.

"A gunner is someone shooting things, and we'll be gunning in goals. So, our team is called the Gunners."

The attentive group of ten and eleven-year-olds murmured approval – except for Benny. He was pretending to be a robot from a television series, waving his arms at a nearby bois d'arc tree, yelling "Danger! Danger!" while kicking fallen psychedelic green horse apples, claiming they were alien brains.

* * *

The chest and back of our jerseys were goldenrod, with blue short sleeves, blue player numbers, and blue lettering.

We looked like a flock of awkward parrots.

* * *

I began the search for my teammates during the pandemic. By the end of 2023, I had accounted for all.

Out of eighteen boys and two coaches, only Danny Edwards and I remained on the field.

I researched Coach King and Coach Timms first and was unsurprised they were no longer living. But when I learned that their sons – who had been Gunners – were deceased, I felt a sense of unease that nearly made me quit looking.

Danny had pancreatic cancer and the clock was ticking. I had received a text message Halloween morning from Annie, his ex, telling me he was near the end at St. Paul's.

I wondered out loud to him, how could all the Gunners die prematurely?

"We're all croaking because those goddamned bloody jerseys were cursed. Our ages prove it. Sixty-one years old and dying. Fucking turning toad before retirement!" Danny's number had been 61. I was well aware of the correlation.

From the hospital's paging system, *Dr. Hobbs, please call the nurses' station. Dr. Hobbs.*

"Dr. Hobbs. Fucking hell," Danny said, grimacing.

He rolled his fierce blue eyes at the ceiling.

"Annie is a treacherous bitch. I knew she wouldn't come."

Then he coded. The alarm was as shrill as a soccer referee's whistle.

Nurses rushed in with the crash cart. I went into the hall.

Dr. Hobbs. Dr. Hobbs.

* * *

Thompson, age 23, jersey 23 – struck in 1985 at a construction site; a steel girder plummeted ten stories. Horrific.

Farmer, age 43, jersey 43 – a drive-by shooting in 2004. He'd just left the airport.

Benjamin Mansfield, age 17, jersey 17 – died of food poisoning in 1979 after a picnic. There had been no robot to warn him about the Danger! Danger! of some tainted canned tuna.

Graham, King, Timms, Kirkpatrick, Mason, Prater, Acker, Heidelberg, Givens, Steele, Adams, Taylor, and Janeka – gone. All ages at death corresponded to their Gunners jersey numbers.

I'm Rick Waco, jersey 99 – the final Gunner.

I couldn't kill myself if I tried.

Blood Follower

Dejan Sklizović

While steaming with hot water, I listened on the phone to a podcast where a charlatan talked about the mechanics of the occult universe. Of course, there were no references, but it was exciting to listen to the guy trying to answer the unpleasant questions of the lively host. He spoke of unknown creatures, so horrible that no human imagination could shape them into a functional form. How do they get to us? One thing is sure: the minds of crazy, dangerously mentally disturbed people are the real catalyst for such creatures.

I heard the distant voice of my fiancée calling me, but I could not recognize the words. Then, it suddenly stopped.

The opened bathroom door let the icy air in. I wouldn't pay much attention to such a thing, but the temperature this low was unusual, especially for the middle of August.

I shyly stared into the darkness, trying to recognize the shapes and familiar contours of the room, but I couldn't. The coldness only gripped me harder so that the drops of hot water on my body were already turning into frost. Then I heard the sound of hundreds of tiny bubbles gurgling uncontrollably, somehow boiling at sub-zero temperature. I stepped into the darkness and found my foot on the still-warm, sticky liquid. I slipped and hit the back of my head on the floor. What was happening above my head, coming from the ceiling blocked all my attempts to rationalize the position I found myself in.

The darkness in the corridor was not of equal density, and a mass of ameboid shape, something pulsating from the supposed centre of eerie existence, encompassed most of my vision. It radiated coldness, yet as it approached, I felt a still-warm liquid seething within the body itself, rippling in the digestive system, vainly seeking a way out.

Several flashing apparitions displayed above me, like dozens of eyes connected by carefully woven threads of light, looking at me and sizing me up. It was like a cosmos full of constellations, only in my corridor, somewhere on the ceiling, and now it was slowly pouring down. The misty cloud thickened and took on a humanoid form. His body's network of tiny stars shone like a ghostly Christmas tree, probably communicating with me that way. He was standing above me, and through the transparent dark skin, you could see the blood that had just been drunk, which had now completely calmed down and merged with the host. It even stopped gurgling and moved into the calm streams of the beast's bloodstream. A Starman full of human blood, that bizarre thought was the last thing that crossed my mind.

Darkness brought a lot with it, and oblivion was the only blessing. For a long time, I was falling into the depths of the unfathomable abyss of some hostile cosmos and experienced things I'm not sure I ever want to remember.

Dungeon Confessions

Sarah Smith

Rope burns replace bracelets as I come to. *Where am I?* Thankfully, alone. Unable to flee, instead, I withdraw, finding temporary solace in the flesh, the bones, the body. My hiding place isn't the corner of this cage, but rather, the skeleton behind human flesh. No one can find me. Not him nor I, as I lose myself to this broken body, cherishing the moments I have to myself, when this body is truly my own. Deep down, in my core, I know it's only a matter of time before I'm consumed once and for all.

In the muddy reflection of my own vomit, bite marks on my face leave bruises in their wake. *Where did these even come from?* The moments blend together; I surrender. No use crying, he'll retaliate. Locked in a cage of my own making. After all, I supplied the key. I let him in, to my heart, to my home, consequences unknown. *I would've held back.* Wrecked by my own naivety, I plead blind devotion to the creature I once called Soul Mate, now, the dungeon master who relishes my perpetual torment. Sounds blend together, yet I can perceive muffled footsteps on crooked stairs. "He's here," I whisper to an otherwise empty room, a single tear falling.

His pointed talon runs up and down the broken scabs, dried blood, and carved tissue, tracing his masterpiece, proof of a job well done. Perhaps they'll become scars, if I'm alive long enough for the skin to heal. He stares deeply into my eyes, glazed over and lifeless. With a smirk, he peels back his layers, and hidden behind his mask is the face of a monster. *I can fix him*— the greatest lie ever told by the wicked mirage of a trick called "love." I'm no longer human, so how could I know love; I barely remember what it means. Held in this psychopath's cage under lock and key, escape is unlikely. *How will I live again?*

Dissociating to flee his abuse, time is lost as I dangle from the ceiling, neck wrapped in cord. Lost to the pain inflicted by a man who has never known love: I am his revenge. Now, a corpse slowly decaying, stuck. *Will I make it?* Scooped up in Salvation's palm, I take back what was mine, all along. In mind, my spirit. In heart, my key. Ears ringing and wrapped in a blanket of warmth, I am greeted by sunshine and epiphany: *I'm free now.* Death brings eternal peace. It's living that's hard.

It Pains Me

Juliette Jarabek

I love my son. I've loved him since before I held him, all wriggling and pink and so, so small. Not that I knew—I'd never *liked* children, rambunctious and crying and needing to be coddled. They were a weakness, a resource, an excuse—all to be exploited and abused. And he was delivered suddenly, uninvited and unexpected. Yet, in the end, I'd welcomed him anyway.

In hindsight, perhaps my distaste rose from misanthropy rather than malice.

Despite his human sin, I developed a sinful humanity. So small, he was, smaller than any child I'd ever seen before and since, his wheezes louder than his cries. It was difficult to care for him in the first days, months, years. Infants are infamous for their disruptive noise, screaming themselves red and blue. But he'd been too blue. He's taught me to hate the quiet instead. Any silence he's left me in has racked me with distress unfamiliar.

But in time, with all my resources, he'd grown.

He's become my pride, so wilful and clamorous. He'd filled my home's labyrinthian halls with unfettered footfalls, no decorum or pretence in his babbles and queries. How did he manage it, inspiring me past common decency into the ignominy of baby talk and pretend play? He'd brought fresh breath to a stagnantly polite society, continuing to fill my lungs over short decades.

I've loved him since before his parents knew him, too; I've loved him *far* past their chance to. Humans considered their own individual survival more important than anything else. Some call it commendable; I consider it obnoxiously tedious. Their lives so short, they try stuffing them with all the self-imposed meaning they can before expiring—a foie gras of folly, though not such a delicacy.

Their veins had pulsed with ego and desperation, the likes of which outweighed any shame as they displayed their newborn offering with bargaining pleas. Their musk was animalic, beastly—a disgrace not worth consuming. I'd let their essence feed the earth instead, leaving them less than another casualty as their village was razed under my heel.

So intelligent and inquisitive, he understands more than I could have hoped—perhaps more than I *should* have hoped. I've never been one for subtleties, though, so what could I have expected? I've had no reason to hide, felt no shame. I stand by my every decision, having no regrets throughout the centuries I've lived.

It pains me that he will not say the same.

I love him. Even as I lie here, my chest crudely caved and blood leaving a vulgar stain on my carpet rather than being savored as it deserves, all I can feel is sympathy for my son. I see the conflict in his eyes, unsure whether he should be accepting or contrite behind the rolling walls of tears. I wipe them away, but they won't cease.

He doesn't stop me.

My pride, the last thing I see; I love him *so much.*

Ari Carrington

I woke at first light, curled on a rock by the running stream. Naked, streaked with blood and mud. I crawled to the water and washed myself as best as I could. Unsteady on two legs, I followed the stream back towards the town once again.

***

I walked into school, stomach turning as the smell of nuclear processed meat wafted from the canteen. Selina sauntered over as I desperately clutched at my sunglasses. “Time of the month?” she asked sympathetically, slipping an arm around me. If only she knew. I nodded, trying not to recoil as I caught the scent of her perfume, taking comfort in the warmth of her embrace.

***

I ran, feet pounding, bounding through the forest, free. A flickering fire in the distance, the stench of young blood. I approached on softest foot. Young people laughing and drinking and then screaming and fleeing as I pounced, ripping throats, tearing limbs, biting down through flesh and blood and bone. Killing for fun, for joy at not being one of them.

***

I woke with a familiar fleshy arm across my fleshy chest. Squinting, I followed it from hand to elbow to snapped tendons trailed in the dirt. I sniffed - though in this form my nose was dulled, I could detect something overlaying the blood. Cheap perfume, much like…

There. A few feet away. Most of a mangled corpse. Selina.

I howled.

The Colour of Promise

NC Maha

The day you carved a rose into my heart, every bone in my body swore to cherish it. Bleach-white bones dug through my grave, leaching damp and strewing ribbons in white-ash glee. Two summers twice, I began to vault blush-pink shoots that bloomed in the dark. Red petals spilled, the colour of blood, the colour of our love. I twined my earthly shell in fronds and grass. A weaver's casket, for the one you'd forgotten. Here I lie, in a bed of my roses.

I rooted into lungs that breathed strange fire; coal-black char that chafes. Strange breath stirred, baring the story of love, hewing off my roses. Thorns-and-leaves-crowned, bare bones exposed; realization bolted through my devoted bones. Your love prism-split yet dripped red alone. In the ruby colour you'd bought for me–but was never mine alone.

I scream. New petals froth, splintering the earth. Finally, I open.

My bones are no more. No more roses.

But I'd promised. I'd promised to cherish your rose, engraved my word in bone-deep ache. The song of a heart rends apart thorns and claws through earth, till cold melts rivulets on a sunny day.

Crawling is all I can do. My limbs have forgotten, but my breath hasn't. The compass tilts: for though doused in rose, I remember your stench. Cordite and grey, on your skin and in my inhale, sharp metal taste on my parched tongue.

"You love me," you'd said once. "That is why I do this."

I love you, I remember, obedient. *That is why I do this.*

I'm at your door, and I knock. Your brand-new wife opens; she's surprised red, blushes a bouquet. She reaches out to clasp me to her breast; a rose-tree from her love.

I entwine her, embrace her close and lift. There *will* be roses. I carry her to my abode; she worms and squirrels, but earth and my tresses hold her warmth close. She finally stills to the listening trees, cold breath stuttering, choked on dirt. I soothe her deep, till she rests.

You'll always have roses; I promise my love. There will always be roses, in our garden.

Jonah

(October's Winner)

Aly Rhodes

It was at night that Toby felt the thing inside him moving . . . its ragged breathing, terrible twists and turns tearing at his innards. Toby lay awake, staring at the star-lit glow-in-the-dark ceiling, a ninth birthday present, and wished he could fly away to a far-off galaxy.

He didn't have a name for what was gestating inside him, for the last few months, but he thought of it as 'Jonah', after the Biblical tale. Toby had tried varied and increasingly desperate measures to expel his 'Jonah' – starting with burning incense and chanting, visits to church, offerings to all and any gods, handfuls of healing crystals (nicked from his mum's room). Then he ramped it up by waving a burning candle over his chest, whilst reciting prayers in garbled Latin. The wax drips burned his skin.

Finally, in despair, he'd prodded himself with a vegetable knife – too blunt he'd discovered. Nothing worked. 'Jonah' lived on. Toby had too, but somewhat battered, singed and grazed.

An exorcism request was next on his list, but he wondered if you had no faith, would that be a handicap? He pressed his right palm hard onto his bony ribcage.

"Push off! Whatever you are, wherever you're from. I hate you. Just go!"

Inside Toby's skinny twelve-year-old body, 'Jonah' rippled as if responding. Toby gasped with the racking pain. He wept, but in silence, snot sliming the pillowcase. No one in the house must hear him, no one must find out his secret.

I'm a monster, he thought. *A freak. I'll be put away somewhere.*

Unable to sleep Toby got up, stealthy, on bare feet, and removed his pyjama top. The moonlight lit his skin revealing the flare of his ribcage and to his shock, how distended it was. He watched the flesh dimple and pucker as 'Jonah' moved.

"What are you?" He thumped his stomach with a fist. Angry.

Then in the wardrobe mirror he saw a shadow emerging from the base of his spine – inky, viscous, surging upwards, smearing the pop group posters and turning the blue-painted walls – black, as tar.

'It' hung over his head, swaying; an alien boa constrictor ready to strike. He sensed its hunger, its need and guessed he had only seconds left to live unless . . . "If I find you food . . . like another person . . ." Toby's voice broke. "Will you, please, please, leave me alone?" Tears welled up.

'Jonah' pulled backwards, hovering near the ceiling, coating it in sickly shadows. Toby eyed his pet hamster curled up asleep hidden in the sawdust nest.

No, don't be ridiculous. Not Harry.

Toby needed something or someone weightier, fleshier, meatier. He weighed up his immediate and nearest choices: - Mum, Dad or . . . his younger annoying sister.

Above his head 'Jonah' oozed and slithered, swaying in agitation. Toby was running out of time. He opened his mouth to call out a name . . .

The Hollow Lantern

Lydia Harrington

Mia discovered the pumpkin on Halloween night, left alone at the edge of her porch, its grin carved with unsettling precision. She glanced up and down the street, but her neighbour's porches were empty, each house bathed in the dim glow of streetlights. She picked it up, surprised by its weight, and felt a chill as she brushed her hand across its rough, cracked skin. The hollowed eyes stared up at her, but something about it felt… wrong. The smell was rancid, a mix of decay and something sickly sweet, almost like old meat.

Setting the pumpkin on her kitchen table, she turned her back to wash her hands, trying to ignore the faint sense of unease prickling the back of her neck. As she scrubbed, she heard a faint scratching, like nails on wood. She turned, eyes narrowing at the pumpkin, half-expecting to find a raccoon or a rat burrowed inside. But it was still, its carved grin eerily wide, its empty eyes watching her.

Shaking her head, she went about her evening. But the scratching began again, louder this time, as if something inside was trying to claw its way out. Her heart pounded, and she crept closer, reaching out hesitantly. Just as her hand brushed the pumpkin, its mouth shifted, the carved grin stretching wider. She jumped back, watching in horror as tiny skeletal fingers began curling out of the hollow eyes, scratching against the table, dragging something small and pale through the gaping mouth.

She couldn't scream, her throat closing as a tiny face pushed through, staring at her with hollow, sunken eyes.

“Thank you for bringing me home,” it whispered, its voice rasping and thin, like dry leaves brushing against each other. Mia stumbled back, hand over her mouth, unable to look away as the tiny figure climbed free of the pumpkin, skeletal hands leaving smears on the table, its dark, empty gaze locked onto her, its mouth twisting into a smile mirroring the pumpkin’s grotesque grin.

It moved closer, each step slow, deliberate. She backed against the wall, feeling the cold press of tiles against her back, her hands fumbling for anything – a knife, a phone – but her mind was blank with terror. The figure reached out, touching her cheek with bony, frigid fingers.

“You brought me home,” it murmured, voice dripping with malice. “Now, let’s carve a smile on you.”

The lights flickered, plunging the room into darkness. She felt the icy touch of those fingers slide down her face, tracing her mouth, her cheeks, and her vision blurred as fear consumed her. When the lights came back on, the pumpkin sat alone on the table, its grin wider, and behind that smile was Mia’s hollowed, frozen face, her eyes wide and filled with terror.

Tocked

Khala Grace

Tick...tock...tick...tock.... The hand of the grandfather's clock trickles down to the next hour. Eager eyes watch the needle sway back and forth - counting away the seconds.

"3558... 3559... " a young boy calls.

Don, Donnn, Doonng...

"3600!" He cheers.

"Daniel, what are you doing awake?" A voice sneaks up from behind.

"Grandpa!" The boy jolts.

"Sorry to scare you!" The grandpa laughs. He places a hand on the boy's back. "Time for sleep."

"Oh..." Daniel sighs. While walking upstairs, Daniel continues to count. 85... 86... 87. He loses his frame of thought. *One... Two... Three...* Daniel thinks while crawling into bed. His grandfather kisses him on the forehead.

"Sleep well." He smiles.

Reluctantly, Daniel falls asleep. He wakes with alarm as the trash cans rattle. Slowly, the boy walks downstairs. He hides behind the grandfather's clock. *Burglars!* He panics. As quiet as a mouse, the boy stands- watching as the thieves plunder his grandfather's belongings.

"Sykes and Werner!" A thief whistles. "How much do these old clocks go for?"

"About a grand!" The other snickers.

"Jackpot!" The burglars gather their haul unaware of the old man in the hall.

"Get out!" Mr. Sykes demands.

He holds a small pistol aimed at the nearest thief. Quickly, the second burglar raises his weapon. Shots scatter in the dark. Glass from the clock litters the floor. The man's mark in the dim room is poor. A fist fight ensues between the three. Daniel sits near the clock in shock. A body flings into the panel and knocks it sideways. Serendipitously, the front of the broken clock lands on top of the boy.

"Thirteen... Fourteen... Fifteen," Daniel whispers.

"Shit you got em!" A thief shouts.

"Come on, before the cops come!" The other insists.

Silence persists. *Fifty... Fifty-one...* The boy counts. Blood and tears fall onto the carpet. A siren blares outside. With a panic start, Daniel begins to hyperventilate. Several shouts enter the room. As the cops approach the clock- Daniel cries out.

"Grandpa!" His voice cracks.

"There's a kid in here!" An officer alerts his squad. Two lift the grandfather clock while a third picks up the child. Despite being told not to, Daniel looks at the bloody mess that's his grandfather. He screams as they bring him to the hospital.

Rest is difficult. Yet, while caught in fatigue, Daniel sleeps in the emergency room. He stirs in the bed as a visitor keeps him company. The boy wakes to see the wispy form of his grandfather. He wants to speak but is interrupted by an embrace.

"You won't be kept alone," Mr Sykes assures him. "I won't allow that."

Daniel cries as the other fades. For a second, he can hear that familiar sound.

Tick...tock...tick...tock

The Silent Choir

Graham Keene

The church was packed with people, all gathered for the annual Halloween service, a tradition that went back generations in the small town, an eerie custom that had faded in importance elsewhere but clung stubbornly here, passed down like an heirloom. Tonight, the air was thick and heavy, pressing down on the congregation as they filed one by one into the old wooden pews, exchanging uneasy glances in the dim candlelight. The choir filed in, their white robes appearing spectral in the flickering light.

The choir members looked different tonight, their faces gaunt, eyes vacant and hollow as they stared ahead, mouths closed in unnatural, tight-lipped smiles. The conductor, usually a vibrant man with an energetic spark, now moved as though in a trance, his eyes glazed and unfocused. When he lifted his hands, a ripple of apprehension spread through the congregation. The candles flickered as a chilling hymn filled the room, a deep almost inhuman melody, one that clawed at their ears and echoed in their minds.

The song gradually grew louder, every note gnawing at the edges of sanity, until the walls themselves seemed to vibrate with the sound. Shadows stretched, coiling and twisting along the walls and ceiling, grotesque faces forming in the dark. People tried to look away, their eyes wide with terror, but their bodies wouldn't obey. One by one, they rose from their seats, their voices reluctantly joining the haunting hymn. They felt their throats seize and move against their will, their mouths opening, adding their voices to the chorus as though an invisible hand gripped their vocal cords.

The song filled them, rooted them to the ground as they knelt before the altar. Trapped, their limbs locked in place, their voices an unnatural extension of the choir's melody. Their own eyes began to glaze over, mirroring the choir's empty stares as the song wrapped around them, echoing in their minds. It was as though their very souls were being drawn out through their mouths, each note stealing a piece of them.

The next morning, the townsfolk who dared to investigate found the church empty, the pews scattered, and the altar candles nothing but puddles of wax. The air was thick with an unsettling silence, and the scent of incense and damp stone lingered. But the true horror lay in the echo that remained – a faint, haunting hum that filled the empty church, a spectral choir continuing their dark hymn for eternity. Those who entered heard their own voices join the melody, unable to leave the church again, bound forever in a song that would never end.

The Cat and The Canary

K.E. Jennings

The lights in the theatre went out, along with the projector. People screamed and George emitted a sound or two. The power for the entire building was out. Flashlights bobbed in the isles below him as movie attendants in uniforms walked towards the front. Their beams shined in an eerie way, giving life to George's fears. He wanted out of there, now.

"Where did she go?"

"Where is he?"

"I don't know, did you see him leave?"

Confused voices shouted from below as George blindly made his way down the stairs in the dark. People were missing. This was the last straw for him, he was done with this motion picture. He followed the beams of light towards the exit doors. In a panic, everyone was bumping into each other, making leaving impossible. Wanting out, George pushed his way through.

Finally, he made it outside into the thick fog. He could barely spot a few taxi cars on the curb ahead, so he walked quickly to one. Rapping on the window, he got the attention of a driver wearing a black fedora and jacket. George couldn't even make out the man's face in the dark, but he was too rattled to care. He climbed in hastily, shutting the door behind him.

"Where to?" a husky voice asked.

George gave the cabbie his address and wiped sweat off his brow from underneath his hat. His heart rate was still elevated.

"Did you like the film?" the taxi driver asked.

The taxi pulled out onto the roadway and began to slowly drive through the thick fog. It played up the fear factor in George's mind.

"Didn't get to finish it. The power went out."
"Is that so?"
The cab driver let the last word drag on a few syllables, alerting George that something wasn't right. Goosebumps prickled upwards at his clothing, spreading across his skin. Something was wrong here.
"Yes." George tentatively answered.
He noticed that the taxi was turning away from the direction of his building. Fear shot through him like a hand touching a hot stove top. This wasn't right!
"Where are you taking me?" George stammered.
"Where indeed?" the man said, dragging out syllables again. "To my house on the hill."
George's mind flashed back to the opening scenes of the movie, where there was a mansion on a hill. Terror spread through his brain. This couldn't be happening.
"You didn't finish the picture, you said. Can't have that."
Violently yanking on the door handle, George tried to get out of the car, to no avail. It was stuck. He felt something by his foot and reached down. His fingers picked up a large clump of damp fur. The smell hit him, a foul odour, just as before.
"Who are you?"
The cabbie looked behind his shoulder, giving George a full-on glimpse at his grotesque face. Patches of fur were falling off where his skin should have been.
"Cyrus West, of course. People call me the cat."

The Mask Room

Evelyn Morley

It was an old carnival, one that drifted into town once a year, bringing with it an assortment of freakish attractions and ominous games. But it was the mask room that drew Felix, a dark booth set at the very edge of the grounds, where a grizzled old vendor sold dusty, twisted masks that looked unsettlingly realistic. They seemed to stare back at him, their hollow eyes filled with something close to malice. Felix, ever the thrill-seeker, chose the ugliest one – a face frozen in a grotesque sneer, the skin around its mouth twisted and unnatural.

The vendor's grin widened as Felix handed over the cash, his eyes glinting with something far too knowing.

"Once you put it on, you won't ever want to take it off," he rasped, his voice gravelly and cold. Felix laughed it off, lifting the mask to his face, feeling its rubbery surface press against his skin. The moment he pulled it over his head, a chill shot through him, cold as ice, spreading like fingers under his skin. His laughter died in his throat, replaced by a growing sense of unease.

As he glanced in the mirror nearby, he saw the mask's expression had changed. The sneer now looked more like a grin, sinister and sharp, and his own eyes stared back at him from its hollow sockets. Panic clawed at his chest. He tried to rip it off, but it wouldn't budge, the edges of the mask seeming to fuse with his skin. His fingers clawed desperately, nails scraping against the unyielding surface, but the mask tightened, moulding to his face, pressing against his bones.

He stumbled out of the booth, gasping, but no one seemed to notice his distress. When he screamed, the sound was muffled, swallowed by the mask. He tried to grab at people, to beg for help, but his movements were clumsy, as if his body was no longer his own. Through his horror, he realized people were laughing, admiring his 'mask,' each chuckle a twist of the knife.

Hours passed, or maybe days. The carnival packed up and left, and Felix was left alone, trapped behind the mask. His mind grew quiet, his thoughts slowed, and the mask's sneer became his own. When the carnival returned the following year, the vendor's booth had a new mask on display, frozen in a lifelike, agonized scream. And somewhere deep inside, Felix's fading consciousness screamed in silent horror, his voice forever swallowed by the mask.

K. L Bexon

Claire's unease dimmed only slightly in the presence of the phone's artificial light. She leaned over the hole, casting the beam under the house. From her position, she couldn't see much.

How come mum never told her about this hatch?

She looked back at the pile of her late mother's things by the door, charity bags ready to go. There could be more down there.

Claire bit her lip. There was just enough space to get in and crawl. She dropped in, falling to her hands and knees. Blackness yawned before her. She whipped her phone out in front of her, holding the light out like a weapon. Spiders skittered as she peered.

The darkness watched her from behind.

Eyes squinted, Claire tried to make out the lumpy shapes from her position under the safety of the open trapdoor. Was it more junk?

The dirt under her palm was cold. The air was dank with rot.

She shuffled along, one hand still outstretched with the light. The floor was full of large bulges; she clambered over each, her back pressing into wooden support beams. As she got closer, she thought she'd made out a squat, straight shape.

Her hand landed on something spongy, sending her off balance. Air sucked in between her teeth as she dropped her weight onto her unprepared elbow.

"Ah!"

Rubbing her bone, she cast the light onto her discovery. A cotton-white face with red cheeks grinned at her. The eyes of the stuffed doll stared emptily. Suppressing a shiver, she turned it face down.

Her nerves were getting the better of her. Claire shook her head and proceeded. She wasn't far from what she could now tell was a box.

It was dusty as she opened it- it clearly hadn't been touched in years.

Faces looked back at her, their youthful expressions frozen in a collection of photos with her mum. Claire swept one child's photo to the side, then another. Her brows creased. Who were they? Mum never mentioned other foster kids. Where had they gone?

She thought of her journey across the dirt. No.

A tightness gripped her gut.

She couldn't help it. Claire cast her phone light across the dirt floor, hand unsteady. She could see now how defined the mounds in the earth were. It couldn't be.

She desperately flicked between the photos, counting. Her throat contracted and released, bile threatening. Her knuckle caught the side of the box; it tipped over.

Forcing breath in and out, hot pools burned behind her eyes. Spilling out from the bottom of the box, littered across the pictures, were hundreds of tiny white chips. The phone light quivered.

Her brain pleaded with her not to look. Not to touch.

Frigid fingers crept forward.

Claire knelt in the dark, clutching one of the small fragments.

A strangled sound died in her throat.

Milk teeth.

The Creeping Shadows

Patrick Langford

Moving into her new home, Sarah felt a strange reluctance, an odd chill that lingered on her skin every time she thought of the place. The house had stood empty for years, shunned by the locals who claimed it was cursed, though none dared to say why. She brushed off their warnings, laughing it away, eager for the peace the countryside offered. But on Halloween night, the peace shattered as the house seemed to come alive around her, shadows flickering at the edges of her vision.

It started as a faint, slithering shape in the corners, barely noticeable. She tried ignoring it, thinking it was a trick of the light or the wind through the old windows. But as the hours crept by, the shadows grew more distinct, almost deliberate. They coiled along the walls, stretching over the ceiling, dark tendrils twisting and creeping closer with each flickering candle she lit. Her skin prickled with unease, each hair on her neck standing at attention as she felt eyes watching her from every direction.

Desperate, she turned on every light in the house, but the bulbs dimmed, then flickered out, one by one. Her breath quickened as the darkness thickened, pressing in, a tangible presence that felt both cold and alive. The shadows began to form faces, hollow eyes and gaping mouths emerging from the dark, each one staring at her, unblinking. She tried to scream, but her voice caught in her throat, strangled by the terror clawing at her chest.

Backing into a corner, she pressed herself against the wall, heart racing as the shadows closed in, brushing against her skin like cold fingers. She could feel them moving inside her mind, whispering in voices that scratched at her sanity, dark promises that twisted her thoughts. Her pulse thundered in her ears, her eyes wide as she realized the faces were hers – twisted versions of her own expression, each one screaming silently.

The last light bulb died, plunging her into complete darkness. For a heartbeat, all was silent. Then, the shadows surged forward, filling her vision, pressing into her until she could no longer breathe. Her scream finally escaped, but it was swallowed by the silence, fading into the darkness as the shadows claimed her. By morning, the house stood empty once more, but the walls bore a new pattern, faint, twisted faces etched into the shadows, their hollow eyes forever watching.

Little Girl

Kate Lake

The tea kettle screamed on the stove. Mariel dashed across the kitchen, phone in hand. Without looking up, she filled her waiting mug with boiling water, releasing the scent of jasmine. Her eager fingers scrolled through images of vintage paintings, all available locally for bargain prices. Mariel dunked her teabag and scowled at the empty spot on her gallery wall. It was driving her batty, that empty spot. Everywhere else, her vintage look was complete. There were mid-century sofas and lamps, pristine examples of coloured glass, a stunning, threadbare Oriental rug, and the art! All original oil paintings from the mid-twentieth century. For weeks now, she'd sought a final piece to complete the arrangement. Something large and eye-catching without being too bright.

Mariel resumed scrolling, then gasped. The image on the screen showed a painting of a small child, maybe four years old. The listing read, 'Little Girl,' and stated it was two by three feet. It would fit the spot perfectly! She made arrangements and brought the piece home later that afternoon, hanging it right away.

The little girl sat calmly. She had cropped blonde hair, a high forehead, and large, deep-set eyes. Her face was gaunt and shadowed. In her thin fingers, she held a doll with pink cheeks and rosebud lips, but the little girl's cheeks were sallow, her lips pale and thin. The effect was striking. Hands on hips, Mariel surveyed her space. Perfection! Though it had not been her habit, Mariel spoke aloud to the empty room.

"I love you, little girl," she declared. "I'm so glad you're here."

Mariel found herself talking to the child often. Telling it about her chaotic job, her disappointing dates. She began calling the child Beverly, which just fit somehow. And Beverly, for her part, seemed quite attentive, compassionate even, with her troubled eyes.

"Maybe I do deserve a raise," Mariel might say. Or "You were right, Beverly. That guy I met online was a real cad." Beverly always responded, and Mariel found her advice to be spot-on.

"No man truly appreciates a powerful woman," Beverly would say. Or "A girl needs to put herself first because no one else ever will."

When Mariel brought a man home in February, he spoke disgracefully and tracked mud across the rug.

"This is an occasion for my special tea," Beverly said. Beverly sometimes called it 'clari-tea,' or sometimes 'tranquili-tea' or 'sani-tea.' Mariel knew just what Beverly meant, and she had to agree. She took a darling vintage mug from the cupboard and served him up a steaming cup of jasmine tea with just enough arsenic to do the trick.

"A happy night is one spent in the company of a friend," said Beverly, and Mariel couldn't disagree. She was never unhappy anymore. She had everything she needed right there in her perfect little condo, in her perfect room, where everything was exactly the way it was meant to be.

The Harvest Feast

Martha Galloway

The Harvest Feast was a ritual older than anyone in town could recall. Every Halloween night, the townsfolk would gather in the old barn at the edge of town, to share a meal and give thanks. Edith had always found it strange, almost sacred, but this year the air felt heavier, charged with something dark and foreboding.

As she took her seat, she noticed an odd smell. It was thick and metallic, almost like blood, mixed with a damp, earthy scent that reminded her of wet leaves and decay. She glanced around, but the other guests seemed entranced, their eyes glazed over as they stared blankly at the dishes set before them. Bowls of stew, crusty bread, and a strange red sauce were passed around, and Edith found herself spooning a portion into her bowl, her hands moving automatically, as though compelled.

The moment she raised the spoon to her lips, she noticed a brittle bone fragment swimming in her stew. She froze, her heart hammering as her eyes darted around the room, wondering if anyone else had noticed. But they were all eating in silence, faces expressionless, their eyes fixed on their bowls. Her stomach churned as she picked through the stew and found more bones, small and delicate – too small to belong to any animal she knew.

Her first instinct was to leave, but just as she tried to stand, two men beside her placed firm hands on her shoulders, forcing her back down. She turned, fear turning her blood cold as she met their blank, unblinking gazes.

“Your part of the harvest now,” one of them murmured, his voice low and empty of emotion. He handed her another bowl, one filled to the brim with a thick, red sauce, its surface slick and dark.

Inside the bowl, something gleamed – a small ring, unmistakably her grandmother’s, one that had disappeared years ago without a trace. A chill gripped her as she realized that the very stew she was eating contained her grandmother, and likely others who had vanished over the years. She opened her mouth to scream, but before she could, the voices around her began to hum a strange, haunting tune.

“Eat up, Edith,” someone whispered, stroking her hair. She tried to pull away, but her limbs felt heavy, her mind clouded with a growing haze of compliance. Against her will, she lifted the spoon to her mouth, each bite thick and bitter, filled with a taste of metal and earth. The taste seeped into her, numbing her thoughts, clouding her memories. Her own reflection blurred in the dark liquid, but something else stared back – her grandmother’s eyes, hollow and accusing.

The whispers grew louder, weaving through her mind until her last thought faded. The townsfolk continued their feast, their faces empty as they ate in silence, honouring the harvest. By morning, the barn would be empty, the earth newly turned, and the townsfolk sated, until next year’s harvest called again.

The Passenger

Khala Grace

Wind whips across the freeway. Heavy rain pours down on the windows of a tractor trailer. The driver puts on his hazards and lowers his speed. After a half an hour, static on the radio crackles.

"Heath! Keep up that pace!" A gruff man's voice breaks through.

"Come on Lawrence!" The young man rolls his eyes. "I know it's all sunshine and kittens over there. But here's a storm. You know me, I can't break my neck or someone else's just because you want me to go faster."

"As soon as that weather clears," Lawrence scoffs. "You better book it."

"Safety is my name," Heath retorts. "You know that and so does old man Mitch. Last I checked, he still owns the joint."

A stream of insults carries along the radio. Heath ignores them.

"Can't... hear you..." He adds while mimicking static. "There's... too much... lightning... gotta go."

Heath hangs up the radio. A truck stop appears on the right. He takes his leave and rests until the storm eases. *A lil nap is needed.* His thoughts ring. Heath falls asleep to the sound of rain. As the melody diminishes, he wakes up with a yawn.

"Time to head out." He stretches his back.

Time passes and the road is landlocked. Cars that pulled over previously are now thwarting the traffic flow as they return to the road. Heath shrugs but doesn't complain. *You can't fix what you can't change.* He concludes.

Suddenly, a series of beats hit the side of the truck. Alarmed, Heath puts the vehicle in park and hits the hazards.

"Who's there?" He cries out while leaning with a pocketknife in hand. Heath's eyes widen. "What the hell are you doing on the road, miss?"

"Help!" A young woman sobs. She has scratches and bruises along her body. "My car crashed, and I need to get to the next exit."

Heath is taken aback. *'Should I trust her?'* He wonders. After a beat, he puts the knife away.

"Hop on in." He pats the passenger seat.

"Thank you!" She smiles.

Traffic clears and it's smooth sailing...

"I gotta call the station," Heath asserts. "This way they know why I'm going to be off course."

The young woman doesn't respond. She wipes tears from her cheeks and glances outside. Heath sighs. *Must be shaken up.* Heath muses. *That's understandable.* He works with the radio only to find nothing but static.

"Come in Lawrence," He calls. "Can you hear me?"

Without a reply, Heath flusters and hits the radio.

"Sorry about that." He turns to the stranger. Heath slams the brakes. "What the hell?"

The passenger seat is empty. Heath pulls towards the side of the road. He readies the truck for a state of emergency. Once the cones are settled, Heath can't help but to investigate.

"Where are you?" He shouts.

Then, his eyes lock onto a figure. Heath hobbles down the muddy hill.

"Fuck!" Heath curses.

There, the young woman's corpse lies in a ditch.

The Living Scarecrow

Jameson Archer

Every Halloween, the scarecrow appeared in Old Man Callahan's field, standing stiff and menacing, its stitched grin and hollow eyes a chilling sight against the moonlit cornrows. No one knew where it came from; each year, it simply showed up in the field, watching over the dying crops with its head tilted at an unnatural angle. The town's children whispered stories about it, but none dared get too close.

This Halloween, Billy and his friends dared each other to touch it. As they snuck onto Callahan's field, the air grew colder, and a low wind rustled the corn, filling the silence with a hushed, eerie sound. The scarecrow loomed ahead, its faded jacket hanging loosely on a thin, twisted frame. Billy stepped closer, squinting in the dim light. Something about it seemed different this year. Real hair poked from beneath the scarecrow's worn hat, and the eyes – they weren't made of buttons or paint; they looked almost… human.

"Go on, Billy, touch it!" one of his friends hissed, barely containing nervous laughter. Not wanting to look afraid, Billy reached out, his fingers brushing the scarecrow's arm. His hand jerked back as he felt warmth – not the cold straw he'd expected, but something soft and pliable. It felt like flesh. His heart pounded as he took a step back, but the scarecrow's head turned, its gaze locking onto him.

In the silence, Billy heard a low, rasping whisper.

"You're just what I need," the scarecrow murmured, its grin stretching wider. Before he could react, its stitched fingers twitched, reaching toward him. He tried to run, but his feet were rooted to the ground, his body frozen in terror as the scarecrow moved, each step slow and jerky, but relentless. His friends, paralyzed with fear, could only watch.

The scarecrow's hand gripped his arm, its straw fingers pressing into his flesh-like nails.

"It's been so long," it hissed, pulling him close, its mouth stretching impossibly wide. Billy struggled, but his limbs wouldn't obey, as if the scarecrow's touch drained his strength. Shadows gathered around them, dark tendrils wrapping around his legs, his arms, until he could barely move. The last thing he saw was the scarecrow's hollow eyes, glinting with a cruel satisfaction.

The next morning, the townsfolk found a new scarecrow in Callahan's field, dressed in a familiar jacket, its head slumped forward, and its mouth stitched into a silent scream. The children who passed by swore they heard it whispering their names, its hollow eyes following them as they walked by, but no one dared get close enough to check. Billy's disappearance was filed away as just another Halloween mystery, while the scarecrow stood watch, waiting patiently for the next visitor.

What Lies Beyond the Door

(November's Winner)

Cedric Rhodes

The parents, Claire and David, never understood why their infant, Lily, was terrified of the basement door. Every time it swung open, her little face twisted with horror, and she'd wail as if something dreadful waited beyond the threshold. They'd searched the basement countless times, finding nothing but dust and storage boxes, but Lily's fear only grew. The crying was relentless whenever the door was open, and their own nerves began to fray.

Desperate, they took Lily to a child psychologist who specialized in early childhood anxieties. After hearing their story, the psychologist recommended an unusual approach:

"Take her home, open the door, leave her in the kitchen alone, and see if she can face whatever scares her."

They thought it sounded strange, even cruel, but they were desperate for something to help their daughter.

So they tried it.

Claire and David sat in the living room, listening to their daughter cry, her screams echoing through the house. Each wail felt like a dagger to Claire's heart, and she fought the urge to rush to Lily, to comfort her.

“She’s scared, David,” she whispered, her voice trembling. But David held her back gently, urging her to trust the psychologist's advice.

“We have to give her a chance,” he insisted, and Claire, though reluctant, nodded in agreement, knowing they were both out of options. Minutes turned into an hour, her wails piercing and desperate—and then, abruptly, silence. Uneasy, they waited, hoping that maybe the psychologist was right, that Lily simply needed to face her fear. After a few more minutes, they cautiously returned to the kitchen.

They found Lily sitting silently, her back to them, staring wide-eyed at the open basement door. But when they drew closer, they noticed her lips moving, whispering something over and over. Her voice, barely audible, repeated, “Don’t look at the man in the shadows.”

Claire’s blood ran cold. Until that moment, Lily had never spoken in a complete sentence, just the usual babbles and single words. Yet here she was, calmly warning them, her words far too clear.

Then, as Lily’s whispers turned to laughter—a laugh that sounded far, far too old for a child her age—Claire’s gaze drifted to the basement door. There, in the doorway, stood a figure as white as bone, eyes dark as midnight, swallowing the light around them, void of any warmth or humanity. The darkness seemed to pulse with malevolence, and Claire felt a chill grip her heart. She blinked, and the figure was gone, leaving only the open, empty doorway.

David, meanwhile, heard a strange noise upstairs and went to check, mutually agreeing with Claire that he should investigate while she stayed with Lily. She stood there, her nerves stretched thin, expecting David to return any moment. But the kitchen remained quiet, save for Lily’s strange, soft laughter echoing around her.

As Claire clutched Lily, she felt a sudden chill—a cold breath against her neck, as if someone was standing just behind her. She dared not turn around, instead backing slowly away from the basement door with Lily in her arms.

The air felt thick, and heavy, pressing down on her.

Just as she was about to leave the kitchen, a soft whisper drifted up from the basement:

"See you soon."

Silent Night Shadows

Arthur Greaves

Snow blanketed Pinecrest Manor, transforming the ancient house into a serene, white sanctuary. Inside, the Hartley family gathered around the grand fireplace, the scent of pine and cinnamon blending with the crackling logs. It was Christmas Eve, a night steeped in joy and tradition.

Emma Hartley admired the towering Christmas tree, its twinkling lights and heirloom ornaments each holding memories of years past. Her children, Lily and Jack, giggled as they unwrapped presents, their excitement filling the room. David, her husband, shared a warm smile, cherishing the moment of familial bliss.

As midnight approached, Emma felt a chill despite the roaring fire. She excused herself to retrieve a forgotten ornament from the attic, a cherished annual tradition. The narrow staircase creaked under her weight, shadows dancing on the walls from the flickering candle she held. In the attic, she found the old ornament box, its surface covered in dust.

When she lifted the lid, a sudden draft extinguished her candle, plunging her into darkness. Emma's heart raced as she fumbled for her flashlight, its beam piercing the gloom. Inside the box lay a delicate glass angel, its wings tarnished yet still beautiful. She reached for it, an inexplicable unease settling over her.

A soft melody drifted down—the familiar strains of "Silent Night." Emma descended the stairs, the angel clutched tightly in her hand. In the living room, the family sat quietly, the room dim except for the tree's glow. Something felt off. The air was thick, heavy with an unseen presence.

"Lily, Jack, come here," Emma called softly. The children obeyed, their faces pale. David stood, sensing her distress.

Suddenly, the music twisted, the notes becoming discordant and eerie. The temperature plummeted; their breaths visible in the cold air.

From the shadows beneath the tree, a figure emerged. Clad in a tattered red suit, its eyes hollow and empty, it extended a skeletal hand holding a broken ornament.

"Another year forgotten," it whispered, its voice like the rustling of dead leaves.

Emma stepped forward, shielding her children. "Who are you?"

The figure's smile was a slash of darkness. "I am the forgotten spirit of Christmas past, seeking what was lost."

Jack trembled, clutching his sister. "We haven't forgotten anything. Please, leave us alone."

The spirit laughed, a sound that echoed unnaturally. "Memories fade, traditions break. Without them, the darkness grows."

Emma felt a pull towards the angel in her hand. Horror dawned on her—it was the key. "What do you want?"

"Restore what was taken," the spirit demanded. "Bring back the true spirit or succumb to eternal night."

Determined, Emma placed the angel atop the tree. Instantly, the room filled with radiant light, dispelling the shadows. The spirit writhed, its form destabilizing.

"Remember," it hissed before dissolving into the air, leaving a lingering chill.

The family stood in silence; the oppressive weight lifted. The music returned to its gentle melody, and the warmth of the fire embraced them once more. Emma hugged her children tightly, grateful for their safety.

As they settled back by the hearth, the angel shimmered softly, a reminder of the night's ordeal. Pinecrest Manor felt alive with renewed spirit, the true meaning of Christmas restored. Yet, in the stillness, a faint whisper lingered: "Remember always."

Emma smiled, understanding that some traditions were kept not just for joy, but to guard against the darkness that creeps in when memories fade. This Christmas Eve had been a test, and together, the Hartley's had ensured that the light would never dim.

The Lynnewood Game: Season One Review

James Fritz

A haunted mansion with 110 rooms, twelve contestants, and $1 million. Stay inside the longest, and you win. Food and drink are provided. No violence allowed. Any contestant can withdraw at any time.

Welcome to *The Lynnewood Game.*

It was touted as the scariest TV show in the world. Thousands applied. Twelve received blood-red invitations in the mail and booked it to Lynnewood Hall in Pennsylvania. Filming wrapped in two months. The entire first season was set to drop on Halloween.

While millions of kids were out Trick-or-Treating, horror enthusiasts binge-watched the show. During the first episode, all twelve contestants were introduced. Alliances were formed, boundaries set, rivalries planted. All twelve made it through the first week. By the middle of episode Two, none of the contestants had any reason to leave. No spooky noises, no flashing lights, no midnight apparitions.

That's when the first disappearance occurred. Dorothy Maher, 72, a retired mortician from St. Louis. Everybody was baffled. Did she withdraw and leave her husband, Russell, in the lurch? Did she get lost? A day-long search by the other contestants yielded nothing… except another disappearance. Winnie Wyn, 27, a collegiate from the West Coast.

Panic set in. Some contestants tried to withdraw but found the front doors locked from the outside. Barring another disappearance, nobody could leave. The remaining ten slept together inside the kitchen that night and took guard shifts.

At the start of episode Four, there was another disappearance. Not of a contestant, but of the food supply. Yet another mansion-wide search came up empty. Blame spread. Near the end of the episode, a brawl broke out in the dining room. Amazingly, nobody from the show intervened despite the fact that the rules seemed to have disappeared, too.

By this point, two opposing factions emerged and occupied separate parts of the mansion: Feast and Famine (F&F), and the Blood Soakers. Some of the contestants forged weapons. In addition to the threat of disappearing, anybody caught wandering into enemy territory risked capture and torture. Each side suspected the other of stealing the food supply. A large-scale conflict seemed imminent.

Towards the end of the season, after weeks without sustenance, the cannibalism started. Russell was an easy choice after expiring of a heart attack in episode Seven. The others proved less willing. Half of the contestants remained.

On the show's final episode, a fire started in the grand ball room and quickly spread to the rest of the mansion. Members of F&F had to cross into enemy territory to escape the inferno and were massacred by the Blood Soakers. After repeated attempts to control the fire, the final two contestants committed suicide in the entrance hall.

Investigations into Irreality, the now-defunct entertainment company that produced the show, have turned up nothing. The police have also been unable to identify the whereabouts of any of the twelve contestants.

Crimson Noel

Beatrice Lorne

Ravens Hollow was renowned for its idyllic Christmases, where snow-covered rooftops and twinkling lights created a perfect holiday postcard. Yet, beneath this festive facade, dark legends whispered of shadows that emerged each Christmas Eve.

Margaret "Maggie" Collins had returned to Ravens Hollow after her husband David mysteriously vanished five years prior. She inherited the sprawling Whitaker Manor, an imposing Victorian mansion on the town's outskirts, cloaked by ancient pines. Determined to rebuild her life and uncover the truth behind David's disappearance, Maggie decided to spend Christmas alone in the manor.

Preparations were meticulous. Maggie adorned the grand hall with ornaments and lights, attempting to breathe life into the cold, empty rooms. Her only companion was Midnight, a sleek black cat with eyes that seemed to pierce the darkness. Neighbours offered cautious greetings, their gazes lingering on the manor with unspoken fears.

On Christmas Eve, a fierce snowstorm enveloped Ravens Hollow, severing all connections. Inside the manor, Maggie settled by the fireplace, the flames casting long, flickering shadows. She sipped mulled wine, the rich aroma barely masking her anxiety. Midnight curled beside her; eyes fixed on the darkened windows.

As midnight approached, an unsettling silence filled the house. The wind howled outside, and the trees groaned under the weight of the snow. Maggie tried to dismiss the growing unease, attributing it to loneliness. Then, a faint, melancholic carol echoed through the halls, its haunting melody sending chills down her spine.

Drawn to the sound, Maggie followed it to the attic—a place she had avoided since David's disappearance. The attic door creaked open, revealing a room bathed in eerie moonlight streaming through a dusty window. In the centre stood a cracked mirror, reflecting not her image but a shadowy figure in old-fashioned Christmas attire.

"Maggie," the figure whispered, its voice hollow and echoing. Her heart raced as memories of David's laughter and his promise to return flooded her mind. "Join us," it intoned, gesturing toward the mirror. The reflection showed a festive gathering, faces gaunt and eyes hollow, mouths twisted in silent screams.

Midnight hissed, tugging at Maggie's sleeve. She turned to flee, but the attic door slammed shut. The temperature plummeted; her breath visible in the icy air. The figure reached out, tendrils of darkness swirling around Maggie's feet, pulling her toward the glass.

Desperate, Maggie grabbed a heavy ornament and smashed the mirror. Shards flew, and the ghostly carol shattered into agonized wails. The darkness recoiled, replaced by a blinding light. The attic door burst open, and Maggie stumbled down, heart pounding.

In the grand hall stood David, his eyes hollow yet alive.

"You broke the curse," he whispered, embracing her tightly. The manor seemed to breathe a sigh of relief, the oppressive atmosphere lifting. Midnight rubbed against her legs, purring in comfort.

As dawn broke, the storm subsided, and Ravens Hollow awoke to a peaceful Christmas morning. Maggie and David left Whitaker Manor, its windows now clear and inviting.

Graveyard Boots

Pip Pinkerton

They were the ugliest shoes she had ever seen.

Hannah Goodridge worked in the gift shop of the Windsor, Connecticut Museum of Witchcraft. She was working her way through community college, getting her generals, but her dream was to become a history major and study pagan European history and folklore. That was a long way away though, so, for now, she just had to stare at these ugly shoes every night.

The shoes were awful. They were of a decomposing black leather that looked like it had reverted partially back to the bovine flesh it had been before. The shoes themselves looked to be holding on by nothing more than a wing and a prayer, or in this case, maybe a devil wing and spell. The stitching was almost nonexistent, and where there were stitches, they poked out through the shoe, all coarse and wiry, almost like the sinewy little fingers of some diminutive skeleton trying to escape from inside. Hannah thought of the little old lady who lived in a shoe and all her children and shuddered.

The shoes, pointy toed in the front and high-heeled in the back, *looked* like they would belong to a witch… or in a Tim Burton movie. Only, these shoes were much grittier than anything you'd ever seen in Hollywood. These shoes were old, worn, and fragile looking, though Hannah thought they were sturdier than they looked.

She had seen these shoes a thousand times, examined them intricately in her off time, and was familiar with all their nuances. There were the scorched bottoms and sides from when their previous owner was burned and reportedly thrashed so wildly that she had kicked both shoes clear off her feet. There were the cemented-on chunks of dirt and crud from untold midnight orgies, which had now become as much a part of the shoes as were the tongue and laces. Today, however, Hannah noticed something she had never noticed before. The left shoe had two drops of what looked like blood on it.

Hannah stared intently at the shoe, and before her eyes, another dark liquid droplet appeared. That is when she realized how cold it had become in the museum, how abnormally dark. The place didn't even feel the same anymore, and Hannah was afraid to take her eyes off the shoes, for fear she wouldn't be in the museum any longer.

Hannah gazed fearfully into the abysmal black leather, watching as more droplets of blood seemed to appear out of nowhere, until it looked like wherever the shoes were really standing, it was raining blood.

Hannah couldn't take it anymore. She was about to look away and make for the entrance door of the museum that may or may be there anymore, but then she heard a noise above the shoes. It was a boisterous, maniacal cackling that made her blood run cold. It was coming from approximately where someone's head would be, had someone been wearing the shoes.

Whispers in the Walls

Nathaniel Crowe

Clara tightened her grip on the flashlight, its beam slicing through the darkness of the Victorian townhouse. The storm outside raged, rain pounding against the windows and thunder rattling the old structure. Every creak and groan of the house amplified her anxiety. She paused, listening as faint whispers floated through the halls, their voices barely audible but unmistakably pleading.

Heart racing, Clara followed the sound, her footsteps echoing in the empty corridors. The whispers grew louder, guiding her to the attic door. It stood slightly ajar, shadows dancing around its frame. Taking a deep breath, she pushed the door open, the hinges groaning in protest. The attic was cluttered with antique furniture and faded portraits whose eyes seemed to follow her every move.

The whispers swelled into desperate pleas, wrapping around her like icy fingers. In the center of the room stood a grand, cracked mirror. Clara approached, her reflection wavering and distorting. The glass rippled, and a pale figure with hollow eyes emerged from her reflection, reaching out with skeletal hands. An invisible force seized her wrist, pulling her toward the mirror.

Shadows twisted into grotesque shapes, pressing in from all sides. Clara's breath quickened as the room seemed to close in, the oppressive atmosphere thick with malevolence. The whispers turned to agonized screams, filling her mind with fear. She struggled against the grip, her muscles burning with effort.

Summoning every ounce of courage, Clara tore her gaze away from the mirror, breaking the spectral connection. The figure recoiled, its icy grip loosening. She stumbled back, racing down the attic stairs as the oppressive energy lifted abruptly. The whispers faded, leaving only the sound of her pounding heart.

Clara fled the house that night, leaving behind the townhouse and its dark secrets. In her new apartment, shadows lingered at the edges of her vision, and faint whispers haunted her dreams. Determined to understand, she returned years later, discovering old diaries that spoke of a vengeful spirit bound to the mirror. Under a waning moon, she performed a ritual of closure, chanting words of peace.

As dawn broke, the house seemed to exhale, the oppressive presence lifting for the first time. Clara walked away, the morning light casting long shadows behind her. The mirror lay shattered, its remnants glistening like broken dreams. She never returned, but the memory of that night lingered—a reminder that some houses whisper secrets meant to remain hidden.

Family Ties

Pip Pinkerton

The baby lay in a pram, dressed in a black, hooded onesie, seeming to stare up at Ronnie with its featureless face, the blank visage almost an exact duplicate of that of its mother, a mannequin dressed in a black evening dress, who also seemed to be staring at him, though neither had any eyes. Worse yet was the mannequin father, dressed in a suit that was supposed to be business-like but looked funerary even in the best of lighting. Ronnie swore he saw the father's head move once.

Ronald 'Ronnie' Wilson worked at Serling's Mega Mall and absolutely loved it. He was alone all the time, could listen to whatever music he wanted as loud as he wanted, and he could even get high. Not only was his job awesome, but it was also full-time, with benefits. The only part of his job he didn't like were the mannequins, especially the aforementioned mannequin family, who just happened to be located in the darkest, creepiest part of the mall.

Ronnie had just gotten back in from a cigarette and a couple hits off his vape pen, so, when he went to go take out the trash in that black, shadowy section of the mall, he wondered if maybe he had gotten a little too stoned, because before he went out, he swore the male mannequin had been wearing its suit jacket, just like it always did, but now the jacket was folded over its arm.

"Why you gotta be all spooky like that and shit? Don't be doing no creepy-ass, mannequin moving when I'm not looking shit. That's not even a little cool," Ronnie said, a little too nervously.

The male mannequin turned his head toward Ronnie, so did the female, at almost exactly the same time. Ronnie could feel his blood get hot and his lungs tighten. He had never experienced fear like this before. He started screaming just as the baby mannequin turned to look at him as well.

Ronnie turned to run away, but not before seeing the male and female mannequins' legs begin to move. He only got a few yards before he heard their hard plastic feet against the cold tile of the mall floor. Worse yet, he could hear the baby mannequin giggling, even though it had no mouth. It didn't make any sense. None of it did.

Ronnie was almost to the gate, which he could've hopefully closed behind him before they reached him, he was almost to salvation. Ronnie reached one arm past the threshold when he felt hard, inhuman hands grasp him turbulently. He made one final lunge forward, giving it everything he had to reach freedom, burning every ounce of energy he had in reserve. Ronnie thought he was going to make it for one bright second, before he was aggressively pulled backward into the darkness, into the shadows. It wasn't long before the empty mall began to echo with screams of agony intermixed with bursts of blasphemously cherubic giggling.

The Midnight Caller

Nathaniel Crowe

Ethan savoured the solitude of his secluded cabin, nestled deep within the whispering woods. The only sounds were the rustle of leaves and the distant hoot of an owl. One night, as midnight approached, the silence was shattered by the persistent ringing of his old landline phone. He glanced around; no one else for miles.

With hesitant fingers, he answered. "Hello?"

"Help me," a voice rasped, sending a chill down his spine.

Ethan's heart pounded. "Who is this?"

The voice remained silent; the line dead before he could respond. Shaking, he tried to dismiss it as a prank, but the calls continued every midnight. Each night, the voice grew more desperate, snippets of a lost family's memories intertwined with pleas for rescue.

Sleep eluded him as obsession took hold. Ethan delved into the cabin's history, uncovering stories of the Millers—a family that vanished without a trace decades ago. Neighbours whispered of unexplained phone calls and sightings of ghostly figures near the property.

Determined to end the torment, Ethan stayed awake one stormy night, the wind howling outside like restless spirits. At midnight, the phone rang again. This time, the voice guided him to the basement. Heart racing, Ethan grabbed a flashlight and descended the creaky stairs, each step echoing in the oppressive darkness.

The basement was a time capsule: old furniture covered in dust; a single landline phone disconnected yet humming with static. As he approached, spectral figures materialized—ghostly apparitions of the missing family, their eyes hollow with sorrow. They reached out, their fingers icy against his skin, pulling him toward the phone.

Ethan stumbled back, panic surging as the apparitions' whispers filled the air. Desperate, he hurled the phone across the room. It shattered against the wall, releasing a burst of dark energy that repelled the spirits. The basement returned to normal, the oppressive atmosphere lifting as silence reclaimed the space.

Exhausted, Ethan fled the cabin, the memory of the haunted calls etched into his mind. Determined to put the past to rest, he documented his experiences, sharing the Millers' tragic story with the world. The narrative brought peace to the restless souls, their presence fading as their story was finally told. The phone never rang again, and Ethan left the cabin behind, forever changed by the night he faced the vengeful spirits of the lost family.

A Great Way to Scare Someone

Greg Beatty

"Do you know what would be a great way to scare someone!" Davy asked, popping up from behind the couch. It wasn't really a question.

"Oh my gosh!" His dad staggered back a few steps and clutched his chest. "Davy, you've got to be more careful. I'm not a young man anymore."

Davy gave a scratchy laugh and said, "Got you. Got you again."

"Yeah, you got me. So, what's your idea this time?"

But Davy was gone, and the room was silent.

Davy's dad searched for his son in a careful and melancholy fashion, without the anxiety that had driven his searches in the first 30 years his son had been appearing and disappearing. He didn't expect to find Davy. He never did. But he had to look, just in case. There wasn't enough space behind the couch for his boy. He moved it anyway. There wasn't enough room for his son between the throw pillows. He split them anyway.

Finally, he gave up, and shuffled off to the kitchen, to microwave his frozen dinner. It was Tuesday. That meant Salisbury steak and creamed corn.

While he tore the cardboard package open with a practiced pinky, he muttered to himself, "Do you know what would be a great way to scare someone?"

The microwave beeped, but did not otherwise answer.

"If you just never appeared out of the blue ever again. That, that would be scary."

And then he blew on his dinner until it was almost as cool as his dim and empty house.

The Silent Room

Nathaniel Crowe

Mark had always been fascinated by abandoned buildings, drawn to their silent stories and forgotten secrets. When he heard about the old psychiatric hospital on the outskirts of town, he couldn't resist exploring it. Armed with a flashlight and his camera, he ventured inside on a chilly October evening.

The hospital loomed before him, its windows shattered and doors hanging ajar. Mark pushed the heavy front door open, the hinges creaking in protest. The air inside was thick with dust, and the scent of decay filled his nostrils. His flashlight beam danced across peeling wallpaper and broken furniture as he navigated the darkened halls.

He reached the administration wing, where a single room stood eerily untouched. The door was slightly ajar, and a faint light emanated from within. Curiosity piqued, Mark stepped inside, finding a pristine office preserved in time. A large wooden desk dominated the room, papers neatly stacked and a rotary phone on the corner.

As he approached the desk, the temperature dropped sharply. Mark shivered, wrapping his jacket tighter. He noticed a door at the far end of the room, slightly ajar. Before he could investigate further, the silent room was pierced by a loud bang as the door slammed shut behind him. Panic surged through him as he realized he was trapped.

Mark rushed to the door, pulling and shaking it, but it wouldn't budge. The room seemed to close in, the walls pressing tighter around him. He turned to the desk, where the rotary phone began to ring, its shrill tone echoing unnaturally loud in the confined space. His hands trembled as he picked it up, the receiver cold against his skin.

"No one should be here," a distorted voice whispered, sending chills down his spine. Mark's breath quickened as he tried to respond, but his voice faltered. The lights flickered, casting fleeting glimpses of shadowy figures standing at the edges of the room, their faces obscured and expressions void of emotion.

Desperate, Mark slammed the phone against the desk, the ringing stopping abruptly. The oppressive atmosphere lifted slightly, and the door creaked open. Without hesitation, he bolted from the room, sprinting down the corridor and out of the hospital into the safety of the night.

Breathless and shaken, Mark looked back at the hospital, its windows staring blankly into the darkness. He never spoke of what he experienced that night, but the memory haunted him. The silent room remained a mystery, its dark secrets locked away, waiting for the next curious soul to uncover its chilling truth.

Ms. Winters Christmas Collection

Emecheta Christian

December was Ms. Winters' favourite time of year. As the holidays approached, she would make her preparations, eagerly anticipating the additions to her macabre collection. An old, ornate snow globe sat at the centre of it all, its brass base etched with strange, unsettling symbols.

This year, Ms. Winters knew exactly who her next target would be—a young boy, no more than seven years old, who she had spotted alone by the toy trains in the bustling department store. With her prize possession hidden in her coat pocket, she approached the unsuspecting child.

"Would you like to see something magical?" she asked sweetly, her eyes gleaming with a twisted excitement.

The boy, drawn in by her kindly demeanour, peered into the snow globe. Instantly, the gentle flurry of snow within transformed into a violent, swirling turbulence. To the child's horror, he began to make out tiny, humanoid figures dancing endlessly through the blizzard. One figure in particular caught his eye—it bore an uncanny resemblance to Tommy, a classmate who had gone missing the previous Christmas.

Before the boy could react, Ms. Winters gently placed the cold glass against his fingertip. At that moment, his world went dark, and he found himself trapped within the confines of the enchanted snow globe, doomed to join the other lost children in their eternal, frozen fanfare.

Back at her home, Ms. Winters carefully placed the newest addition to her collection on the mantel, its occupant desperately pressing against the glass, his muffled cries for help going unheard. Eleven other snow globes lined the shelves, each containing the frozen forms of children who had met a similar fate over the past years.

Ms. Winters smiled, savouring the satisfaction of her macabre hobby. The police had been investigating the disappearances, but they would never find the bodies or traces, not when the kids had been trapped in snow globes.

As Christmas drew nearer, Ms. Winters knew she needed just one more to complete her set. She had her eye on a little girl with rosy cheeks and a bright, pink scarf—the perfect addition to her growing collection.

The police would continue their futile search, unaware of the true horror that lay hidden in plain sight. For Ms. Winters, the holiday season was a time of dark celebration, a twisted ritual where she could indulge her insatiable desire to capture the innocent and imprison them in her twisted version of a winter wonderland.

The Forgotten Dollhouse

Isabelle Keene

Emma had inherited her grandmother's antique shop, a quaint store filled with relics from bygone eras. Among the treasures was a meticulously crafted dollhouse, its intricate details and lifelike dolls captivating visitors. Emma loved displaying it prominently, a favourite among the shop's patrons.

One rainy afternoon, a mysterious woman cloaked in black entered the shop. Her eyes were piercing, and she moved with an unsettling grace. She approached the dollhouse, her gaze fixed on the miniature figures. Without a word, she handed Emma an old, weathered key and whispered, "It's time."

Curiosity and unease mingled within Emma as she examined the key. It fit perfectly into a hidden lock beneath the dollhouse's foundation. Heart pounding, she turned it, and a section of the floor slid open, revealing a narrow staircase leading downward. Despite her fear, Emma felt compelled to explore.

She descended the steps, the air growing colder with each step. The passage led to a hidden basement, lit by a single, flickering bulb. The room was filled with lifelike dolls, their eyes following her every movement. In the centre stood a grand table, covered in dusty parchment and strange symbols.

As Emma approached the table, the dolls began to move, their tiny hands reaching out as if trying to grasp her. The air thickened, and the temperature dropped further. Whispered chants filled the room, the words unintelligible yet filled with malice. Emma felt a presence pressing against her, the dolls' intentions clear—they were not mere decorations but guardians of a dark secret.

Panicking, Emma turned to flee, but the door had vanished, replaced by a solid wall. The dolls surrounded her, their movements synchronized in a nightmarish dance. One doll, larger than the rest, stepped forward, its glassy eyes gleaming with malevolence. It raised a tiny hand, and the symbols on the table began to glow with an eerie light.

Emma realized too late that she had unleashed something ancient and malevolent. The room seemed to warp, the walls closing in as the chanting grew louder, transforming into agonized screams. Desperation surged through her as she tried to back away, but invisible forces held her in place.

In a final, frantic effort, Emma grasped the dollhouse above, pulling it back into the shop. The basement collapsed, sealing the dark secret once more. Gasping for breath, she found herself back in the antique shop, the dollhouse now silent and still.

Shaken, Emma decided to hide the key and never speak of the incident. Yet, late at night, she could hear faint whispers emanating from the dollhouse, a haunting reminder that some secrets are better left forgotten. The dolls' eyes seemed to watch her, waiting for the day they could once again reach out and reclaim what was theirs.

What Happened to Mr Vespers?

(December's Winner)

CJ Hooper

Lying on the floor he'd watched the dust fall slowly and settle around him. All of his energy long since spent in trying to open the trap door or reach the shutters. There was no furniture to aid his escape, no handle on this side of the trap door, what purchase he could get was meagre, painful and futile. A few weak shafts of moonlight had made it between the shutter slats, so he could see the dried blood on what remained of his nails and the paper-thin skin that hung loosely over his brittle bones, wrinkled and torn in places where his attempts to escape had taken their toll. Moving was now an agonising act that involved grating his weak limbs across the rough floor, and the last time that he'd tried to stand his knee had fully collapsed underneath him. The pain shot up his leg and his spine, but his cry was as weak as his joints, even the sound of his body crashing to the ground was more of a clatter. Devoid of tears he wept only pain, and his eyes ached with the strain of trying to cry. Whether his leg was broken or not was irrelevant, he could not use it now.

This final night was cold, but he'd ceased shivering as his body had given up the fight to stay warm. The only sense he could really trust now was smell, and he had soiled himself for the last time yesterday. Anger had long since given way to fear after he realised that he had no way out of the tiny attic room without help, and no such aid was coming. Last night he'd thought that he could hear people in the house below and try as he might he could not raise sufficient breath to cry out or strength enough to raise a hand and knock upon the floorboards. He strained his eyes to focus as he looked up to the sliver of the moon that was just visible between the shutters. In supplication he uttered the name that had come to haunt him, trap him, and keep him here forever,

"Lampwick…"

His pupils grew large with the dying of the light and remained dark in their dilation. Those dry eyelids were locked open, and his face had frozen in an open-mouthed grimace, showing his remaining teeth, and bloodied receding gums. That dry husk of a throat rattled as the last air of his lungs vacated his body, like a spirit leaving an empty house. The chest collapsed as all tension left his form and appeared to deflate gently against the cold wooden floor beneath him. With a last move the emaciated head turned towards the shuttered windows and faced a thin beam of moonlight. In the cold attic room, away from anyone, beyond the help of friends, and without comfort, Mr Vespers died.

Silent Night

Laura Whitaker

The snow fell soundlessly, cloaking the streets in an unnatural stillness. Beth's boots crunched as she trudged home, her arms loaded with last-minute gifts. The houses lining the street glowed softly with Christmas lights, but one stood dark at the end—a looming silhouette that made her quicken her pace.

She hadn't noticed it before. New neighbours, maybe? She looked away. The sooner she got home, the better.

The lights in her own house welcomed her, spilling warmth onto the snow. Inside, she set the gifts down, brushing flakes from her coat. The tree stood by the window, its ornaments glinting faintly in the firelight. Something about it seemed off.

Beth frowned. She'd decorated it that morning, hadn't she? The angel on top tilted awkwardly, as though something had jostled it. Shaking her head, she reached to fix it.

A knock stopped her.

It was faint but distinct, coming from the front door. She glanced at the clock—10:15. Too late for caroller's, too early for the neighbours who might drop by on Christmas morning. Her chest tightened.

Another knock. Louder this time.

Beth crept to the door, peering through the peephole. The porch was empty. She opened it a crack, cold air biting at her face. The street stretched silent and empty.

Shutting the door, she locked it, double-checking the bolt. Her unease grew as she turned back to the tree. The ornaments shimmered, reflecting her face back in fragmented pieces. The angel leaned farther now; its head almost crooked sideways.

Beth's breath hitched. One of the ornaments—a red glass bulb—had moved. She was sure of it. It had been near the bottom earlier. Now it hung eye-level, turning slowly as though unseen hands had set it spinning.

The knock came again, this time at the back door.

Her stomach dropped. She hadn't locked it. She ran, her socks sliding against the hardwood floor. The kitchen door stood ajar, swinging gently. Outside, the yard was empty. No footprints in the snow.

Heart pounding, Beth locked the door and backed away, her eyes darting to every shadowed corner. She grabbed her phone, the screen lighting up her trembling hands.

The tree crackled behind her.

She turned slowly. The firelight illuminated it fully now, casting long shadows on the walls. The ornaments seemed wrong—faces pressed against the glass from inside. Not reflections. Faces. Twisted, screaming, mouths open in soundless agony.

The angel on top straightened with a snap.

Beth stumbled back. The lights on the tree flickered and went out, plunging the room into darkness. Her phone slipped from her grasp as the shadows shifted, thickening, moving toward her.

The last thing she felt was cold fingers brushing her neck.

The Missing, Found

Stacey Michelle Warner

"So, Dr Shrink, what does it say about a perp if this is their hideout?"

'*Dr Shrink*.' *Detective Mendez's wit is unparalleled*, Susan thought as they descended into the basement, the smell of damp rising to meet them.

"Likely, they have a pretty big secret."

"Duh."

So intelligent. As a criminal psychologist, Susan was happier behind her desk. But everything about this case had been, well, odd, and when the offer was made to go into the field, she felt compelled to say yes.

Susan's heart raced as Mendez nudged open the nearest door. The room was pitch black, silent pierced only by a repetitive ticking noise. She switched on the torch on her phone and immediately dropped it with a startled shriek as it landed on a blank face staring into the distance.

Shaking, she picked up her phone and looked about the room. Sat on hospital gurneys glassy-eyed and bolt upright were people she recognised. They had stared back at her in the precinct as 'the missing'.

Mendez took the pulse of one then frowned, waving a hand in front of their eyes.

Tick. Tick.

The noise continued. It scratched at something inside of Susan, unsettling. She scowled and aimed her torch at the source. A metronome sat on a side table, tapping out a regular beat.

Susan swallowed. "Hypnosis."

"Nah, that's fiction."

"It's not widely considered effective, but it's real."

She approached the nearest patient, studying his features. She couldn't imagine that Dr Folkes, their suspect, would have aimed to create these vacant dolls. Surely, he'd had bigger plans…

Suddenly, the patient turned to stare at her. Her blood chilled. Every pair of eyes were fixed on hers.

In unison they spoke, "Dr Folkes will see you now." Susan swallowed hard as Mendez unsheathed his pistol and moved into the next room.

Dr Folkes smiled, wide. An itchy feeling of unease tickled Susan's brain.

"Why -?" Mendez started.

"It's a classic profile, someone who *believes* they're a genius with something to prove."

"Oh," Folkes said, "but I am a genius."

"Yes," Susan agreed, then frowned disagreeing with herself.

Tick. Tick.

And why could she still hear that damned metronome?!

"A perfectly compliant army. The potential."

Snarling, Mendez raised his gun but before he could pull the trigger, a dozen arms clung to him. The patients were no longer next door. He wrestled for control as the gun went off. Blood pooled at the stomach of a patient, a fleeting moment of hope. But if the patient felt pain, it didn't register as his fingers grabbed at Mendez. The fight seeped out of him.

"Thank you, Susan, my favourite patient, for bringing him to me."

Tick. Tick.

Argument rose in her throat but instead calm settled over her.

Tick. Tick.

Her mind cleared.

She would do anything for this man. Mendez's screams bounced off her as he was dragged out of the room, flesh twisting in the grasp of her fellow patients.

She only stood. At His command.

The Crimson Carol

P.N. Harrison

The snow fell silently, covering the world in an untouched veil of white. Lucy stood by the window, watching the street as Christmas lights flickered and blinked in cold rhythm. Her fingers pressed against the glass, leaving a faint trail of condensation as she traced the outlines of snowflakes. The air inside was warm, but her skin prickled with an unease she couldn't quite place.

The street outside was deserted, the only sound the occasional rustling of the wind through the trees. And then she saw it—a figure at the end of the street, just outside the glow of the lampposts. A man in a tattered Santa suit, dragging a heavy sack behind him. His movements were slow, deliberate, and something about the way he moved made Lucy's breath catch in her throat.

Her phone buzzed, breaking the silence. She hesitated, then reached for it. A message lit up on the screen: **"Let him in."**

Lucy froze. She stared at the message, her thoughts scrambling. It was late, too late for a visitor, especially someone wearing that grotesque costume. Her fingers hovered over the keyboard, then typed back: **"Who is this?"**

The reply came instantly: **"He knows what you did."**

The words made her stomach turn. She felt her throat tighten, a cold chill creeping up her spine. She glanced out the window again. The man had stopped directly beneath the porch light. He stood still, staring at her house as if waiting for something.

A knock echoed from the front door.

Lucy's pulse quickened. She hadn't heard anyone approach. She had made sure the door was locked. She hadn't even heard footsteps on the snow. Still, she couldn't shake the feeling that someone—or something—was waiting just outside.

The knock came again, louder this time, more insistent.

The phone buzzed once more: **"Let him in. You don't want him to come in on his own."**

A wave of nausea hit her. What was happening? Her mind raced to that night—her eyes stinging with the memory of the icy road, the headlights blinding her as the figure darted across the street. She could still hear the sickening thud, the shattering of glass. She had driven off in panic, not even checking to see if the person was okay. Not even stopping.

Her fingers trembled as she typed: **"What do you mean? Who is he?"**

Another reply: **"The child."**

The doorbell rang; the sound too loud, too final in the otherwise silent house. Lucy stood frozen, staring at the door. The sack outside—she had barely noticed it before, but now it seemed impossibly large. And the man in the Santa suit, his face obscured by the shadows, had started to hum a soft, chilling tune.

"Silent night… holy night…"

The words froze her in place. That was when the door creaked open, slowly, the draft of cold air sweeping in. The sack began to shift. Lucy's heart pounded as the figure stepped into the dimly lit hallway.

She tried to move, but her feet felt like they were cemented to the floor. The sack dropped with a heavy thud at her feet.

Something stirred inside.

A small, pale hand reached out, fingers curled and stiff, and Lucy felt the weight of her actions crashing down on her, the guilt, the denial, and the icy realization of what she had done. The snow continued to fall outside, but the world beyond her door was now as cold and suffocating as the grave.

Seasons Past

P. N. Harrison

Whitney sighed as she finished wrapping a Holiday Barbie. This year's line seemed to be a homage to years' past, and the figure was, down to the style of its packaging, just like one she had asked her mother for when she was little. Her mother didn't get her the Barbie, of course. She said toys like that gave girls bad ideas. She doubted her mom would approve of her seasonal gift-wrapping job, either. But it didn't matter now. Her mother had been dead for eight months, and Whitney didn't have to care about what she thought anymore.

She reached for the next toy in the pile – a Teenage Mutant Ninja Turtle "Turtle Van." Vintage throwback toys must be in style this year. One Christmas season, long ago, she had brought the Turtle Van to her mom's shopping cart and begged for it. "That's not a girl's toy," her mom had snapped. Whitney remembered her dejection as she carried the van back to the toy aisle. She had been so upset that she had dropped the toy and left a sizable dent in the corner of the box. She had worried no one would ever buy it with the packaging damaged.

She sighed and began to wrap the box. She didn't see it at first, but her fingers felt it as she traced the paper across the box. Just like the one long ago, this toy's cardboard box had a dent in the corner. As she touched the corner, she thought she heard her mother's voice whisper the words, "For you."

As she heard the voice, Whitney's mind went back to a Christmas season twenty years before. She had visited the pet store every day that month. She loved the white Pomeranian puppy in the cage closest to the door. Every afternoon, she would drop by during her walk home and talk to the dog through the bars of its cage. She even liked its name, "Lucky."

It took some doing, but Whitney gathered the courage to ask her mother for a special Christmas gift. She would take care of Lucky herself, and it could be her only present that year. She remembered how her mom had scowled and said, "I'm allergic." Whitney was sure this wasn't true, but it didn't matter. Her mother had spoken.

She put the newly wrapped van aside, then reached for her next box. She tried to ignore that the boxes around her seemed higher, closer, than before. The box in her hand wasn't a toy's box at all, just a plain, brown cardboard box that rattled when she moved it. Black dirt clung to its outsides. She knew she could lose her job for opening it, but the familiar voice again echoed, "For you."

Very little remained of the canine skeleton inside, just a skull, some ribs, and a tarnished metal collar bearing the name "Lucky."

All around her, boxes – relics of seasons past – loomed taller than ever.

Serial Thriller

V.M. Sawh

Every horror story you've ever read starts with some kind of warning, something simple and unambiguous, like 'Don't toy with forces you don't understand', but that's just for fiction.

I grew up on a steady diet of real horror, the kind that makes you lock your doors at night. Netflix has made a fortune off it; you know what I'm talking about: True Crime.

Oh yeah, the real stuff, like the Springville Slasher, the Maryland Murders, or the Tokkaville Terror. When it comes to actual chills and honestly, thrills, real life beats out anything Hollywood can come up with. Even better when the killer is in your town. He doesn't have a name yet, but he's carved up a couple of other girls around my age. I wonder if he targets us because we're still in high school. Maybe he thinks we're too stupid to lock our bedroom windows.

Now, granted, I am a sucker for the occult, too. For sure there are dark forces at work in our daily lives. But that they can be exposed and purged with a whiff of burning sage is kinda comforting. So when I heard about this Black Crystal, that could be used to talk to the dead, well, come on sign me up already, right? Couldn't have been more excited. Yeah, it's sketchy ordering off the internet, but that's how it's always been. I saw on TikTok where this girl used the Black Crystal to talk to her dead mom. I mean, my mom's still alive, so that sucks, but I have a much better idea.

I'm gonna use it to see his next victim. See who he is and how he does it! Then I'll track him down, live stream me exposing him and boom: instant clout!

So, I get the crystal, and I turn out the lights in my bedroom. The instructions say I have to use incense and candles, but after a few minutes, I'm gagging on smoke. I don't want to set off the smoke alarm, so I open a window to air it out. It's fine, there's a breeze. Mom won't wake up. I get back to the Black Crystal, light the candles, and get the chant going.

"Speak To Me. The Dead Don't Rest. Speak To Me. Show Me The Next."

I keep it going so long that the words don't even make sense anymore. My eyes droop. I think it's not gonna work, but then the crystal gets warm.

This is it!

Wait, this doesn't make sense. I don't have a mirror there. Why am I seeing me?

There's a shape behind me, moving in the candlelight. I see it raise a knife.

It comes down in the back of my neck and my mouth fills with blood.

But the chant keeps going. I look up and see the Black Crystal in the mirror. There's another girl holding it, watching me die, her face bright with delight.

Daniel Forsyth

The snow fell heavier than usual that Christmas Eve, blanketing the streets in thick, silent layers. Clara stood at the window, her breath fogging up the glass as she watched the lights blink from nearby houses, their warmth flickering like a distant memory. Her parents had promised they'd be home in time for the holiday dinner, but the storm had other plans. They were stuck at the airport.

The tree, lonely in the corner of the living room, sat unadorned, its needles dry and sparse. The gifts beneath it were few, all wrapped neatly in festive paper. Clara's eyes lingered on a single, unusually small box near the back. It had appeared out of nowhere earlier that evening. Her mother hadn't bought it. Neither had her father. The tag was simple, with no name—just the words: *To Clara.*

She kneeled down and hesitated. The wrapping paper was strangely soft, almost fabric-like, and the box was unnaturally light. Her fingers trembled as she pulled back the paper.

Inside was a small, delicate porcelain doll. Its face was pale, cracked in places, its eyes a shade too wide, too knowing. The expression frozen on its face was a twisted semblance of a smile, but something in its eyes made Clara's skin crawl. She could've sworn it blinked.

A sharp knock at the door startled her. Her heart thudded in her chest as she quickly stood, clutching the doll in her hands. No one was supposed to be out in this storm. She peered through the peephole, but saw nothing—just darkness, thick as ink.

The knock came again, louder this time.

"Who is it?" Clara called, her voice shaking.

No answer. Just the knock again, rhythmic, persistent, as if whoever it was already knew she would ask.

Slowly, Clara opened the door. There was no one there. Just a dusting of snow on the doorstep and something else—another gift, this one wrapped in deep red paper.

The tag had her name on it.

She pulled the gift inside, closing the door behind her with trembling hands. The storm howled outside, but the house seemed colder than before. She set the doll down and turned to the new package.

Her breath caught in her throat as she unwrapped it. Inside was a second porcelain doll, identical to the first. Only this one was grinning. And as Clara stared at it, the air around her grew frigid, her fingers stiffening, too cold to move.

She turned, the hair on the back of her neck prickling.

The dolls were no longer sitting on the floor.

They were standing.

And they were smiling.

The Unseen

Tim Kaney

He stepped out of the shower and listened again for what he thought was a rustling sound. Did it come from his bedroom? Maximillian thought someone was on his bunk bed. Not a single source of the sound could be found after a thorough investigation. Quickly, he got ready for bed. Little Maxi, who had the start of a cold, and was only 11, tried to forget about it and leapt into the top bunk.

An odd, green light spilled in through his bedroom window. Cold chills suddenly shot across his backside, and he instinctively wrapped himself in his cozy, dinosaur quilt. After nestling into bed, just as his mind crept closer to sleep, he became aware that he was not alone. A strange poking and prodding fouled the sanctity of his red bunk bed. It started lightly near his hips and alternated sides as it got harder towards his head. Then it jumped to his feet. He moved ever so slightly to try to avoid being touched. Side to side. By now, he encased his whole body in his blanket. It should keep him safe; he thought. Maxi's little mind raced. His heart thumped loudly in his ears. Muscles all over his body shivered.

Maxi's mother was upstairs, and he knew that if he screamed, she would come to his rescue. These things would have to deal with the wrath of 'Mom'. Sucking all the energy from his bowels, and even from the tips of his toes, he prepared to let out a holler. Releasing all the energy and air produced no sound. Dreadful terror must have rendered him speechless; he wondered. Maxi quickly flipped down his covers and held his breath again. While dark, his room was partially lit by that eerie light. His heart doubled its pace. It took a few seconds for his eyes to adjust. Nothing. No sound. No one was in his bed. Maxi scanned several times. Something touched his foot. Without a sound, Maxi shot under his covers again.

The invisible things continued their torment.

Pounding on the wall, he thought, would surely get his mother's attention. Maxi slammed the wall with his fist. A few layers of skin were lost to the rough texture. Soon after, he heard the slow, but promising, footsteps of his mother start above his bedroom. She proceeded down the squeaky stairs. The old metal railing creaked as she gripped it for support.

As he hoped, the prodding quickly stopped. His mother's footsteps had vanished. Maxi was still under his covers. He felt a new presence beside his bed. Maxi had the image of his mother standing beside his bed in his mind. Excitedly, he yanked the covers from his face.

Poor Maxi's little heart sank.

His mother never came that evening. Only a deceitful, mom-shaped form did. Instead of his mother's warm, reassuring face he gazed upon a grotesque, featureless oval of winkled flesh.

Little Maxi could finally speak but only managed a blood-curdling shriek.

The Gift of Bells

Margaret Holloway

Snow fell thick and heavy, muffling the world in silence as Elsa trudged along the narrow forest path. Her lantern swayed, casting jittery shadows that flickered among the skeletal trees. Each breath fogged the icy air, but the sound of bells made her shiver far more than the cold.

It had started faintly, a distant chime carried on the wind, almost melodic. At first, she thought it might be sleigh bells. But as the night deepened and the forest grew darker, the sound crept closer.

"Just the wind," she whispered, clutching the lantern tighter.

The path seemed endless, the trees pressing in like watchful sentinels. Snow crunched underfoot, but the bells rang louder, their tune irregular, almost deliberate.

A shadow flickered at the edge of the lantern's glow. Elsa froze, the hair on her neck prickling. She scanned the trees, heart pounding, but saw only twisted branches and snow-draped silence.

"Who's there?" she called, her voice trembling.

The bells answered.

They were louder now, their tone no longer cheerful but sharp, grating, wrong. The sound burrowed into her skull as she spun in a circle, the lantern throwing wild shapes that clawed at the dark.

And then, she saw it.

A figure stood at the edge of the light. It wore a cloak of red, trimmed with white, and a wreath of holly crowned its head. But its face—its face wasn't human. Hollow black pits where eyes should have been. A mouth twisted into a grin far too wide.

The bells dangled from its fingers, small silver spheres dripping crimson.

Elsa stumbled back, her heel catching on a root. The lantern fell from her grasp, its flame sputtering out. Darkness rushed in as the figure stepped closer. The bells' discordant jangle filled her ears, piercing and relentless.

In the suffocating black, something cold pressed into her hands. The bells. Their sound was unbearable now, a maddening jangle that seemed to echo inside her skull.

Far away, the forest grew still once more, save for the faint, unending chime.

Kris Van

I landed headfirst into the water with a smack. My arms failed out, reaching for anything to grab. I contorted my body twisting in the water. My lungs stung; the impact of the water had caused me to expel all the air from my body. I only saw darkness.

Which way is up?

In my thrashing, my thigh hit stone and mud, and I swung my foot down, pushing myself to the surface. I gasped emerging from the water, shifting my stance to stand in the chest high water. I claw at my hair where it has matted to the front of my face, coughing, and spitting water and grime.

It's so dark

After gulping several deep breaths, I look around. Rubbing my eyes with one hand and reaching out in front of me, my hand smacks into a stone in the black void in front of me.

I don't know what I expected.

Rapidly blinking until my eyes adjust to the emptiness, I shuffle forward until my outreached hands are pressed against the damp cold stone wall. I wince as a sharp pain shoots from my fingertips. I gently place them against my cheek feeling the ragged broken tips of my fingernails.

I hope it hurt.

My hands are shaking as I feel around the smooth wall, side stepping, searching for something unknown. I realize I'm shivering. I put my hand to my chest and felt the cold skin and my rapidly beating heat. Will I go into shock? Could I freeze to death? It's only early fall but the water here is freezing. Macabre thoughts race through my head.

There isn't a way out.

I finally look up, at the bright sphere of light above me. A scream bubbles up out of my throat with unexpected intensity. Anger flashes and adds to my fear as I pound at the wall screaming and swinging my arms wildly in the water.

How could you?

I sob, pressing my face and shoulders against the wall, as exhaustion weakens me. Pleading into the void, for hope. I wrap my arms around my waist in the water. The sequined fabric of my dress scratches against my skin. The image of him complimenting the colour just an hour ago flashes behind my closed eyes.

The Blue brings out your eyes.

I flip around so my back is pressed against the wall. Tears are still streaming down my face. My head lurches forward as I suck in air through my teeth. My hand gingerly probes at the source of the throbbing hot fire at the back of my skull. He probably thought I was dead. Before he pushed me into the well.

The Whispering Frame

Elliot Hartwell

Martha found the antique mirror at a flea market, buried under faded quilts and tarnished candelabras. Its frame, carved from dark mahogany, was adorned with intricate swirls that seemed to ripple when she looked at them too long. The vendor claimed it was Victorian, and something in its cold, glossy surface called to her.

She brought it home and hung it in the hallway, opposite her bedroom door. It fit perfectly, as if the house had been waiting for it.

That night, she woke to the sound of whispers.

At first, she thought it was the television. She padded barefoot into the living room, but the screen was blank, and the house was silent save for the faint hum of the refrigerator. Returning to bed, she passed the mirror and paused. Its surface seemed darker than before, almost liquid, reflecting the dim hallway in unsettling detail.

The whispers started again as she stood there, faint but insistent, like dozens of voices murmuring just below the edge of comprehension. She leaned closer, her breath fogging the glass.

"Martha," they sighed, and she froze.

Her name slithered from the mirror, soft as silk, followed by faint giggles. She staggered back, her pulse pounding. For a long moment, she stared, waiting for the voices to return. They didn't. She convinced herself it was exhaustion and hurried back to bed.

The next morning, her reflection didn't feel quite right. It followed her movements too precisely, her eyes lingering in the glass half a second too long. She avoided the mirror after that, draping a sheet over it and telling herself it was silly to be afraid.

But the whispers grew bolder, louder, slipping into her dreams. They weren't calling her name anymore—they were laughing, taunting, mocking. And they were growing angry.

One night, she woke to find the sheet crumpled on the floor. The mirror stood bare, its surface rippling like a pond disturbed by a stone. The whispers rose into a cacophony, and something moved inside the glass—a hand, reaching.

Martha tried to scream, but the mirror swallowed the sound.

By morning, the hallway was empty. The mirror hung silently, its glass smooth and dark, waiting for the next curious soul.

Should've Listened

(January's Winner)

Emily Jones

Breath pounding, I run. *You're on my trail; you're on my trail.* Deep in the foreign woods, I stay. *Keep going, keep going.* Scratched. Nipped. Scraped. My feet are bleeding, cheeks stinging from cold. You're a kilometre behind me. You. The woman I love. I'm without a guide or prayer; my muscles cotton, my heart overworked. The past twenty-four hours have been a nightmare. I've been bitten, burned and bludgeoned. Half-drowned and stabbed. Damn you. Damn that boat and damn everyone that drowned. They were lucky.

We weren't supposed to be here. We should've been miles away; married, drunk and frisky in our overpriced hut. But I had to spot this island. It'd be romantic, I said. To escape the noisy tourists and have you all to myself. I cringe as I remember the captain's face, forcing too many notes into his hand as I insisted. He warned us. I laughed in his face and took you onboard, his tale absurd.

At first it was perfect. The ocean was calm, no other boats under the blushing sky. We were the only ones in the world. We danced. You twirled. And we kissed to the sound of distant songbirds. The island crept into view. The untamed trees towered over the water like an Eden paradise, the rugged cliffs wild with waterfalls and swinging blossoms.

Then the water changed. It thickened and bubbled like hot slurry, blacker than soot, the smell putrid. It tossed us about like a child's toy, waves so strong the first mate was thrown overboard. Something dragged him under. The captain fought the wheel, trying to turn us around, but the boat took control and drove us closer to the island, hurtling towards the cliffs. The crew drowned one by one, blood foaming to the surface. You were shaking in my arms. I didn't know what to do! A split second before we crashed, I grabbed your hand, and we jumped. I washed up on a narrow beach, sand whiter than starlight. You were nowhere to be seen. I screamed your name until I was hoarse, heart pounding like the tears down my face. You couldn't be dead; you just couldn't be.

Ten minutes later and I found you in the water. You'd come back to me. You were OK! Aside from a nasty gash. Were those *claw* marks? I rinsed the blood off. A word was carved into your leg. *Kill.* For the first time, I didn't recognize the woman looking at me. There was something dark behind her eyes, something dangerous and feral. Like an animal. And it made me fear for my life. As quickly as the water had changed, you snarled and lunged at my throat.

***

I don't know what the hell happened or what's making you do this. But you'll never stop. I know that now. I've lost you and it's all my fault. I should've listened. Now there's only one question left. Which one of us dies first?

Fuel for the Shadows

Evelyn R. Blackwood

The gas station sat alone, swallowed by the encroaching woods. Its neon sign buzzed erratically, spilling weak light across cracked asphalt. Dani gripped the steering wheel, knuckles white. She hadn't planned to stop, but the fuel gauge hovered on E, and the road ahead stretched black and endless.

The attendant's booth was empty. A single bulb swung above the pump, casting jittery shadows across her car. Dani stepped out, the night swallowing her in its damp chill. Somewhere in the distance, cicadas hummed. Closer, the woods whispered, leaves shivering though there was no breeze.

She swiped her card and lifted the nozzle. The pump clicked but didn't start. She glanced toward the booth again, but it remained lifeless, the windows smudged and opaque.

"Need help?"

The voice came from behind her. She spun, her pulse kicking against her throat. A man stood just outside the glow of the overhead light. His face was slack, expressionless. His eyes—flat, grey—reflected no light.

"No, I'm good," Dani said, forcing a smile. She pressed the nozzle back into place and opened her car door.

"Tank's empty," he said, stepping closer. "You won't get far."

She hesitated, one foot inside the car, hand hovering over the ignition. "I'll figure it out."

The man tilted his head, a slow, unnatural movement, like a puppet pulled by invisible strings. "You should come inside. Got cans of gas in the back."

The booth. She swallowed, glancing at the smeared windows. They weren't smeared—they were streaked. Bloody handprints, faint but unmistakable, dragged down the glass.

"No thanks," she said, slamming the car door shut. She turned the key, but the engine coughed, sputtered, and died. Panic coiled in her chest as she tried again, her hands trembling.

The man moved closer, stepping fully into the light. His face was wrong. Too smooth. The edges of his mouth pulled up, splitting his cheeks in a grotesque grin. Teeth glinted—long, jagged things that jutted unevenly from black gums.

"Come inside," he repeated, his voice deeper now, a wet, gurgling rasp.

Dani lunged for her phone, but it wasn't in the cupholder. It wasn't in her bag. She glanced at the passenger seat—empty.

A soft tap on her window made her freeze. She turned slowly. Another face, identical to the first, peered in. Its grin stretched wider, the skin cracking like old paint.

Behind it, more figures emerged from the woods, dozens of them, their mouths leaking dark, viscous fluid. They surrounded her car, the air filling with the sound of their jagged teeth clacking together in unison.

The pump light flickered and went out.

In the suffocating dark, Dani screamed.

The woods swallowed the sound.

Strawberry Moon

Gregory L. Steighner

Tonight, I became my true self.

I'll always remember being Jim, living in a small hamlet nestled among the forested rolling hills of Western Pennsylvania. I lived in a valley, buried by old oaks and maples trees. I took true pleasure walking in those woods, nourished simply by listening to nature. Night provided tranquillity, as few dared traveling the forest paths at night I knew well.

In the deepest part of the forest was a pond, fed by a spring that ever flowed. A haven for animals and those willing to enjoy the moment of being. Yet, there were some that didn't care for the forest as it was.

Last month, at the township meeting the commissioners approved of a development plan. It would be transformed into a park, with marked trails, open fields for soccer and baseball. People applauded the naming of the water park. Some voices spoke out against these changes. I added mine as well, but we were ignored. The first trees would be cleared at the beginning of July, that suggestion was greeted with brilliant fanfare.

In sorrow, I entered the forest this Midsummer's Eve, as the Strawberry Moon rose sailing low over fated trees. I approached the pond, as wisps of fog started drifting in the grey light.

Someone was singing an aria that blended into the nocturnal sounds. I then saw her, standing on the water's edge. She was a lithe figure clothed in a delicate gown that gleamed in the moonlight. An ethereal beauty that enraptured me.

Her silver hair danced over her shoulders as she turned towards me saying "Hello."

I asked who she was, and she answered, "Athenia, I have come for you."

Confused, I asked, "Why me?"

Her smile was like a crescent moon, soft and stunning, "We have been watching you since a child. Your heart and spirit are with the forest. You're in the autumn years.

I felt the weight of ages, "I'm dying?"

She shook her head once, "Does it matter? Come with us to see the forest as it once was in the dreams of Faerie."

She reached out her left hand; I grasped it firmly, "I'm ready."

We passed beyond the water, under gates of living trees into the realm of dreams. My youth restored in the lights of silver and gold. I place some called Avalon.

Athena looked at me and said, "Welcome home."

The Hollow Guest

Marcus Dellinger

The farmhouse had been empty for years, its windows dark and boarded, the fields around it long overrun by weeds. But tonight, light seeped through the cracks in the shutters, a dim, flickering glow that caught Amy's eye as she drove past. She shouldn't have stopped—she knew that—but something about the light felt wrong, like it didn't belong.

She left her car on the shoulder and climbed the sagging steps to the porch. The wood groaned under her weight, her breath fogging in the chill. A faint sound reached her ears, like whispers carried on the wind. No wind blew.

Her flashlight caught the front door—it hung slightly ajar. Amy pushed it open, the hinges wailing. The air inside smelled damp, faintly metallic. Shadows leapt across the walls as her flashlight beam danced over peeling wallpaper and splintered furniture.

"Hello?" she called. Her voice was swallowed by the dark.

The glow came from deeper within, from the living room. She stepped closer, her sneakers crunching over glass shards. The whispers grew louder. They weren't carried by the wind—they came from the room ahead.

She rounded the corner and froze.

A figure sat at the centre of the room, hunched over in a chair. Candles surrounded it in a rough circle, their flames trembling as though afraid. The figure's back was to her, its head bowed. It didn't move, didn't breathe.

"Hey," Amy said, her voice trembling. "Are you okay?"

No response. The whispers, too, had stopped. The only sound was the crackle of the candles.

She stepped closer, her flashlight beam landing on the figure's hands. They were pale, too pale, the skin stretched tight over long, thin fingers. They twitched.

"Are you—?"

The head turned sharply, too sharply. A neck shouldn't move like that. The face was wrong. Hollow eyes stared back at her, black and endless, the mouth stretched wide in a mockery of a grin, its teeth too many, too sharp.

Amy staggered back, the flashlight slipping from her hand and spinning across the floor. The shadows leapt; the room alive with movement.

The figure stood. Its limbs unfolded, impossibly long, the joints bending the wrong way. It stepped over the candles, the flames snuffing out as it moved.

Amy turned and ran, her sneakers sliding on the glass-strewn floor. She made it to the porch, her breath coming in panicked gasps, but as she reached the stairs, the farmhouse door slammed shut behind her.

She didn't look back. She didn't need to. The whispers had started again.

They were coming from right behind her.

The Beast in The Cellar

CJ Hooper

The smell of damp was the first thing he noticed, musty yet wet, and clawing at his lungs. Breathing deeply through gritted teeth Clive struggled not to gag. Had it not been necessary then he would never have gone down there, but 'needs must when the Devil drives' he thought to himself, and so he went further down the slight steps which felt as though they had too much give and could collapse under his weight at any moment. His children had sworn that they'd seen, Salome, the family cat, going through the cellar doors that led to the basement of the pub from the street.

Clive had been unable to force the beer cellar door from the outside, naturally this would have been locked from inside the building to prevent kids from breaking in, but ironically it meant that he found himself forcing open the back door accessed from the overgrown beer garden. The Dunthorpe Arms had been closed for nearly two decades now, and any thoughts of it reopening as a gastro-pub were becoming increasingly unlikely as it fell into ruin.

The steps down into the cellar were easily accessed, as the internal door to the floor below was long since rotted and collapsed in on itself. Trying to be careful he had the choice of using both hands to steady himself on his dark descent or use one hand and carry a torch.

There had been the sound of something scratching around in the dark and pausing for a moment he tried to squint into the shadows. As this was no good, he balanced himself precariously on the third step from the floor, not wishing to scare off Salome, if it were her. Fishing out his torch was easy enough but typically it wouldn't light, and he cursed himself for not checking the batteries. With a deft flick he suddenly had a brief connection, but the light shone directly into his eyes, and then he heard the scream. It was animalistic and raw, and came from a throat that was dry, as he swung the torch light in its direction, he saw the dark mass of hair and rags fly at him and the weight of it caught him off balance. He went with it though the decrepit banister and onto the filth encrusted floor. The torch went spiralling off into the cellar, still lit, and landing just before the chewed up remains of Salome, her glittery collar shining in her blood matted fur.

The beast in the cellar reared up again, and its breathing, heavy and ragged, gave way to a growl as uneven, jagged teeth fell down upon their victim's throat. Clive tried to resist but he had fallen badly, and pain shot down his back and leg as it bit into his neck severing the nerve. The figure above him, a feral woman, clad in rags and dirt, would dine well for a change.

The Husk

Clara Whitaker

The first sign something was wrong came when Darren woke up scratching. Not a little itch—this was frantic, clawing-at-his-skin kind of scratching. The kind that left trails of red streaked down his arms and chest. His sheets were damp, his skin slick with sweat, and under the overhead light, he saw it: a fine, pale dust coating his pillow, his arms, even the bed.

He thought it was skin, dead flakes peeling off from a sunburn he didn't remember getting. But it wasn't. It was finer than that, softer. Almost like powder.

He vacuumed it up and told himself he'd been dreaming, that it wasn't anything to worry about. But by that evening, the itching was back. Worse. Deeper. It wasn't just his skin anymore—it was inside him, burrowing beneath the surface, tickling at places he couldn't reach. He stood in the shower for an hour, the scalding water doing nothing to soothe him. The soap lathered in strange, greyish streaks. When he checked the mirror, he realized why.

Tiny holes, just under his ribs. Pinpricks at first, almost like bug bites, but more symmetrical. Perfect little rings, like someone had pressed a tool into his skin.

He covered them with gauze and duct tape. He told himself it was nothing, that it would go away, but the holes deepened. By the next day, there were more of them, trailing up his sides, his chest, even the backs of his thighs. They didn't bleed. They didn't hurt. They just... grew.

The powder was everywhere now, falling in faint, constant drifts from his body. He swept it up, but it never seemed to stop.

It clung to his clothes, floated in the air, settled on his furniture like ash.

And then came the smell.

It was faint at first, almost sweet, like old fruit left out too long. But by the third day, it was rancid. Something sickly and sharp, a stink that followed him no matter how many showers he took. People at work noticed. They gave him a wide berth, their eyes darting to the yellowed bandages under his shirt.

He stopped going in after his manager pulled him aside and whispered, "Maybe take a few days to... recover."

On the fifth night, the holes began to move.

Darren didn't see it at first, but he felt it. A shift, deep beneath the surface of his skin, like something turning over in its sleep. He tore the bandages off and saw them—tiny, segmented legs, pale as bone, twitching inside the holes. They were burrowing deeper, their movements slow but deliberate.

He spent the night with a steak knife and a bottle of whiskey, cutting into his flesh, trying to dig them out. But for everyone he pulled free—long, white, writhing things that squealed like newborns—two more appeared.

By dawn, he was covered. His flesh was no longer his own. The holes had spread across his body, a network of tunnels and canals. He could feel them inside him now, crawling through his veins, nesting in the soft tissue of his organs.

He didn't scream. What was the point? No one was coming. No one could help.

When the sun rose, Darren stood in front of the mirror and looked at what was left of him. His skin sagged, pale and translucent, his eyes sunken into black hollows. A thin trickle of powder fell from his mouth as he breathed.

And beneath his skin, they writhed.

They were hungry.

And they weren't done.

The Reclamator's Final Notice

Devin James Leonard

When the school bus dropped him off, Timmy checked the mailbox and shuffled through the postage on his way up the driveway. Among the normal white envelopes of monthly bills and ads, an onyx black package grabbed his attention. He didn't know what it contained, but he'd seen this type of mail twice before. The first one came two months ago, the next a month after that, and both times his mother had snatched them from his hands and held the obsidian postage close to her chest, telling him it didn't concern him.

Since his mother wasn't home when he went inside, he opened the letter and read it:

> *Dearest Debtor,*
> *Infinity Corp has begrudgingly advised you of your long overdue balance as payment for their services. Since you have repeatedly failed to comply, the enterprise has turned your account over to me, to which I have been instructed to proceed with your demise without further delay.*
> *However, there is still time to avoid your execution if you contact IC within the next five days. This is your last opportunity before I handle this matter internally.*
>
> *Sincerely,*
> *The Reclamator*

Everybody knew who Infinity Corp was, including ten-year-old Timmy. If you found yourself with a deadly illness, the IC treated you. No matter the severity of your disease, whether it be stage four lung cancer or if you had a tumour the size of a tennis ball growing inside your brain, the enterprise could and would cure you. There was nothing they couldn't treat. *Inoperable* was not a word in the enterprise's vernacular. But once the IC fixed you up, you were indebted to them for the rest of your natural-born life. Pay the monthly fees and keep living. Fail to pay, and the company sends an assassin to take back the life they gave you. Like a repo man reclaiming a car because you were late on the payments. You got three warnings, and according to this statement, Timmy's mother was on her third and final notice.

He wasn't even aware she had been sick, and now, according to the letter, she had a measly five days to get into contact with the company about an extension.

Timmy flipped the envelope around. Checked the postmark. Saw it was five days old.

The doorbell rang.

What Crawls Below

Julian Crowhurst

The basement door shouldn't have been open.

Ethan froze at the top of the stairs, gripping the banister, his pulse a slow, measured thud in his ears. He never left it open. Not after last time.

The darkness beyond the doorway gaped like a wound, swallowing the dim hallway light. A scent drifted up from below—earthy, damp, tinged with something sharper. Coppery. The old pipes leaked sometimes, rusting at the joints, but this was different.

His wife, Claire, was in the living room, curled under a blanket, half-asleep with a book in her lap. If he called for her, she'd come running, her worry magnified in the reflection of his own. He didn't want that. Not yet.

His fingers flexed, the cool brass of the banister grounding him. A few steps down, the wood groaned beneath his weight. He held his breath, listening.

A wet, dragging sound—just for a second. Then silence.

Ethan's mouth went dry. It was probably an animal. Something that had crawled in through the crawl space. That's what he told himself. His foot found the next step. Then another.

At the bottom, the pull-string for the light dangled in the dark. He reached for it, the thin cord brushing his fingers. He yanked.

The bulb flickered, humming weakly to life.

Something was wrong.

His workbench was bare. The toolbox, usually shoved against the far wall, lay open, empty. The shelves, once cluttered with paint cans and dusty jars, stood skeletal, the contents gone.

A faint, rhythmic clicking filled the space. Soft, deliberate.

The air thickened, cloying. A shadow shifted near the foundation wall, deep where the light couldn't reach. His skin tightened as his eyes adjusted.

It was a hole.

A jagged, gaping cavity had split the cement wide, raw earth stretching beyond. And something inside it moved.

A limb unfolded—thin, pallid, too many joints bending the wrong way. Another followed. A hand, if you could call it that, stretched long fingers toward the concrete floor.

Ethan staggered back, knocking over a paint can. The noise sent the thing into a frenzy. It slithered forward, unfurling more of itself from the hole, its body pulsing with slow, unnatural breath.

The clicking wasn't coming from its limbs. It was coming from its mouth. A jagged seam in its face, edges peeling apart, teeth like needles glistening in the dim glow of the bulb.

A whimper rose in Ethan's throat. He hadn't made the hole.

Something had been making its way out.

And now it knew he was here.

The Tale of Edwin Gill

John Leahy

My friend Edwin Gill was a most annoying person. The reason I found him annoying was because he was good at everything he tried. An excellent athlete, gifted handyman, a guy who could bag a woman with only a few simple lines, and a brilliant stock trader who infuriatingly only spent about half the time at his desk that I spent slaving at mine. He was also a fan of various high-octane activities like big wave surfing, hang-gliding and rock climbing amidst a host of others. The man was fearless. So, when the terrifying hands erupted from beneath London's tube tunnels, snatching random tube carriages and whisking them back down into whatever unimaginable location in the bowels of the earth that they had emerged from, it didn't surprise me much when Edwin said that he was going down into the hand-hole left between Liverpool Street and Bank. He wanted to see for himself what that hand was attached to.

Edwin was also a brilliant mountain-climber and caver.

***

The first-hand tore through the ground on the Northern Line between Kentish Town and Camden Town. The second one appeared between Elephant and Castle and Kennington, the first one returned (forensic analysis of CCTV footage had determined that it was indeed that same one as had emerged on the Northern Line) between Knightsbridge and Gloucester Road. By the time the second hand burst forth again between Bank and Liverpool Street, crowds on the tube had diminished by nearly seventy percent. Edwin hadn't been scared, he'd been curious.

So down he'd gone.

***

I'm looking at two giant things, their huge maws open to receive the screaming people tumbling from the tube carriages that the unspeakable behemoths are holding in their hands. The camcorder footage zooms in on the head of one of the impossible beasts and I can see its dreadful jaws working as it chews on the unfortunates that its mouth contains.

The screen goes black.

I look at my old friend in his bed, his hair pure white, his once handsome thirty-year-old face now that of a wizened septuagenarian. His eyes are open, the fear that drove him to his suicide still present in them.

The tube stopped running yesterday after the sixth hand incident, which occurred between Bayswater and Notting Hill Gate.

So now the monsters have no more food.

I close Edwin's eyes. I wonder how long it will be before the things under the city can no longer contain their hunger.

I imagine it'll be more than their hands that will be coming up out of the ground.

Meat

Samuel Renshaw

Randy pulled into the diner parking lot, tires crunching over loose gravel. The neon sign above the entrance buzzed, its glow flickering red across the hood of his truck. *Miller's Fine Eats.* He'd never heard of it before, and he'd driven this stretch of highway a hundred times. But the hunger gnawing at his gut didn't care.

Inside, the place smelled damn good—grease, grilled meat, something rich and slow-cooked. A lone waitress behind the counter, lean and long-limbed, smiled at him as he took a stool. She had high cheekbones, dark eyes. Her name tag read *Lila.*

"What's good?" he asked.

"The meat," she said, already pouring him coffee.

Randy glanced at the menu. No details. Just *The Meat*—$12.99. He smirked. "What kind of meat?"

Lila's lips curled at the corners, not quite a smile. "Specialty house cut. Fresh."

His stomach twisted with need. "I'll take it."

She walked into the back, hips swaying in a way that made his mouth dry. A minute later, she reappeared with a plate, sliding it in front of him. A thick, red steak, glistening under the diner's lights. No sides. No garnish. Just meat.

The first bite melted on his tongue, rich and buttery, juices dribbling down his chin. Best damn steak he'd ever had.

He finished it too fast. Licked the plate. Looked up at Lila. "Another."

She grinned, sharp and knowing. "Told you it was good."

A door swung open behind the counter. The kitchen. A man stepped out, heavy-set, bald, wearing a stained apron. He carried a slab of raw meat, crimson and marbled, cradling it like something precious.

Randy swallowed. Something was wrong. The cut was too smooth, the muscle too familiar.

He looked past the man, through the swinging door.

The kitchen wasn't a kitchen. It was a butcher's room, tiled walls glistening wet. Hooks hung from the ceiling. And on one of them—

A leg.

A human leg.

Randy staggered back, bile rising. Lila tsked. "Shame. Most folks don't look."

The butcher sighed and wiped his blade on his apron. "Guess we need more meat."

Randy turned to run, but Lila was already moving, grinning as she reached for the knife.

R.G. Halstead

Almost ready to finally slash his own wrists to end it all, a lost and desperate Tommy Bradford was safe for now. In his locked bedroom. Trying to stop trembling and hopefully forget the jolting hell that he had gone through and somehow endured at school today. Again! He could not forget Miss Watson and her homework assignment, though, it sat right there in front of him.

That yappy bitch always gave out homework. Always! Probably when she finally died and went to hell, too. Oh, the Devil would get her, he hoped.

Taking in a deep breath and slowly letting it out… his young heart eventually began to beat normally again. That changed suddenly when his mother yelled out from the kitchen for Tommy to check up on his grandfather who now lived in their basement.

The old guy was either deafer than usual, more stubborn or dead when the woman had called out to him minutes ago.

With his mother being his only real respite here in the home, Tommy had no choice but to leave his warm bedroom sanctuary and go downstairs to see what the old guy was doing. Considering the ancient fart's non-sensible ramblings at the dinner table every night, he was probably going more nuts.

His heart was almost pounding out of his chest.

Taking in a deep breath did not help Tommy with what he was seeing as he nervously stood in the basement, wide eyed.

Grandpa Dave had Miss Watson, Mr. Abernathy and that witch Mrs. Harper tied up and gagged. Plus, there were the school's two worst bullies incapacitated, too. Butch Adams and Billy Collins. Oh, he absolutely loved the looks of sheer horror and shock on their faces. They were mumbling under the gags. Pleading for Tommy to help them.

Yeah. Right.

Tommy smiled when his grandfather suggested that he get closer and join in on the satisfying torture. Handing Tommy a sharp knife.

Tommy was gonna use it to slash the wrists of the teachers who gave out too much homework and the bullies who had made his life hell. All of them pleading for mercy while wetting themselves.

Tommy Bradford had every intention of sadistically making their lives a slow-dying, blood-spurting living hell.

The boy with a new life started with the very deserving Miss Watson, before the Devil got to her.

If there was anything left over for the Devil to deal with.

Shadows in the Fog

Vivienne Ashcroft

Jacob noticed the fog rolling in as he took out the trash. Not the usual mist that clung to the town's riverbanks this time of year—this was thicker, heavier, moving like it had *intent.* He stopped on the porch, trash bag dangling from one hand, and watched it swallow up the streetlamp at the corner.

Something about it didn't sit right.

The air felt *too* quiet. No crickets. No cars. No distant hum of the highway. Just the sound of his own breathing and the *drip, drip, drip* of condensation sliding off the gutters.

Then came the footsteps.

Soft at first. Steady.

Jacob squinted into the swirling grey. "Hello?"

No answer.

He could barely see the curb now. Just a dull orange glow from the lamp, diffused into nothing. But there was something *moving* out there. A shape. A shadow in the fog, just at the edge of his vision.

The footsteps stopped.

Jacob held his breath.

A long inhale drifted through the mist. Wet. Deep. Like something breathing him in.

His spine went rigid. He turned and hurried inside, shutting the door harder than he meant to. He threw the lock, slid the deadbolt, but he didn't move away. Not yet.

He listened.

Nothing.

He exhaled, ran a hand through his hair, and laughed under his breath. Jesus. Just the fog messing with him. Probably some drunk stumbling home from O'Malley's.

But as he turned from the door, a faint *tap tap tap* echoed against the window.

Jacob froze.

The blinds were closed, but he could see the shape through them—tall, thin, standing right outside.

Another tap.

His mouth went dry. He took a slow step back. The fog pressed against the glass, swirling, writhing. The shape didn't move. Didn't knock. Just stood there.

And then… it leaned in.

Something dark spread across the window. Not a hand. Not exactly. The fingers were too long, too thin, pressing into the glass like they wanted to *sink inside.* The nails scraped downward, slow, deliberate.

Jacob stumbled, knocking over a chair. His brain screamed at him to *run*, but his legs wouldn't move.

A voice—low, guttural—hissed through the door.

"Let me in."

Jacob bolted for the bedroom. Locked the door. His heart slammed against his ribs. His phone was still in the kitchen, but he wasn't going back out there. No way in hell.

Silence.

For a moment, just the sound of his ragged breath.

Then…

Another inhale. Deep. Wet.

Right behind him.

Jacob turned.

The closet door was open.

The fog *was inside the room.*

Infinite Closure

Nicole Nevel-Steighner

Talia found her office a sanctuary for her thoughts. Thinking over her years of giving therapy, she hoped her patients felt the same. It was taking longer to clean out then she imagined. Lingering on the names on the files was the hold up. The progress stalled completely, landing on a particular one. Thumbing through the notes, she imagined Clarice, sitting in that chair across her desk, complaining about the cigarette smoke wafting about the office. Now, confined to a small room, she was barely able to speak. Not ideal, but what can you do with those that can't handle themselves? How could she continue to serve the public at mass when she couldn't help her own girlfriend?

She hadn't planned on caring about her, let alone loving her. Their sessions started out professional, yet there had always been that spark. The way Clarice would focus on her with those blue eyes. The tendrils of red hair that fell like corkscrews over her shoulders rendered her appearance ethereal. She looked as if from another time.

The framed photo inside her bottom desk drawer told the tale. Clarice was a muse. Only she couldn't share her with the world. It was against the law. Who ever said love was lawful?

Sighing, Talia placed a leopard print ashtray into a cardboard box. Leaving her practice would be infinite closure.

There was a storage space in the basement of the aged house that she needed to clear as well. Would the world be ready for what she'd kept?

The rats had chewed through some wiring, so armed with a flashlight she descended. It was cooler than she remembered and the smell of years of neglect flooded her nostrils. The owner of the house lived in Florida and was fine with a monthly check for the space. Talia would empty the place before departing, as the end of the space she'd leased for years, was now two days shy.

Pulling her key from her jacket, she shined the light on the small oblong hole. How odd that something so small could hold her entire world?

The door creaked open with regret. Was that the sound of tiny demon claws scattering by? Yes, she'd sat out poison yesterday, but it hadn't seemed to quell them.

"Clarice." She called out, shining the light about the dank room. The walls ensconced with faded peacock paper; she couldn't imagine staring at all day.

"I've nearly finished with the office. It's time for us to close the place up and leave the keys."

The silence mirrored the chill. As she aimed the beam in the corner, there was her love, her muse. Staring blankly ahead, vomit smeared on the sides of her cherub mouth.

Dropping to her knees Talia crawled towards her.

"It is wrong to shut away the things that disturb us." She whispered, pushing away the rats that danced around them as she held Clarice.

"I see you've eaten their dinner."

Waterworks

Thomas Henry Newell

When he knocked on the door of Reedmarsh Flat 409, there was no answer. But the door opened, inviting him in. Jeffries walked in, calling out, "Anyone home?" He saw a light under a door down the hall, and he walked towards it.

When he opened the door, it took him a moment to process what he saw. A figure was on the toilet. "Sorry!" said Jeffries loudly, going to close the door. But he stopped when he realized that the figure was not actually on the toilet. Instead, it was perched predatorily on the seat. Something shimmered in the room.

"Stay" the figure said, and Jeffries did. "You're from the waterworks," the figure said.

"Er, no," Jefferies said. *Did the little person know about his contact?* Jefferies had to get that signature. If the residents signed, no-one would question the waterworks. "I'm from the council." He tried to smile.

"Would you like something to drink?"

Jefferies stared at the figure, smiling incredulously. In the dim bathroom, he really, really didn't want a drink. Besides, he knew exactly what the waterworks were doing here. But if the residents signed the council inspection, the waterworks could pass the buck, and they'd never know.

"I'm really just here for the signature. The council's had complaints about water quality, and I want to make sure everything's above board." If he got it, the council could condemn the place as sewage runoff, blaming Reedmarsh's residents. *Why not? They were dirty enough,* thought Jefferies, taking in the dim council flat facilities. And he would get what his contact promised.

"Our water doesn't spring from that well," the figure said. Reedmarsh, Jefferies had heard, had once been known for its pagan ways and water burials. And it was known for its lamprey pies.

The room shimmered again. Jefferies turned to see a full bathtub glowing a sickly green. When Jefferies looked back at the figure, he truly saw it. Its hair was eel-black and shimmered and writhed. It spoke in a voice drowning in mud. "Be my guest. Drink deep," it pointed to the tub.

The Reedmarsh inhabitants left offerings for the spirits of the marsh, praying for bountiful catches in their traps. That had been a long time ago. Jefferies knew this in an instant. He saw it in the water. He saw the history of old gods and dark bogs. Then he blinked.

His eyes stung when he opened them. He looked up at a dim bathroom, and he realized he was submerged in the bath. His head screamed despair, and his mouth opened, drinking deep. His muscles seized, frozen in the cold, ancient water.

He saw the creature perched on the toilet seat. The figure stared hungrily at him with green eyes. Its round mouth opened revealing the maw of a lamprey.

The Start of a Beautiful Friendship

(February's Winner)

CJ Hooper

The water tower was tall and rusty, with some of the finest examples of local graffiti adorning the exterior. These exhibited the local kids' insecurity and also their own ignorance of anatomy. Urban explorer Thomas Machenall had climbed the tower to have a look at the view from the roof. Feathers were scattered all around. The old iron roof had, in part, given way to time, oxygen, and the acidic effluence of pigeon crap. This had left a jagged hole. Cautiously Thomas cleared a way through them to the aperture and spread his weight evenly to avoid causing another collapse. By a clearer panel Thomas was able to lean over and peer in. The smell of stagnant water assailed his nose. Then came the after stench of ammonia. He gagged and went to pull his scarf over his mouth and nose. It was then he noticed the eyes in the dark. Thcy were bulbous shining eyes, and, like a fly, cross figured. Mystified he leaned in. The staring eyes seemed to grow wider. Entranced, Thomas, forgot himself, and peered into darkness. Arms moved, and long fingered hands grabbed his wrists. He screamed. Thomas' was pulled sharply forward. His body lurched. He fell down into the hole, crashing down into the fetid uncool water and into darkness.

When he awoke his shoulders were in agony, dislocated at least. His trousers had shredded on the torn metal, and his legs felt as though they were bleeding, but in the murky water he could not tell. The only light was the sun which shone in a single beam through the broken roof. Thomas had fallen almost twenty feet and had landed in about half a metre of scum encrusted water. Mould was growing around the edges and had begun climbing up the sheer walls. There was no escape. Then he saw it.

The great green eyes stared at him from the other side of the water chamber. They glowed in the midst of the gloom. The creature was humanoid, the eyes large and wide. Then it moved, spiderlike climbing down the wall, and into the water slowly, as if trying not to disturb the surface. Long splayed fingers rested upon the broken crust of scum then scraped up some of the mould with its nails. Its cupped hands reached towards the terrified and stricken guest. Unable to move or scream Thomas was force fed the grimy repast. The creature's fingers stroked his throat bidding him to swallow the offering of food. Nonetheless Thomas choked and brought it all back up, vomiting over his half-submerged chest. The creature then offered him something feathered and red, and though in pain he tried to wave it away. The pigeon remains were pushed into his mouth. The creature angled its head mournfully as this too was rejected. It didn't matter, its new friend would need to eat soon, and the creature was willing to share. This is how friends are made.

Bigger Brother

Kyle Bolan

Mommy says that I'll have a baby brother soon, and I'll have to be a good bigger brother for him.

Mommy has gotten a lot bigger too. Her belly is big and really bumpy. Sometimes she shows me her tummy and lets me feel it. I've felt the baby move and every time he does, mommy looks hurt in her face. I put my face on her tummy and yell at him to stop hurting her, but mommy says it's okay and to leave him alone.

Daddy has been gone a lot too. Mommy says he is on a trip and will be home soon. I miss daddy. It's been a long time since I've seen him. Mommy told me to write down what I want to tell him so I don't forget. I'm writing that I hope he gets home to help mommy and tell my brother to stop hurting her. I think he could make him go away.

I don't really want to be a bigger brother.

I told my teacher at school about mommy and how I hate my brother. She says that I shouldn't say that, and I need to be a good bigger brother.

I don't care what she says. I just want the brother inside mommy to go away.

Daddy needs to come home.

***

Yesterday, I was home from school and wanted to find mommy because I was hungry. I cried when I called her, and she didn't answer.

I had to go potty, so I went to the bathroom and found her there on the floor. There was red all over the tub and floor and also all over mommy. I wanted to hug her, but I was scared and didn’t know what to do.

Then, mommy talked, and I saw that it wasn't mommy, it was daddy. He told me that it would be okay and to give him a hug. Even though I was scared, I did anyway because I was happy to see daddy. I got all red and sticky from him.

I asked where mommy was, and he said not to worry because I would have a baby sister soon. Then, he showed me his tummy. It looked like mommy’s did and I felt it. My sister moved like my brother did in mommy. Daddy said I would have to be a good bigger brother for my baby sister.

I yelled that I wanted mommy to come home and yelled and yelled until daddy told me to stop. He said she couldn't come home because she was busy, and I cried.

He told me to write down what I want to tell mommy, so I don’t forget. I’m writing it down while I’m waiting to be the bigger brother they want me to be.

The Mist's Touch

Marinda Kotze

Dusk crept into the forest.

Tinges of purple started to bloom amid thick banks of grey clouds overhead.

Cal and Angela thought they still had time to catch a glimpse of the lake. But by the time they got there the lake was already tucked in under a plush blanket of mist. At the edges of the lake, swirling tendrils curled up and around the fir trees, as if to caress the rough texture of their trunks.

Cal suggested that they turn back. Weaving through low hanging branches and batting away at spiderwebs, they headed west through the quiet forest.

Then the darkness enveloped the forest seemingly all at once. And the mist…the mist started crawling in behind them.

The rhythmic drum of a pair of flapping wings echoed above them. Angela stopped to look up at the tree canopy. When she turned her gaze back to the path, a silvery wall of mist hung where Cal was supposed to be.

"Cal!" Angela called. The mist absorbed the sound of her voice.

Cal's footsteps were now almost inaudible. Muffled by the soft carpet of dried fir needles on the forest path.

Cal felt an icy tinge at his ankles.

"Let's walk a little faster," Cal said and turned his head to check on Angela.

That's when he tripped on a moss-covered rock. His flashlight bounced out of his hand and tumbled into the thick underbrush.

The coarse surface of a tree trunk scraped the length of his arm and grabbed at his shirt as he went down. Disoriented in the dark, amidst hairy ferns, Cal quickly got back onto his feet. Something soft pressed against the back of his leg. He jerked his leg away.

Cal fanned his arms around him.

“Angela?” He heard his own voice in his head, but it didn’t project out into the air.

His arms caught onto something – threads, thin and sticky.

Cal tried to wipe the fibres off, but they matted around his fingers and arms like velvety wool.

Something tapped the nape of his neck. Just once. Cal recoiled and swiped at it. Now the back of his head and neck were also coated with something silken to the touch.

Cal felt a gentle pull at his shoulders, then a soft thud.

“Mmph.” Angela was there, right next to him. But a layer of cotton wool separated them.

Cal tried to pull the cloth apart. Angela’s body jerked and twitched on the other side of the dense fabric. But the more they struggled the more the fibres tangled up in between their fingers, their arms and legs. It became tiresome to grapple with it. So eventually, they stopped.

After a while, Cal and Angela felt the gentle patter of tiny paws scuttling and scurrying, weaving and spinning their bodies into elliptical cocoons. Then they joined the larder with the rest. Suspended in silent stillness.

Still Life

Sara Jordan-Heintz

My limbs feel so stiff as I lie on my back at a twisted angle. I can feel every bump and hiccup in the road as the truck barrels down the highway. No one has checked on me since we left the city.

Looking down I notice one of my slip-on dress shoes dangles halfway off my foot. And damn the luck, the nail polish on my left index finger is chipped. I shudder to think what my hair must look like, and my pillbox hat sits askew.

How I ache having to hold my handbag in the crook of my arm. But at least it's Chanel's latest out of Paris. All the others will be so jealous when they see me flaunting it.

I must admit to having felt trepidation when I learned I'd be moving from Cleveland to Cincinnati. I kept reminding myself that the spring Couture collection would soon hit the shelves, and I always relished the fact I was able to get a sneak peek due to my position within the company.

I wouldn't mind a facial and new makeup. I've been wearing this berry-coloured lipstick and cat eye-styled liner a season or two past what's proper. Fortunately, it will be after closing by the time we arrive. No one will see me.

The truck pulls into the back alley and comes to a halt. Two men step out and open the rear door. They grab some floor lamps, rolled carpets and crates. I'll be last on the list to bring inside.

After a few minutes I feel burly arms grab me by the waist. I'm carried sideways through an open doorway, helped to a standing position, and then plunged into total darkness.

In the morning, before the sun is even up, I hear footsteps coming down the hall. It's show time.

I stand inside the department store window, now attired in a green paisley patterned dress and hot pink pumps — my cheeks and lips similarly hued in that same springtime tone. My hair is long for the first time in decades. It'll probably take some time to adjust to being blonde, but as I admire my reflection in the glass, I feel a sense of accomplishment, of newness and change. Of triumph.

No matter where I'm moved, where I'm placed, or how I'm dressed, I'm always the most beautiful mannequin in the store. Bend me, shape me, pose me. Lingerie, ready-to-wear, a smart raincoat and galoshes — no one tops my versatility.

Rearranged displays, movement out of the corner of the eye, disembodied murmurs — decapitated mannequins. The activity has increased, the shop girls whisper among themselves after closing time each night.

My brain is developing more each day. And when no one's looking, I can make my wrist flick or a toe tap. I'm feeling more — what do the mortals call it? Alive.

Freak Show

Alan Dark

Kyle knew he had made a bad decision coming here. The barker had told him that the show was only for adults, and despite his pleas, he had been forced to leave. But that hadn't stopped him. Kyle snuck around the back of the building where it was taking place, an old barn on the McGregor farm, and slipped through an opening hidden by a weak board.

He smiled at the thought of taking her virginity like the many girls before her and made his way into the dark interior while doing his best to keep his erection at bay. The barn had been converted from its typical wooden beams and rusting tools to include steel struts, a wooden Dias-like stage, and numerous curtains that cast awkward yet flirting shadows across the area meant for the crowd.

Kyle watched as an overweight man wearing a too-tight white suit stepped onto the stage to introduce the performers. The first act was a human with fish-like features; too big eyes and thick lips topped a bent body covered by scales and the occasional fin. The next act was a woman dressed in flowing robes concealing the extra set of arms that revealed themselves once she began doing a magic trick. The third act featured a muscular acrobat who was able to remove his limbs and spray blood over the crowd.

Everything built up to the fourth act, Lady Despair. The curtain slowly raised from the floor to reveal a naked woman with a tight, sensual body. The veil she wore dropped to her bare breasts which appeared to glisten as though water was lightly misted on her bare skin. Kyle felt himself growing as his eyes focused on her hard nipples and barely noticed the hooked knife she carried in her right hand. Kyle heard her singing and, though he couldn't understand what she said, he felt himself calm and believing that the mostly naked woman could do no wrong.

She stepped forward and pressed the tip of the blade against another man in the audience. Kyle watched her and swore that the veil hid red lips curled into a smile and a pair of sharp teeth. The man appeared hypnotised and didn't react as the blade pierced his throat and a spray of blood coated the woman's breasts and dripped from her nipples. People screamed and tried to run but nobody knew that the barker had already locked the door. People banged on the door as the woman walked into the crowd and cackled as witnesses of death fell to her wicked blade.

Kyle ran back to the hole in the barn, relishing the feel of grass under his palms as he crawled to freedom, freezing only when he saw the pant legs reaching like twin towers in front of his face. He looked up to the barker who smiled and showed Kyle the heavy hammer that he carried.

"I told you; the show wasn't for you." He chuckled.

Idol

Ivan K. Conway

"No, don't!" pled the panhandler strapped to Nancy's garage table.

She hadn't wanted to. But her phone barely functioned these days. Even after she'd sacrificed two cats. It clearly wasn't satisfied with such small offerings anymore.

"Nothing personal," she tearfully told him while raising her axe.

It was true. Altar Wireless gave Nancy free internet, calls, and texts. However, she was expected to give her phone monthly sacrifices in return. Initially, she simply had to kill insects to appease it. Yet, it grew dissatisfied with that within half a year. Next, she provided rodents as offerings. The phone grew displeased with that within another six months. She then resorted to murdering stray cats and dogs. Now, even that wasn't enough.

Nancy swung as hard as she could at her captive's neck. Her arms weren't that strong, though, so it took several strikes to finally sever his head. He died by the second swing. At least, she hoped he did.

He'd taken her bottle of drugged booze without question. Dragging his unconscious body into her wheelbarrow proved much harder. She then covered him with a black tarp and pushed him home. Thankfully, none of her neighbours had been curious enough to ask what she was doing.

"Please accept this humble offering," she habitually recited to her makeshift shrine beside the table.

Her phone stood in judgement on its plastic tripod set on a pine stump. White candles burned merrily around it.

For half a minute, Nancy stared at her phone expectantly. Her eyes then narrowed. "Well?"

Nancy then winced and peered around. She still didn't fully understand what her status was in relation to her new phone. Part of her worried about possibly offending the device.

Finally, a familiar apple logo appeared against her black phone screen. Nancy relaxed and wiped her bloodied brow. "Thank God."

Fortunately, the large rainhat and coat she wore for these ceremonies were both easily cleaned. The gore staining her face and hands would come off in the shower. Any other blood slid into a drain in the garage's cement floor.

The phone screen fully activated to display everything in perfect working order. Seeing that made Nancy weepingly jump in bittersweet celebration. "Yes! Yes! Yes!"

She'd vowed to get a normal plan if the animal sacrifices ever failed. But not having phone bills kept her financially afloat this year, and she still hadn't found the third job she needed.

"It'll just be for a little while longer. Just until I can get my head above water. And I'll draw the line at kids," she swore uneasily. "If keeping this phone running means having to sacrifice children someday, I'll switch to a normal plan."

The tallest bar in the upper corner of her phone screen flickered threateningly before returning to normal. This made Nancy look around anxiously and shiver. "Okay, I'll stop at babies."

Two bars flickered this time. Nancy swallowed hard and blew out her ceremonial candles without saying anything more.

Only From the Shadows

K.A. Schultz

Seeing my love again on the night of his funeral—just as he had looked on that gurney at the coroner's – forehead flattened, hair matted, his left mandible crudely bridled to the bony underside of his exposed cheekbone – had filled me with an all-too familiar shock of horror.

The first time had been when the phone call had come.

The second, when I had entered the coroner's office and laid eyes upon him.

This was now the third time, when I had flipped the switch in the hall.

And there he was, still staring at me.

The next night he was there again when I turned the light on in the cellar, a limp marionette draped over a stack of bricks.

Such a sad, sad horror. My love was manifesting to me as he had been when I had gone in to identify his body. Broken and bloodied despite the best (albeit cursory) efforts to clean him up.

His ghost never spoke, nor did it blink, but looked me straight and deep in the eye. The pain and heartbreak in its gaze echoed mine, so much so that the shock of this brutish apparition was also always accompanied by a searing sadness, which would wash over me, paralyzing me where I stood.

In any unlit, shadowed space into which I passed, there he would be, the moment I turned on the light.

Never moving, never uttering the first word, only watching me, there he would hover, stagnant and silent, until I exited. The apparition would disappear promptly without a lingering trace.

I soon learned, I could walk out of the unlit room only to immediately re-enter it, and he would be gone, and I could remain – subsist – in the room with some semblance of a more peaceful solitude.

Before the second week passed, I had out of sheer exhaustion intuitively figured out how to avoid these harrowing visitations. I learned to pause before crossing the threshold, and to reach around the doorjamb to locate the switch and to turn on the light before entering any room or windowless space, for he, it, manifested only from the shadows.

By the third week I could locate every light switch without having to see it.

By the fourth week, I'd decided to simply keep every light on in the house. I ordered a thick satin sleep mask online – even had it overnighted – but I couldn't sleep. I had not slept in I don't know how long. I was still trying to process the loss, and the gruesome way my love had left me.

It came to pass, that one day – or was it night? – something else set in. I resolved to stand in the hall, at the door to my bedroom, and to reach around the doorway to shut off the light.

As soon as I flipped the switch, I could feel cold fingertips touching mine. I then felt a withered, hard hand grab my own, and I let it pull me into the darkened room.

After the Prayer Circle

Benjamin Kardos

It was early evening when we returned home from church after the prayer circle for our abducted child. He'd been missing for a week, snatched from his stroller while the nanny was taking him for a walk in the park. As the police conducted their investigation my wife arranged the prayer circle of close friends, family and the local priest. Angela figured if worldly authority was unable to deliver our son, then perhaps the divine authority could.

"Dear God," droned the priest, "we ask you to hold baby Brian in your loving care, in your mercy keep him safe until he is returned to his family. Please God, bring him back."

I parroted "Amen" with the rest of the circle, although I'd never believed in prayer. It was all wishful thinking for the delusional as far as I was concerned.

Angela was still crying as we went to bed. I managed to maintain stoic silence, holding her until she fell into a fitful sleep. I drifted off soon after her. The house was eerily quiet without Brian in the crib next to us. I still half expected to hear his ear-splitting cries in the night, demanding a bottle or a diaper change. I fell into the deepest sleep I'd had in months.

I was awakened in the darkness by a strange weight on my chest and the feeling of tiny hands in my mouth, forcing my jaws open.

Crying out, I thrashed in the bed, wrapping my hands around the mysterious intruder, attempting to throw the small body off me, but it gripped my sides with legs like iron bands. My ribs cracked under the vice-like pressure.

Startled by my screams, Angela awoke with a jolt, switching on the bedside lamp. She shrieked in disbelieving horror, staring wide eyed at my attacker, frozen with shock.

Brian sat on top of me, blue faced and dripping wet, glaring at me with raging eyes. Scowling demonically, he forced my mouth open and lowered his lips to mine, vomiting a stream of dirty water down my throat.

I squirmed and choked as the liquid poured into my swelling lungs. My chest burned as I swallowed the violent torrent jetting out of our infant. I stared into his eyes, pleading for mercy, desperately trying to comprehend what was happening to me. Struggling against his terrifying unnatural strength I felt myself growing weaker as I began drowning from the inside.

I couldn't believe it. The prayer circle had worked. Brian had actually returned to us.

Images flashed through my head. The day Angela told me she was pregnant… the day Brian was born… his relentless screams of hunger… the day I followed our nanny to the park and snatched Brian from the stroller… that short walk to the river…

My final moments were full of regret. I shouldn't have drowned our child. I should have burned him. Its unlikely ashes can seek revenge from beyond, no matter how many prayers are offered up.

The Teddy Bear

Dawn DeBraal

"He's a little old to be sleeping with a stuffy, isn't he?" His mother's boyfriend's voice made Patrick wince at the tone. Tom was always trying to make him "toughen up."

"Mark, he's only eight, cut him some slack. Why would you want to take that away if Farley makes Patrick feel secure?"

"Because he looks like a dork."

"Stop it!" His mom swiped at her boyfriend's arm, who grabbed her hand and pulled her in for a kiss.

Mark turned to see the little boy snug in his bed, with a nightlight making the bad things disappear.

"Look, Patrick, I'll allow Farley to sleep with you tonight, but you must grow out of this. Tomorrow, we will burn Farley in the fireplace before you go to bed, and you can prove to your mom that you are a man now."

Burn Farley? Never! Patrick pulled the covers over his head and hugged Farley as hard as possible. He would find a way to save his dearest friend.

"Psssst, Patrick." The bleary-eyed boy blinked, rubbing his eyes.

"Hello?"

"It's me, Farley, kid."

"You can talk?"

"Yes, you used to talk to me long ago, but then you stopped believing in me."

"Farley, I still believe in you. What are we going to do about Mark and the fireplace?"

"Here's what you're gonna do, listen carefully."

Patrick wandered downstairs as Farley told him to. He pulled the big knife from the block on the counter and walked back upstairs.

"Now go in their room." Farley encouraged.

"I'm not supposed to go in the room if the door is closed," Patrick argued.

"Did you do everything the way I told you?" Patrick nodded his head up and down. "Okay, I'll be with you." Patrick had the knife in one hand and his teddy bear, Farley, tucked under his arm when he opened his mother's bedroom door.

"Hey, pissant, what are you doing in here? You know this room is off-limits!"

"There's someone downstairs!"

Tom grabbed the knife from Patrick and ran down the hall, tripping on his dump truck at the top of the stairs and rolling to the bottom, where he lay on the floor moaning with the big butcher knife poking out his belly.

"Come on, Patrick, let's go back to bed," Farley said. "Remember to pick up that truck."

When the door closed, Patrick's mom came to search for Tom.

"Tom? Tom!" She called an ambulance.

"I'm scared, Farley; I don't want to go to jail," Patrick said, pulling his best friend closer.

"Nonsense, kid. When the cops come, they will peek in your room and see you sound asleep with your teddy bear wrapped in your arms—the picture of innocence. They won't even wake you up."

"Now go back to sleep. This has been a bad dream, is all. Good night, Patrick."

"Good night, Farley."

Night Terrors

FL Journey

The third hotel on this business trip, and all I wanted to do was sleep. However, at some point in the night I jolted awake. I looked around the room to see if something had awakened me, but nothing moved. The meagre light coming in from the half-opened curtains showed no disturbances. As I scanned the room, I noticed a figure standing near the customary hotel desk and chair, as I looked a car passed by the window lighting up the room. Instead of a figure, it was my jacket hanging over the handle of my luggage.

I closed my eyes, chiding myself for seeing figures where they weren't. It was my overactive imagination, and I knew it. As I fell back asleep, I chuckled to myself at how overdramatic I was being. It didn't seem that long before I was jerked back awake. This time it was because it felt like something was dripping on me. On the ceiling a pattern started to form and at first, I thought it was water from an upstairs unit. If it got worse, I would get up and let the clerk know. For now, I had to sleep, I had a long drive to another town in the morning.

When I woke up, I figured it was all just a horrible nightmare. I scanned the room, seeing if anything was out of place. The morning sunlight pouring into the room helped me relax. I looked up to the ceiling fearing what I may see, however there was no writing, not even a mark from last night's dream. Too many nights in hotel rooms will do that to a person. As I got up to use the restroom I placed my foot on the floor. It felt wet and tacky and when I picked it up, I noticed a number of what appeared to be fresh blood drops on the floor next to the bed. *It was just a dream, right?*

Walking into the bathroom, I looked at myself in the mirror only to see the words “Help me” written in what I could only imagine was blood. That is when I noticed the shower curtain closed. I looked down at my hands to see them stained red. Turning around I slowly opened the curtain not knowing what to expect, but what I found was worse than I could ever have imagined. There was no body, no clothes, nothing but a tub of blood. Shaking my head I turned on the shower head and washed away all the blood.

After showering and cleaning the blood off the mirror I packed and walked to the door. Looking back, I said to the empty room, “Clean up after yourself next time, you are getting careless.” I jumped into my car and drove to the next meeting, a town two states away, the smell of blood faint but ever present.

Original Fears

CJ Hooper

There was no shortage of monsters in this town and none of them sought to hide their actions any further. The drug dealers were open about their business and the pimps flaunted their wares for sale at all times of day and night.

The rest of the town lived in fear and did their best to mind their own business lest they become another statistic. Despite the crimes of Layston being an open secret still few people knew the true source of evil in the town. There were deals made every day, and each night, but as the sun went down the sharpest fools would gather on the corner, just as the lights came on.

At the in-between time of twilight, the 'Scarecrow Man' would walk the streets from east to west, gathering the secrets whispered behind the closed curtains and bolted doors. Then at the corner of the street the tall figure would let his supplicant's step forward, one by one, and listen to their pleas for succour. Few walked away disappointed, though each would soon learn that their side of the deal was strongly weighted against them.

Dennis Harrison was a family man; he held the safety of his daughters closest to his heart. So scared was he of their suffering at the hands of some thug that he too was prepared to seek out a deal with the proverbial devil. He waited with the others for the Scarecrow Man to appear and as he did, so he patiently held on for his chance to approach. The request was hurried but heartfelt, that his daughters would be safe and not suffer as others had done in this town.

The tall dark man with the face shrouded by hair, winked one of his glinting eyes in the dark and said, "No daughter of yours shall suffer, I promise you this. In time I shall recoup my cost, do you accept?"

He did.

Relieved Dennis returned home, and went on with his life, and began to forget his original fears.

It was just over a year later when PC Tracey Stirling came to the door of the Harrison household. Winona and Shirley Harrison had been found dead underneath the motorway bridge. They had suffered terribly, and the details were kept from Dennis until the coroner's full report.

In his rage Dennis stormed out that evening, just as the lights were coming on, and he sought out the Scarecrow Man as he beat the bounds of Layston before arriving at the corner where he would be expected.

"You gave me your word! You said that they would not suffer, and now they are dead! You lied to me!"

The shadowed face turned to look down at the raging man, "No daughter of yours suffered, as promised. Look to your cuckolding wife Mr Harrison. Then, you must honour the deal."

The Cold One

Michael Bertolini

"This isn't like her." Jason fumbled with the key as he unlocked the door and rushed up the stairs. He pushed the door to Lisa's apartment open, struggling against something pressing against the door and dropped to his knees in horrified revulsion. Lisa, his beautiful girlfriend who had given him a key to her apartment to take their relationship to the next level, was dead on the kitchen floor. He started to cry as he reached out and tilted her head, he felt a thin layer of ice that coated her skin. It wasn't out of the question for a cold wind to engross the city in May, but she was dressed appropriately and this, he thought, looked intentional.

He struggled to stand, to get his feet under him, and call the police. Maybe they could do something, he mused and stopped in his struggles as he saw the ethereal creature floating on the other side of the kitchen. It resembled a man, he knew as much, with the stereotypical robes of the grim reaper flowing from its shoulders. But Jason could see through it as the unknowable creature shifted so that he could see the skeletal face with a blue hue. It opened what could only be considered a mouth and a wail Jason had never experienced escaped.

Jason felt his ears bleed as sound rippled through him, vibrating his bones as he dropped to his knees. He screamed, at least he thought he did, and struggled to get away. He climbed over Lisa's frozen body as the creature floated closer, the blood from his ears freezing as it passed. A skeletal hand reached out to Jason and gripped him by the shoulder.

He felt the cold tear through his body as pain blossomed from his shoulder. His back arched as his body reacted, trying to retreat from the pain. Jason instinctively kicked back, and his foot met no resistance yet more cold ripped into him. He cried as he lost feeling in his leg.

“Please.” Jason pleaded as the creature, inhuman in all but appearance, released another wail that made Jason recoil as it touched his face. The skin turned blue, and blisters erupted. He screamed again as the ethereal creature leaned closer and tore into his body. Jason felt incredibly cold as his body was consumed and he thought of the phrase “the icy claw of death” as his vision went black.

Luc Dantes

It's 3am. My digital alarm clock says so. It gives off a crimson haze against the black canvas of the night. I don't remember waking up, but here I am—lying in bed, staring at those ominous red numbers.

I haven't been afraid of the dark since I was a little kid. I'm 15 now, nearly all grown up. Michael Benowitz has been saying he's a man since his bar mitzvah nearly two years ago.

No, I'm not afraid of the dark—the fear weaving around my spine is even more primal; it numbs my nerves and makes my heart beat slower as I consciously take each breath. My body's not my own, so I pray, just like mum used to do whenever I had a nightmare as a kid.

"Our father, who art in heaven," I hear footsteps creeping up the spiral stairwell leading to my room. The house is kind of shaped like a fishing boat, so my room is the only one upstairs. Someone's coming and they're definitely coming for me, "Hallowed be thy name."

Their steps are getting louder as they near the door, like a drum beating to my lagging heart "Thy kingdom come." The door creeks open, ever so gently—almost—tenderly?

I can't see who it is, I'm unable to move; I open my mouth, yet my scream doesn't carry, "thy will be done," they're beside my bed now. "On earth as it is in heaven—" my soul cries out to the Lord God almighty! A hand is thrust into my gut and what I can only imagine are my intestines are excavated.

The pain isn't like how they describe in the movies. It's not my body, but my brain that's scorched by electric fire. I feel a warmth oozing down my sides and realize it's my blood pooling beside me; I can feel the nothingness of where my innards once were.

Visceral slurping—a familiar fragrance—mum?

Busy Signal on The Reincarnation Hotline

Ken McGrath

Hello.

Thank you for calling the Reincarnation Incorporated hotline.

This is an automated message.

We understand that this can be a difficult, confusing and a traumatizing time. Rest assured that our team of dedicated customer service agents are available to ensure that your transition goes as smoothly as possible.

As such we request that you please remain calm and stay on the line to maintain your place in the queue.

If you know what your Karma Credit score is please input the number now followed by the hash key, otherwise please press zero.

0

We appreciate your patience and co-operation.

Please select one of the following options:

1: if you have used the Reincarnation Incorporated service before.

2: if you have been reincarnated previously and used a different service provider at that time.

3: if this is your first reincarnation or you cannot remember the details of any previous incarnations you may have had.

3

Thank you.

This is an automated message: We understand that this is a difficult, confusing and traumatizing time. One of our customer service agents will be with your shortly.

Thank you.

This is an automated message: Please hold the line to retain your place in the queue and remember that your call is important to us. At Reincarnation Incorporated we are here to help you achieve the very best next life that you can.

Please hold the line.

All of our customer service agents are busy at the moment.

Please continue to hold the line.

This is an automated message: Due to a recent earthquake in the South Pacific we are at present experiencing a higher-than-average number of calls. This is resulting in unfortunate delays to our service. Thank you for your patience.

If you were affected by this recent event, please press 1 now.

If you are unsure of the circumstances surrounding your current situation then please press zero.

0

Thank you.

This is an automated message: We understand that this time of transition can be difficult and thank you once again for your patience. Your call is important to us, and we hope to have a customer service agent available to assist you shortly.

Please continue to hold the line.

This is an automated message: We are experiencing an unexpected higher than average volume of calls and unfortunately cannot deal with your query at this time.

You will be allocated a random short-lived reincarnation to hold you over while we process this backlog.

We apologise for this inconvenience and thank you once more for your patience. We understand that this can be a difficult, confusing and traumatizing time.

Please note this temporary reincarnation will not affect your overall Karma Credit Rating.

If you do not agree or would like to appeal this decision, then please press 1 now.

1

Unfortunately, due to the high volume of calls we cannot process your request at this time.

Goodbye.

Beep. Beep. Beep.

Bad Penny

(March Winner)

Jim Donohue

From the moment he got the phone call, he'd been dreading this. *Why does she want to meet with me? It was nice for a while, but I ended it. There's no going back.* But yet, there she is. Like a bad penny you can't get rid of. He steps out of the shower, towels himself off, and begins the grooming process. *Just because I don't want to see her, doesn't mean I can't look and feel good, right?* Dressed and out the door in record time, he heads for his car and the drive into town.

I really don't want to do this. And yet, he seems to be rushing to get there. Maybe he does want to reconnect after all.

No freaking way! He pulls into the parking lot of the agreed upon place, walks into the diner, pretty empty at this time of the night. *Hmmm, never been here before. Looks nice enough*, he thinks. The booth he chooses feels very comfortable. He's a couple of minutes early, so he waits.

The waitress comes over and says, "Hi Freddie, same as yesterday?"

"Sure," he says, confused as to how she knew his name, "I'm expecting someone".

"I know", she replies, and walks off with a smile, disappearing into the kitchen.

That's when the lights go out in the diner.

To say it was pitch black would be a slight overstatement, because the streetlights offered what little they could to the only person now sitting in the otherwise empty diner. Freddie heard the little bell ring as the front door was opened.

And there she was.

Her matted brown hair hung down in front of her face, like the girl from that horror movie, The Ring. She wore the same tee shirt and jeans that she wore the last time he saw her. The day he killed her.

But...she's...

Freddie's breath caught in his throat, as he watched in terror as she sat opposite him.

"Hello, Freddie," she croaked, her voice reflective of the maggots that coated her vocal cords. Freddie couldn't speak. He just sat and stared at the dead girl, as chunks of skin fell freely from her face.

"Not so pleasant, is it?" she said, noticing his discomfort. He managed to agree by shaking his head, still not sure what was happening, yet knowing exactly what was to come.

"Well, this is our hell, Freddie. The hell you created for us. I'm doomed to walk the Earth like this, and you are doomed to meet me here. Over and over again. Freddie barely found his voice, "F-For how long?"

"Until you DIIIIEEEEEE!!" she growled.

Freddie screamed. "NOOOOOOOO!!!!"

That's when he woke up.

From the moment he got the phone call, he'd been dreading this.

Why does she want to meet with me? It was nice for a while, but I ended it. There's no going back.

But yet, there she is. Like a bad penny you can't get rid of...........

After / Birth

(Reader's Choice)

Secret Geek

Strip-lights trembled an embryonic darkness as Kyisis cut through a pungency of offal-stink and the line of anxious hospital staff. Every face battling with it-couldn't-happen-here acceptance.

"Excuse the mess, Detective," the uniformed Corban joked, lifting the crime scene tape.

Kyisis' feet broke the white, powdery line at the threshold to the old operating room.

"Salt," Corban revealed. "She spread a circle of it round the room."

Kyisis fed his gaze on the corpse in the centre of the dimly lit chamber; a distraction from the horror show on its walls.

"Suicide?" he asked, frowning.

"Come see," Corban directed.

Kyisis stepped through the pooling blood, cradling his nose. The body wore hospital orderly robes, was young — even pretty — once. Her abdomen was ripped open.

"Looks—"

"—Like somethin' ate its way out, right?" Corban said, grinning sardonically. "And what's with all that shit on the walls?"

Kyisis forced his eyes upwards. Someone had woven a copper-lattice hemisphere onto the central ceiling light, reaching down on all sides like the crinolines of some vast, antebellum dress. It gave the room a domed feeling that belied the once-straight tiling of the blood-spattered walls. But it was what was grafted onto the copper dome lattice that compelled Kyisis to cover his nose again.

Flesh. Black and brownish yellow. In places, some chunks fought to retain their rounded, disk-like shapes; elsewhere, others had succumbed entirely to the pull of time and rot. They were the source of the offal stench: the corpse-reek that delivered the room to his sickening pall; Kyisis' stomach itched with it.

"Near as we can figure, she's been bringin' 'em down here for months," Corban said, gesturing to the bound flesh.

"We know what they are?" Kyisis asked.

Corban nodded over to the two forensics officers in coveralls snapping away with the expensive camera.

"Lizzie Borden over there says they're placentas," Corban declared, running his hand down his fat gut. "Wild, huh?"

"Why would anyone do that?" Kyisis asked.

"Might have something to do with this," the female forensics officer replied.

Lizzie Bordan, Corban? Asshole.

Kyisis stepped around the corpse, trying not to see the reverent anguish imprinted on her face. The forensics guy groaned, then flashed another shot and the room was birthed in an oversaturation of unforgiving light.

"What we got?" Kyisis asked, stooping down to see.

It was a journal of sorts. A decoupage of newspaper articles and hastily scrawled notes. Stories of pregnant girls bleeding out in parking lots; doctors dealing in illegal, backstreet abortions; the summoning's of some insane, revenging pen in many scripts and languages. But — on the open page, in English — ritualistic words screamed out: ‘Five Must Die to Bring Its Birth.

“What do you think it means?” Lizzie asked, massaging her abdomen and wincing slightly.

“You eat a bad burrito too?” Corban spouted, doubling over and clutching his gut.

The tormented squeal of an oversaturating flash gave form to shadows. It was then that Kyisis felt the itching of his stomach start to bite.

The Fortunate One

Robert Herold

I laughed and withdrew my hand from the old fortune-teller's gnarled grasp. I glanced at Angie, whose own fortune moments ago promised adventure.

"The fates have spoken. They think you should have me over for the night. That'll be the start of your adventure."

Angie blushed. This was, after all, our first date, though we'd known each other for years.

The fortune-teller grabbed my hand again, and her raspy voice said, "I'm quite serious. Do not go home if you value your life." Chuckling, I gave her twenty dollars, telling myself if I got lucky, I might return tomorrow and give her a hundred. I drove Angie home, and she invited me in. "It's the least I could do when you're in such danger," she said with a flirtatious smile. I made a worried face. "Thanks, Angie. You're a lifesaver."

Inside, we had drinks. A spark became a blaze, and before I knew what was happening, she was in my arms, and we kissed with abandon. Then, Angie took me by the hand, the same hand the fortune-teller had grabbed—and led me to her bedroom. The following day, though part of me just wanted to camp in her bed, we decided to have coffee and croissants at a local bakery.

Angie smiled at me over breakfast. "The fortune-teller was right. That was a great adventure."

I returned her smile. "It was to die for."

"Is it safe for you to go home in the light of day?"

I said I thought so, and Angie insisted on accompanying me. At my place, three fire truck crews were stowing their gear. My former home was a mass of charred timbers, twisted metal pipes, and ash.

“What the hell happened?” I asked a uniformed man, the fire marshal.

“Isn’t it obvious? You the owner?”

I said I was, which led to a series of questions. After providing identification and contact info, he transcribed my statement and had me sign it.

Noticing smouldering patches across my front lawn, I asked about them.

“Damned if I know. Let’s have a closer look.”

Angie and I followed the fire marshal into my yard. A series of burned tracks, shaped like giant cloven hoofs, ran from the street to where the house had stood and back again. *A demon?* My head spun with the possibilities. Who might I have pissed off who had that sort of power?

I grabbed Angie’s hand. “Come on!” We ran as fast as we could to my car.

I drove to the waterfront, where the fortune-teller had her booth on the boardwalk. We raced up and down the carny area but saw no fortune-teller, so we stopped at a caramel corn booth and inquired.

The proprietor, a heavy-set woman with pink hair and a nose ring, laughed at my query and said, “The old gal who used to tell fortunes died in a fire twenty years ago.” She chuckled again. “I guess she didn’t see *that* coming.”

Coffee Break

Ivan K. Conway

"You don't have to do this!" urged Chelsey while trembling in Mike's arms. "We've got new sedatives on the way as we speak!"

Mike's bloodied head shook before he pressed the scalpel slightly deeper into her neck. "How many times do I have to tell you? Your damn drugs aren't working! Give me oil and a lighter! Now!"

Stabbing pain struck his chest with every heartbeat. He was pretty sure his ribs were cracked from the intense pounding. And this agony was nothing compared to the burning bullet wounds in his head, torso, and stomach.

Tears were dampening Chelsey's lab coat. "Mike, you're not thinking clearly! It's sleep deprivation! Just let us keep trying! The coffee's bound to—"

"I haven't slept in five goddam days! I can't take it anymore! Give me some damn oil and a lighter! I know they're in this lab somewhere!" Mike roared. He would've also been crying if his eyes weren't so dry.

"Mike, I'm saying this as your friend. You don't want to incinerate yourself."

Mike's eyes clenched in misery. "What I want is to rest! Drugs won't let me do that! Bullets won't let me do that! Burning myself to ashes is the only way out now!"

Dr. Charles's voice sounded over the laboratory intercom. "Michael, please calm down."

Mike's laugh was hollow. "Calm down? Calm down?! Do you think I'd be doing all this if I could just calm myself down?! My heartrate is probably faster than a hummingbird's right now!"

"Michael, if that were true, you'd likely be dead," Dr. Charles observed cooly.

Mike poignantly tilted his head. A chunk of red brain matter slid out of it. "Doc, I don't think you've been paying attention! I can't die! Your goddam coffee won't let me!"

The pistol he'd used on himself still lay smoking on the lab's tile floor. Two of its six bullets remained lodged in his body. Yet, any of Mike's self-inflicted gunshots would've killed an ordinary man.

Chelsey warily eyed the intercom on the adjacent wall. "Doctor, please tell me you got those new sedatives!"

"They're on their way, Miss Bradly. Just be patient," Dr. Charles answered with nonchalance.

"Like you give a damn!" snarled Mike at the one-way window in front of him. "Probably taking notes as we speak! Thinking of ways to market this poison you've developed! Well, I'm done being your lab rat! You hear me?! I'm done!"

Dr. Charles was as unshaken as ever. "I'm afraid the contract you've signed says otherwise, Michael."

Mike's head dipped in despair. It didn't matter how expensive college was getting. He never would've participated in this experimental trial had he known what awaited him.

Suddenly, the lab door burst apart as men in riot gear stormed into the room. There then came a pricking in Mike's neck from a fired tranquilizer dart. To his immense relief, his heartrate slowed before he finally lost consciousness.

That Corner of The Ceiling

Ron Schroer

We call them dark shadows and the darkest come by night.

And what is night, other than an absence of sun?

The world remains whole, but that temporary absence allows certain things to move safely about.

I see that corner of the ceiling, *there*, where the folds of night are darkest. Most solid.

God, I've never seen it so black. That corner overhead, nearest to my bed.

I watch this blackness with tired eyes and fancy that it moves, that it has sensed me watching and now slides slowly from its corner, oozing down the wall until it has passed from my sight. Surely some delusion!

And then a strange thrill sweeps through me as I imagine I can hear it, down there on the floorboards, the soft, slippery sound of something inching its way across my floor. This is some fabulous dream, I tell myself, as my bedsheets are eased away by the weight of something hauling itself up to greet me.

Yes—I swear that I can feel the presence of something here with me. If this is a dream, then the dream has body.

Its first touch is delicate, tentative; the gentle exploration of a new and nervous lover. It caresses my neck, searching, its tapping of my skin like the brushes of a feather.

Tapping, tapping, to the beat of a throbbing pulse, there within my virgin flesh. And there and then it rests, as if it simply wishes to nestle there, to nuzzle me.

But then the needle—the sweetest prick—sure and sharp, and a sudden warmth like red wine in my belly. There's a dissipation of something complex and exotic, a kind of love, I think. My limbs lay helpless, my organs alive and yet subdued, oddly compliant. The heart beats and the lungs breathe and the blood flows, yet these acts of life are no longer my own.

And now a fresh embrace, as my shadow lover mounts me, sliding over me like a second skin. I am enfolded, I am joined, I am wedded, as magical thoughts now come to me, as my rich, warm pulse flows outward.

I see such wonderful things! I see the signs and wonders of glimmering visions. I feel the joys of shining memories, of only the best days. I feel the weight of my sunlit happiness. Or is that my second skin, filling slowly with a flowing treasure?

But who, or what, is my lover? I open my eyes (or perhaps they were never closed) and look down, along my hooded body, and I can't help but laugh.

Its skin is black, like that corner of the ceiling, but it glistens thickly, it has gloss, an oily sack, my hungry body-bag, its mouth held fast against my throat. My lover, my last caress, my false paradise.

I laugh; I laugh. I am leeched, I am emptied, I am filled with *joy*.

The Toy

Stacey Michelle Warner

Kate reached for the wrong cupboard. She blinked in silent confusion before reality caught up. With a sigh, she opened its neighbour and retrieved the coffee she was looking for. Damn. She really needed a proper night's sleep. Dreamless. Preferably.

The remnants of the nightmare clung to her even in the daylight. A chill in her veins. Bones heavy and weary. It had been the same for weeks now.

She "woke" in her dream, sat bolt upright. She turned, slow, held back by dread, to see the doorway to the bedroom warp and widen. A summons, felt deep in her core, called her through. The hallway stretched out; pitch black aside from the attic hatch which emanated warm light. Her stomach knotted as she reached for the pull-cable, but she couldn't fight the inevitable.

There, in the darkest depths of the attic, was a toy. An old-fashioned robot, with a wind-up mechanism. Paint peeling. Broken.

Kate knew that the toy needed fixing, and she needed to do it. Through her sleep, she would toil and slave, often with such intensity that bone started to show through papering skin. She handled the clockwork mechanisms, the cogs ripping at her. She had given so much that each tear drew no blood. Her eyes, pulled taut with exhaustion, sat in black caves.

Though every night she seemed to make progress, every morning she woke up to the grim knowledge. The toy wasn't fixed. It wasn't like she was dreaming of zombies or monsters and yet she woke up nauseated, chest heaving against cold sweats.

She sipped the bitter brew then stood with resolve. *I should just see what's up there, put this to bed once and for all...*

She stood underneath the attic panel, staring upwards. Her stomach clenched with foreboding. Some part deep inside of her screamed: RUN. But it was at war with the same voice that tells your fingers to pick at a scab you know you should leave well alone…

In the end, it wasn't really a choice. She climbed into the attic, each rung cold and biting into her skin. There, sure enough, was a toy robot. Every muscle clenched as she turned it in her palm and realised that, somehow, the toy was fixed. All that was left was to turn the clockwork.

Click.

Click.

CLICK.

The robot juddered at first, as though it might not move at all. She leaned in, curious, desperate to inspect the strange little thing.

Then suddenly it leaped, it's claw shaped hand shoved into her throat. She fell to the floor clawing at exposed vocal cords. There was no scream, just a blood curdling gurgle punctuated by the clicking noise of clockwork. The toy marching to the open hatch was the last thing she saw as the world went black.

The Looks on Their Faces

R.G. Halstead

Knowing that he was going to die eventually, old Walter Holt set hundreds of snap traps in his house. To kill the damn mice. Snap! Snap!! Their little necks and spines were viciously broken. When he was really lucky, the vermin killer was able to run up in time to see the damn thing struggle, let out unreal sounds, shudder... and then die. Oh, he loved the looks on their whiskered faces just seconds before the end.

It was what he lived for now... after murdering his five wives over the years. And somehow getting away with all of them. Walter did not need to worry about any cops now. Ha! Murdering hundreds of mice was not illegal.

To help him be able to afford to keep the lights on in his house for so long to witness the violent, snapping deaths, he collected the dead mice into a bag once a week and took it down to the local meat shop. The guy there ground them up and sold it as mystery meat to the unfortunates. He gave Walter ten bucks for every bag full of dead mice.

Money for the monthly electricity bill.

It seemed to Walter that his luck was increasing. There were more and more snapping deaths that he was able to run up to and see the little bastards' look of upcoming death. A unique, horrific look on their faces. Much more pathetic than before. And as a real bonus, the sick old man was now seeing live mice feast on dead mice caught in his traps. Holy shit. How low was that? he thought.

He liked this. He did not question how these rodents' faces could now show emotions when they never did before.

His prey made more spine-chilling death rattles while in the process of dying. But it was the looks on their faces that really got him going.

Walter and his 495 traps wanted more.

He did not mind having to wash off the smell of death from the snap traps that had caught another one of them. A small price to pay for so much enjoyment.

After witnessing five death rattles in one morning, Walter and his racing heart decided to take a break by reading a book. He selected a heavy hardcover novel and pulled it from the bookshelf. Jammed in there too tight, Walter was soon falling backwards. And the bookshelf came slamming down on him.

Damn it. He was stuck under the heavy bookshelf. Yelling for help did no good.

That was when he saw the thousands of mice come towards him from all angles. He could see them licking their lips. Smiling. Snarling. Their many bites into his flesh hurt like hell. Non-stop.

And to make his slow, painful death even worse… several mice dragged his bathroom hand mirror and positioned it so that the mouse killer could see the look of upcoming death on his own face.

The Urge

David O'Mahony

What harm could it do? It'd just be a little scratch, wouldn't it?

The itch is driving me crazy. All day every day, all night every night. Even when I'm asleep I'm dreaming about it.

But it's not the same part of my skin all the time, you understand? It moves. Sometimes it's my stomach. Sometimes it's my leg. The worst is when it's my back – I couldn't reach it even if I wanted to.

I can't, you see. I mean, my hands work and all. That's not the problem. The problem is that I don't want to let it out. The thing that's under my skin. You have it too, don't you? Yeah? I mean, it can't just be me, right?

I think I can see it sometimes, when I'm looking in the mirror and the light is just right. The colour just drains away and I'm in black and white, a sketch and not a watercolour. But then it's like there's two of me, only the other one is just beneath me – and it doesn't move like me. When I look left, it keeps looking forward for half a second. When I look up, it looks down. Sometimes I swear the skin is bubbling, like a cat playing under a blanket. The bubbles are in colour, full oil painting colour. And I know, right in that second, that I could be in colour too if I gave in to temptation.

That's when the itch really gets to me. That's when I get the urge to just drive my nails in and pull the skin apart. That's when I think to myself, it's just a shell anyway, why not let the real you out?

And after all, what harm could it do? It would just be a little scratch.

But then I stop myself. Because what if it's not the real me? What if it's worse?

So, I'm stuck in this little halfway world, going mad from the itch and mad from fighting the urge to scratch it.

What was it Augustine said, we're all just olives in the press? Being crushed by one thing and then another at the same time?

And I'm so tired. I've never even tried rubbing the skin where it itches, isn't that crazy? Or maybe I have, and I've forgotten. I've lost track of time. Everything is the same all the time. I wake up, I go to sleep, I wake up, I go to sleep, but I don't even know if it's night or day.

But I need something, anything, to change.

And I'm looking at myself in the mirror, watching the thing inside me looking right back. It's nodding at me, like it's giving me permission.

The itch is so bad. I think I'll do something about it tonight.

After all, what harm could it do? It'd just be a little scratch, wouldn't it?

Omnivores

Scot Ehrhardt

Caridea salted the water a second time, as instructed. Realistically, she thought, it shouldn't make any difference. Just put it all in at the beginning.

Pandal, her son, leaned around her to peek into the pot. She curled her body over the tiny screen of her phone. A young chef on CrusTube with bright cherry pigmentation was speaking. "In one movement, bring both claws up toward you in a snapping motion."

"Eww," Pandal said.

Caridea ignored him. On the screen, the spine pulled from the cavity like a drain auger. She hadn't considered the violence of cooking before, but—

"—They have heads?!" He grabbed the phone from the counter. "Yuck, look at the hairs!"

"These are packaged without heads." She held one up. "Split and cleaned."

Pandal shuddered.

She plopped several into the water. They sunk; the water bubbled. She returned to the attractive chef, who recommended only four minutes.

Indeed, their colour was already changing. A deep pink spread inwards from their little appendages, muscles blossoming through the sliced-open backs. Their tightened shapes spun slowly in the frothing water, like dancers, Caridea thought. "You liked them at the restaurant, Pandal."

He flung open the kitchen door. "I'll eat whatever's in the yard."

“Opportunistic omnivore,” Caridea murmured to the CrusTube chef. “He looks grown, but he mopes like a shrimplet.”

The chef suggested horseradish.

She scooped one human out with a slotted spoon and watched the steam rise from its body. Her maxillipeds worked the pink meat to her mouth. Salted twice—lovely.

Reptilian

Tom Folske

Brittany didn't consider herself a conspiracy theorist by any means, even though she didn't believe politicians or the government, but who did? She figured plenty of people were cheating and lying on every tier of life, it was human nature, the rich just got away with it easier. Still, they were probably just buying more yachts, not trying to deviously manipulate humanity, well, at least no worse than anyone else with wealth and power ever had. Besides, what could she do about it anyway?

Brittany was waiting for her boyfriend Kent outside the bar where she worked. She just finished her shift and had stepped outside to have a cigarette while she waited. At some point, Brittany had begun to pace out of boredom mostly, and her inability to sit still. When she passed the dumpster, however, she heard something move and it startled her. She was barely able to suppress a scream.

"What the…" Brittany whispered, before quietly creeping closer and craning her head to listen. The thing moved again. Something large was shuffling around inside the dumpster. Brittany crept closer still, goosebumps popping up on her arms and the hairs on the back of her neck standing up progressively more with each step she took. She felt a tingling tightness in her spine as she reached out with great trepidation and put her hand on the lid, preparing to investigate. Brittany involuntarily held her breath as she lifted the lid and peeked inside the garbage dumpster.

At first, her mind couldn't comprehend what she was seeing, she thought she was looking at one of the velociraptors from *Jurassic Park* having its way with her boss Randall. It took a moment to process that the torso of what she was now sure was not, in fact, a dinosaur, was actually protruding from the waist of her employer, while his limp and vacant flesh lay empty across the garbage pile in front of its lap.

The thing was legitimately wearing a Randall suit. The thing was Randall.

The Randall-thing jumped in surprise, looking up at Brittany like a deer caught in headlights. Brittany stared back at him in just the same fashion.

A moment later the thing moved, and Brittany wasn't sure if she had really seen Randall start to lunge at her or not, but she slammed the lid down as fast as she could and took off running.

Thank the fates, Kent pulled up just as Brittany emerged from the alleyway. She ran and jumped into his truck, slapping the door violently behind her. She commanded Kent to get the hell out of there and the look on her face prompted him to do exactly that without question.

When they got back to their apartment, it took two hours until she was finally able to tell Kent, who believed her, what she saw, and he was the only one she told. Needless to say, Brittany never returned to bartending for Randall. She never went to that bar again.

Under the Knife

Russell Mickler

My cardiothoracic surgeon enters the O.R. "Morning, sorry I'm late."

"Bout time." Her assistant, Dr. Michael Thompson, waits to my left. "Was there a run on Iced Caramel Macchiatos?"

Ethan, the anaesthesiologist, sniggers behind me. "I'm pretty sure Hermès handbags went on sale again at Saks."

"Neither" the doctor says, retrieving a clipboard at my feet. "Your wife insisted on cuddling before I left, Mike."

Dr. Thompson flinches as everyone chuckles.

"Hello again, Mr. Keenan."

I reply from the table. "Doctor Patel."

She examines my vitals. "You've already met my team, so we'll get started. State your full name, please."

"David Kyle Keenan."

"Birthdate?"

"June 7, '62."

"Occupation?"

"Deputy Director of Operations, EPA."

Ethan pats my shoulder. "A V.I.P."

He smells like vinegar.

Dr. Patel whispers to the perfusionist before addressing me. "And the procedure you're undergoing today?"

I swallow, my mouth dry as a dustbin. "A coronary bypass."

"Good." Dr. Patel approaches from my right. "I'll have you under for five hours. Questions?"

I hesitantly glance at Dr. Thompson.

"Oh, don't worry," he assures. "I've double-checked her medical degrees and board certification. She's legit."

I grumble, avoiding the doctor's eyes. "No."

"Everyone?"

"Ready, Doctor."

Dr. Patel turns to her instrument tray. "Ethan."

"Just relax," he says, slipping a pair of earbuds into my ears. "These will keep you entertained."

Testing 1-2-3.

"Did you hear that, Mr. Keenan?"

I nod. Ethan wears a weekend shadow — stubble crawls down his throat. Soft, drifty music plays as he secures an anaesthetic mask over my nose and mouth. "Alright. I'll have you count backward from ten."

"Ten," I say, muffled behind the mask.

Sweetness fills my lungs.

"Nine."

Ethan calibrates a dial. "Very good."

"Eight."

The music layers in a distant, breathy flute.

"Seven."

"Breathe in deeply."

"Six."

My extremities feel weightless; my tongue stills in my throat.

"Mr. Keenan?"

I'm unable to speak.

Ethan gives a thumbs-up to Patel. "Roger-Roger."

"Prep the patient." Dr. Patel lifts a scalpel.

Ethan smiles upside down at me from behind his mask.

Hi, Dave.

A recording of Ethan's voice overlays the music while a technician sponges cold antiseptic across my chest.

By now, you've realized you're paralyzed yet retain full sensation.

Dr. Patel leans over me to position the knife with her forefinger.

There are no words for what you're about to experience, but before that, Minister Wei Zhang conveys his deepest regrets.

I try to lunge, sit up, or pull away, but I can't.

If only you hadn't rejected those lithium mining permits in Nevada.

Searing pain blinds me as the blade scores my sternum.

He paid good money for your approval.

I try to scream — blink, twitch. Nothing.

Ethan rests a palm on my shoulder.

As for myself, I so rarely get to explore this aspect of my job. Thank you.

Drowning in agony, I barely comprehend what he's saying.

But don't fret.

Ethan closes my eyelids.

She'll chalk up your demise as a routine complication.

"Sternotomy retractor," Dr. Patel commands.

Babalon

CJ Hooper

Six candles flickered barely resisting the unnatural breeze around the circle. The darkness beyond was not so opaque that Sheila could not see the figures that shifted rhythmically to the syncopated beat of a drum. The acidic taste of blood was around her lips and on her tongue. Dry heaving she failed to vomit but her guts persisted in trying. She couldn't remember how she got to this place, just some drinks and party atmosphere in that huge room overlooking the sea. The night had promised to be one to remember. She screamed though it hurt her throat, it felt torn and ragged, but still she cried out. Her limbs felt like dead weights with no feeling in her extremities. As she attempted to stand her head span, and she collapsed down onto the floor. The lines of a star were visible on the floor with each point leading to a beeswax candle. Her hands reached out to one of these, but her strength failed again, and she rolled sideways, knocking something that made a metallic sound as it fell. It was a chalice, simple and pewter, and it spilled red upon the floor. There was no mistaking the viscosity of blood as it poured around the cup and stained her hands as she struggled for stability. Laughter emitted from the darkness, mocking her attempts to stand. Crying and screaming, she begged them to help her, but this encouraged more jeering.

A voice laughed, "I've no sympathy for you."

"Why are you doing this?" She yelled, "Why?"

Then the voice spoke, closer this time, "You wanted to learn. We showed you. Now you get the highest honour of all."

There was a change in the air, the smell of beeswax candles and blood was overpowered by the scent of leaf mould, and an animal odour. It was like sweat and wet fur, a dirty foetid smell of an unclean cage. Sheila tried to turn as she felt breath on her bare neck but was held by fear. Something close behind her snorted, it was bestial, but the hands that gripped under her arms were human, articulated, and strong. They gripped her under her arms and lifted her up into the air. Her sinews screamed with pain and the strain of her own weight pulling her down, her shoulders were wrenched by the strength of the beast that hoisted her up. Above the ground and high over the candlelight she could see beyond the magic circle. The figures were robed, six, maybe seven of them, continued to move around her.

A high-pitched woman's voice called from one of the hoods, "Receive your blessing, Babalon!"

Whatever held her up pulled her in close and she could feel the roughness of animal hair and muscle against her naked back. She tried to scream again but her voice failed, the candlelight's blurred. The deep darkness from outside the circle closed around her and she returned to unconsciousness.

Sacrifice

Kay Hanifen

The wailing cries of the dead surround me, ice cold fingers groping, tearing at my dress, digging their grave dirt nails into my flesh. The God who watches with cold, golden eyes impassively at the ant colony we call Earth turns its hungry gaze upon me as I chant the words to bring about my apotheosis. I hold the ceremonial dagger in one hand and a book in another. Centuries ago, the worshippers of the Old Ones had bound it in human flesh, flayed from the still living sacrifices. They made ink from their blood and wrote the ancient words in an impossible tongue.

Love requires sacrifice, and to feel her in my arms once more, I'd give the Old Ones the world itself. Her name is etched in the grave before me, the vibrant life attached to it reduced to cold, grey letters on dreary stone.

"Hjila henaoba B'alant Nok!" I shout above the wailing din and wind so fast it tore away my breath. "K'nath'uhl, The Watcher in the Sky and Guardian of the Dead, I invoke you. Grant me your power so that I may restore and join the one I love. I give you my eyes in exchange." Without hesitation, I stab it into one eye and then the other, screaming in agony as the world plunges into absolute darkness and silence. I fall backwards into the dead grass with a gasp, viscous fluid dripping from my now empty sockets. The groping hands of the dead no longer tear into me, and all I can hear is my own agonized breathing.

Then I hear her voice, and it's like the first birds of spring. "My bride?" It was her voice. Her lovely voice that I thought I'd never hear again, and my only regret for cutting out my eyes is that I couldn't see her face.

I wish I could see her, to once more gaze into those deep brown eyes, braid her raven hair, and trace the red cupid's bow of her lips. "Is it really you?"

"I think so," she replies, and a hand appears on my face. It doesn't feel like her hand. Where her hands are soft and warm, this is cold and slimy, like a raw steak. Something shifts under her skin before burrowing into mine. "I've wanted to sleep by your side for a long time. Come, we'll rest in my bed."

A hand wraps around my foot and pulls before I can even think to struggle against it. And then I'm falling. I land on top of something hard and my ribs crunch, making every breath agony.

"No," I cry, struggling to get away from her unnaturally strong grip. She pulls me into her casket, and the smell of decay and formaldehyde fills my nose, making me cough. The top of the casket closes above us, and she holds me close as the sound of dirt patters from above.

Asunder

(Aprils Winner)

Lars Rook

My eyelids creak apart.

I have no memory of arriving here.

I don't even know where here is.

Last, I recall, I was in my cell, drifting into a jittery sleep, awaiting my final sunrise. Darkness took me.

Then I was here.

I stand barefoot, on the damp forest floor. For a second, I'm elated. I'm free. I feel dew on my toes, fresh air on my cheek.

How I got here isn't important. All that matters is that I'm safe.

Far away from the hangman's noose.

Then I see them.

I squint, forced to rely on what few spots of daylight pepper through the thick canopy. Blurred shapes solidify in the gloom.

My eyes begin to see.

My brain begins to understand.

My blood runs instantly cold.

My moment of ecstasy is cut short. I'm frozen, rooted to the spot by a cocktail of terror and disgust. I can't tear my eyes away. I can't even blink.

Corpses, everywhere.

I count dozens, maybe even hundreds. I can't begin to guess how many more there may be. Some dangle limp from the trees, like pale, fleshy ribbons. Others lie bloated on the ground.

Most have been torn to pieces.

And the damp underfoot? That's not morning dew.

It's blood.

My heart stops. My mouth goes dry. I'm suddenly all too aware of the absence of birdsong. The forest spins, the stench of raw, rotting meat overpowering my brain. It's so potent I can taste it, like rusty tin on the tip of my tongue.

Something warm and moist condenses on the back of my neck.

It growls.

A shockwave runs through my body. I launch forward, diving into a frenzied sprint. I don't look back. I don't want to see what pursues me. I hear the steady thud of feet in pursuit.

I must go faster. The forest is a blur. Branches whip my flesh, and thorns tear through my clothes. Blood and sweat stream down my face. I taste salt and iron. I'm half-blind, maddened by terror. A stitch sears my side, but I can't rest.

Stopping would mean death.

I only know I've tripped when my chin hits the ground. The impact knocks me for six. My teeth rattle. My brain slams into my skull.

Groggy, I struggle to bring my eyes into focus.

I instantly wish I hadn't.

I'm locked, eye to eye, with a corpse, only inches away. My gut contracts. I scream.

I know that face.

It's mine.

My eyes dart around. Every single corpse is the same. Each one is me. I remember now. Thousands of deaths, each one excruciating. Every sensation is raw, fresh. I experience the unspeakable agony as my limbs are ripped away, as my sinews are severed, as my skin tears like paper.

The creature is upon me now.

A fresh wave of pain begins.

Darkness takes me…

My eyelids creak apart.

I have no memory of coming here.
I don't even know where here is.

Mother Mercy

(Reader's Choice)

Dan LoBrace

Sister Cecile cut her prayers short, eyes drifting back to the warped window across the chapel.

Outside stood the sign—wooden, weatherworn, and humming with dread.

ABANDON ALL HOPE.

It marked the edge of the woods—thorny trees cloaked in fog thick enough to slice.

"It will always be close," said a stern voice behind her.

Sister Cecile hung her head, caught again.

Mother Mercy approached from across their crumbling convent outpost, her ancient face drawn tight with disappointment.

"We must not let its presence distract us."

"I know, Mother," Sister Cecile sighed. "Our duty is sacred."

Mercy's spine stiffened. "We guard the gates of hell, Sister. There is no higher task."

The trembling nun nodded. "Forgive me, Mother. I'm just… so tired."

Cecile's limbs were weak. She had arrived months ago and had been stationed here ever since.

Mother Mercy placed a hand on her shoulder. "Being near hell… drains us. Those woods are filled with abominations hungry for your life force. That is why you must remain steadfast."

Cecile hesitated.

"When will the other Sisters arrive?" she asked softly.

Mercy didn't answer at first. She turned to stir a pot of gruel—slow, deliberate. Cecile winced at the wet, slopping sound.

Then, without looking back, Mercy said, "They wandered too close. Beyond the sign. They are now lost forever."

Cecile blinked back tears. Mercy didn't flinch.

"If they call out to you from the woods, do not listen. It is but an unholy deception."

"Get back to your prayers now, Sister," Mother Mercy said as she continued stirring the gruel.

Cecile returned to prayer, forcing herself to focus. But her mind slipped. How long had she really been here? What was she doing before she arrived?

What exactly was on the other side of that wooden sign?

Outside, the wind sent it creaking.

Cecile tilted her head. The warning pulsed with new weight.

Abandon all hope.

Then—like a veil lifting—the outpost unravelled.

The stone walls surrounding her became screaming skulls. Benches contorted into corpses locked in mock-prayer. And Mother Mercy—

Cecile gasped.

Beneath Mother Mercy's black habit grinned a demon. Its eyes were viscous and boiling. It smiled rows of rotten teeth, dipped a claw into the pot, and pulled up a human face—Cecile's face—slurping it like soup.

Cecile screamed—

And it was gone.

The wind howled. The sign creaked again.

"Are you alright, child?" Mercy asked, once again perfectly human, sipping from her ladle.

"I… I think I need to lie down," Cecile whispered.

"Of course, dear," said Mercy, smiling. "Rest well. We need all our strength to fight this evil."

Cecile turned toward her room, one hand against the wall to steady herself.

She looked back once—at Mercy.

Then at the sign, visible still through the warped glass.

And then she wondered:

Was the wooden warning keeping her out?

Or was it keeping her in?

A Foggy Forest (Reader's Choice)

Michael Ajogwu

A foggy forest, twisted trees stretching like skeletal fingers, a decrepit sign that reads: "Abandon All Hope." The wood is silent, save for the shifting mist curling around the trunks like grasping hands. The air is thick with damp rot, the scent of earth long undisturbed.

Emily shivered at the sight of the notice, her face was pale and drenched with fear, as she pulled her jacket tighter around her. The fog and cold were really weird. She shouldn't have wandered this deep, but curiosity had gnawed at her, pushing her past the point of reason. The stories about the forest had always seemed like local folktales, crazy warnings meant to keep children from straying too far. But now, standing here, the silence felt unnatural. Like the world itself was holding its breath.

Just then, a whisper blew into her ears. They slither through the air, too low to make out words, but familiar. A voice from the past. A lost loved one. A secret only she should know. They beckon, tugging at curiosity like a fishhook through flesh.

"Emily..."

Her breath caught in her throat as she sharply turns around to locate the voice. That voice. It sounds just like her mother. But that's impossible. Her mother had died three years ago. And yet, the whisper carries the same warmth, the same soothing cadence she remembers from childhood bedtime stories.

"Come here, sweetheart. I've missed you." The voice added.

The fog thickens, shadows pooling between the trees, growing darker, deeper.

They are not men, nor beasts. They are the absence of light itself, gliding between the trees like liquid voids. No eyes, no faces, just unimaginable figures stretching unnaturally in the shifting mist. They flicker, like candle flames in a dying breeze, and yet they never vanish completely. Always at the edge of sight. Watching and waiting for you alone.

Emily takes a step back, her pulse hammering. The ground feels unsteady, her legs shaking rapidly, like the earth beneath her feet is no longer solid. She swallows hard, trying to convince herself it's just a trick of the mist. Just her mind playing games with her in the dark, she tried to run, but to no avail.

Then she hears it, a heavy breath, too close behind her.

Spinning around, she finds nothing but the swirling fog. But she knows she's not alone. Her skin prickles, a heavy weight pressing down on her chest. The whispers grow louder, voices layering over one another, pleading, laughing, sobbing as it grows louder. And beneath it all, a voice that is unmistakably her own, speaking words she does not remember saying.

"Help me."

A shadow detaches from the others, drifting forward, slow, deliberate. The whispers stop. Then, a single word in her voice said:

"Run."

Branches claw at her arms, snagging her clothes as she bolts through the trees. The shadows move with her, shifting like ink spilled into water, closing in, closing in. Her breath comes in ragged gasps, her legs burning with effort. She stole a glance over her shoulder.

And sees them.

Hundreds of them. Silent. Flickering. Hollow. The ground beneath her vanishes. She falls, and the fog swallows the scream.

The Suicide Woods

(Reader's Choice)

CJ Hooper

She passed the sign with barely any notice given to it. She had seen the photos of it before, in books and on screens, and she was not shaken by it. Keiko considered the instruction unnecessary.

The sign was supposed to be a warning, but it was ill heeded but for the few who understood its true meaning. Those had 'abandoned all hope' before they set off for the forest. They had succumbed to despair long before they had even heard of the Suicide Woods. Once they'd gained the knowledge of them, and their location, however, they set out on what they thought would be their final journey.

Keiko was one of those who had decided to end their life. Everything had become so dark that no thing and no one could redeem her existence. She would walk into the trees as so many had done before her, and, if her knots were correct, the fall and jerk would snap her neck. Death would be instantaneous. Her pain would be over.

The trees creaked as she passed, and the fell wind carried the stench of decay before her. The deeper she went the worse the smell became. It was like foul and heated rotting meat. The natural exothermic reaction of entropy destroying the remains of the former victims of suicide. It was strange to use the term 'victim' Keiko though when the sentence of this illness was self-induced and terminal. In previous months and years, she had been more charitable in her considerations, but now here she was, joining their ranks.

Shadows before her, suspended from the boughs, became more definite. The long elliptical shapes became human shaped. These were the bodies of the recent dead, she assumed, too soon to have decayed and petrified against the exposure to time, and nature.

The first body she saw was that of a nurse, like Keiko, but the uniform here was turning green, blue, and black with mould. The next was of an elderly man, with a face lined with age and scars from some torment visited upon him by life. The third she saw was a woman, a recent mother judging by the deflating swell of her tummy. Keiko had failed to save ladies like her, both during and after the birth of their children.

The physical reality of the corpses left hanging, and unredeemed in the woods brought her planned act into sharp relief. While she had no hope, it seemed she still had doubt, and her resolution wavered.

The mother's eyes opened, and the corpse began to wail, her eye holes gushing blood as she did. The cacophony was an unholy sound, which was joined by that of the noise of the corpse of the old man, which simply began muttering, trying to speak through its strangulated trachea. Her life had no hope, but it could never be as bad as this, eternal torment suspended in despair.

The Bee-ginning of Revenge

Dawn Colclasure

My eyes opened and I gasped. My mouth felt different. Not human.

I reached up above me and felt a satiny covering. It's too dark to see anything, so I had no clue what it was.

I only knew I must get out.

My hands pounded against it and soon it broke into pieces. Dirt fell onto me, and I realized I was buried.

Roaring with fury, I tore away the covering. I managed to break free of this thing and dug my way out of this grave.

Finally, I reached the surface, and I threw myself higher, hungrily gasping for air as I landed on the ground.

I got to my feet, shaking dirt from my face and head.

A buzzing sound occurred behind me. I cocked my head, listening. The sound grew louder right behind me.

Surprise flooded through me when discovering I had wings on my body! As the buzzing intensified, I reached above my head and felt antennae.

I looked down at my body. I had the body of a bee! Normal human arms and hands, normal legs and feet, but the rest of me was a bee.

I looked around this graveyard to see hundreds of other mutant bee creatures looking just like me standing over the graves they had just crawled out of.

I detect a variety of scents. My eyes suddenly glowed with evil. A command from our queen came to our minds: "KILL THE HUMANS! GET OUR HONEY!"

Our wings buzzed loudly as we prepared to take flight. We took to the air, our group growing in number by the hundreds as more of our brethren emerged from their graves.

As we drew closer to the town, our bodies morphed into smaller sizes, and we broke into groups.

I zeroed in on a house and flew inside through an opened window. I flew straight to the kitchen, where I knew our honey was kept.

A human sitting at the table in the kitchen looked up and screamed when it saw me. It swatted its arms through the air. I zoomed at its neck, furiously stinging again and again. My mutated stinger with its razor-sharp edges cut deeper and deeper into the human with each strike, blood squirting out.

I felt the poison from the insecticide that had made me what I was leak into the human's neck with each sting. It soon dropped dead.

My body mutated back to a human-sized adult. I found the honey and carried it out of the door. I looked to see my brethren also stationed on a front porch, where they had killed to regain what was rightfully ours. Each of our stingers dripped with blood and remnants of human flesh.

Once we had all gathered on the street, we took flight, returning the honey to our queen in the abandoned hive, the lone survivor from when the humans had sprayed our source of food with their poisons.

The Nightmare

CJ Hooper

Emma woke with a start, she was not in her bedroom, but she couldn't see or hear anything, She was alone in a dark place. The floor was smooth and polished. There was a smell of cooking fat and something not far from crispy bacon, but instead of tantalising her taste buds it made her gag. It was the odour of decay that she smelt underneath it all that caused her to retch. The only sound was a ringing in her ears, the high-pitched whine that came when she was exhausted or dehydrated, or after a night at a rock festival with her parents. Her sense of touch was the only way to find her way out at present and so she kept to the ground, sliding her hands along what felt like wooden flooring. There was a patch of dust in front of her, and her left hand had disturbed it. It irritated her sinuses as it clouded into the air in front of her and she stifled a sneeze with her forearm. With her right hand she reached out and touched some more but carefully she felt along where it lay. She realised it was in a rough line before her and extending around in a curve. It was a circle. When Emma brought her hand back to her face she could smell a distinctly alkaline odour, this may have been chalk-dust or something similar, though it was hard to tell with the overpowering stench of rotting meat assailing her senses.

That gag inducing smell was growing stronger and just as she edged forward past the line of dust her right hand slid into some nearly solidified wax and the remains of a candle. It was still hot and molten in part; she quickly withdrew her hand and held it to her mouth to blow on it. This was where the putrefying smell of dead animals was coming from, or at least from here and from other candles like it. It was an effort, but she managed to rise to her feet and began stepping warily out of the circle and into the space beyond. Her foot recoiled as she trod upon something wet and clingy, it wasn't blood she realised wiping her toes with her bare hand, but from the smell it was some bodily fluid and quickly she went to wipe her hand on her pyjamas. She flinched again as her hand touched her side. She was naked. Emma gave a short scream and reached down to the floor to wipe whatever this disgusting excreta was, it felt like mucus but smelled like something more revolting.

There was a sudden snort in the air. Something animal was in the room with her. A new smell reached her, it was the scent of animal's cages at the zoo, and there was something like leaf-mould in the air.

Her stomach heaved, and she dry retched, her quick breath became sobs.

The beast was just behind her.

The Box

Patrick T. Luce

I stood, staring into the crowd of relatives and self-proclaimed "friends of the family", not seeing them but looking through them at a painting on the wall of the funeral home. It featured a large barn near the left side of the frame and an old, discarded tractor with vines growing up and into its rusted grille. That painting caused me to think about my parents' belongings. Now, with both of them gone, what did they have that would become old and rusted and overgrown with neglect.

Someone was standing in front of me, telling me how sorry they were. I hadn't even realized that this person, a woman I'd never seen before in my life, had taken my left hand between both of hers and caressed it with her old hands that seemed to be wrapped in cold, wrinkled tissue paper rather than skin. Not meaning to be rude but feeling numb to the plight of everyone else in the room, I pulled my hand away and walked out of the funeral home. I'm sure some had been confused by the action, but it didn't matter.

I drove, not really thinking about anything, and ended up at my parents' home. The house whose door had opened and closed upon every chapter of my childhood—at least a far back as I could remember. I parked in the driveway and walked, not up to the front door but around the side and through the gate into the backyard. I left the gate door open and heard my mother's voice telling me that doors left open had a bad habit of slamming on you at the worst possible moment. I smiled a little at the memory and continued through the yard to a massive, broken-down shed that rested in the far north corner.

I stood in front of the large double doors and realized with astonishment that I had never been inside. A rusted combination lock hung motionless from a chain which had been strung between the two door handles. I could have looked for a large rock or something, but what was the point? I reared back and slammed the bottom of my shoe squarely on the old lock. It hurt, but the lock crumbled, and the chain fell away. The doors swung open half-way without being touched, and I reached forward to open them the rest of the way. I expected tools and gardening supplies—maybe some weed-be-gone, or an old watering can. Instead, I found a single large wooden box almost as wide as the shed itself and maybe three or four feet tall. The lid was one solid piece and did not appear to be secured down in any way, so I leaned forward and lifted. The lid came up easy enough but when I saw what was inside, I dropped it. Two questions formed in my mind. How long had my parents been locked in this box? And who, or what, had taken their place?

Hidayat Adams

She's back, standing silently in my bedroom doorway. Her blood-filled, shattered eyes stare at me hungrily. I'm transfixed, as on every other occasion of her visitation. I'm desperate to move, to switch on the light, but my body is paralyzed.

She hisses a name. Vapor issues from her mouth like a snake slithering towards me. The cold wraps its coils around petrified me, squeezing, tightening, cutting off my air. I know I'm about to pass out, but I fight it. I don't dare close my eyes.

Sheri and I met, fell in love and got married all in a span of three and a half months. A whirlwind romance if ever there was one. Too late I discovered her flaw: she was sickeningly cloying. She started to smother me with her constant need to touch me, message me, call me. Not an hour could pass without her reaching out to me.

I don't recall when the idea came to me to kill her, but there it was. I saw it all so clearly – how I could take her away for a weekend to some remote Air B&B, preferably one in the country where there'd be many places to bury her corpse. I acted on it that weekend. Luckily, we had no close friends, and our marriage was never advertised. Killing her was simplicity itself. When I dropped the cinder block on her face as she lay sleeping on the picnic blanket, her eyes shattered, crimson blood spurting like twin geysers.

I buried her under a tall pine tree, covered the ground with fallen needles. Returning to our flat, I immediately packed up our things and moved out. I left a note for the landlord, saying I had to return home for a family emergency. I left an extra month's rent to assuage any suspicions he might have.

Nobody ever came looking for me or Sheri.

I had escaped without any repercussions. Until the nightly hauntings started. Night after night I dreaded closing my eyes.

My eyes flick open, dart toward the doorway. But there's no doorway. Only the cold embrace of my dark grave above me. I open my mouth to scream. Dirt fills it. A whisper next to my ear intensifies my already heightened horror.

"Now we'll never, ever be apart again, darling Caleb."

My Mother Before Me

Eden Esquibel

The first time They knew my mother was dying was before I was born. Something unusual brewed in her, a systemic attack on her own flesh and vessels and organs. The treatments that were available were invasive, something They were unable to counter, even with all of Their intelligence and awareness. When I was nothing but cells, I latched onto the hope of survival, something of perpetual usefulness now.

The second time They knew she was dying was when I was born, and upon my early arrival, kept me in an incubator like an animal for slaughter. Her form barely survived, her cells collapsing constantly, as she shed her own skin like a snake. She could not stand for that long. They provided enough sustenance for her to maintain her form. When I was only four pounds, I was thrust into her arms, and she looked upon me with terror. I was something unknown to her, covered in hair.

She was not recognizable to me as my mother for many years. I knew her as a lady, a woman, which is something I wish I could take back now. She spoke to me of what life was like before, of her youth, of her last days of enjoyment. She could not bear the truth without her body becoming a useless, dying thing. My mother was something They could not consume. Even as her daughter, I could not understand her.

It was right before she died that she told me the truth. I was fifteen. When the door shut behind us, and she lay in bed, she grabbed my hand and held it. "You must continue to live. You cannot trust Them. They do not care about you." When I asked her what They were, she shook her head frantically. "They are those without names. We don't have a word for Their kind in our language."

I squeezed her hand, and she whispered, "You cannot show them fear. You have the same opportunity for the Growth. They will take you in and tell you that They can cure you. It will not show itself for another five years. You have to escape before then." I looked at the door behind us. She looked past me, eyes wide with terror. "I was so young when they came down to earth," she whispered. "Now I don't remember what life was like before. You have a chance before it grows."

Suddenly her hand went limp. A scream escaped, but her mouth was closed. Whatever it was, it launched out of her so quickly, the blood barely flowed. I looked back at the door and heard it lock. I looked at my mother's corpse, and the thing that crawled out of her. It smiled at me before it jumped down my throat.

The Dare

CJ Hooper

There was a long tunnel that went under the railway bridge, and it came out onto the fields beyond the town. It was a popular jogging route when the day was bright, and the summers were long. At night and in winter though it was avoided. Graffiti adorned the inside, though none of it was the shabby tagging which one mostly saw in the towns. This spray paint here was called 'artistic' by the generous, and 'grotesque' by the prudish. The first depiction to appear was that of a simple white figure painted around a protruding broken pipe which had previously drained water from the spoil around the bridge. The next was a hanged man, not the inverted symbol of wisdom from Tarot but the figure of a naked male strung up by its contorted neck. The rest were more gory and bloody, the work of a twisted mind, the local press had described it.

Jenrick was braver than most, and he ventured out there often with his friends from school, but never did they stay beyond twilight. This time, however, he had been dared by the other lads to go out there, and to film himself walking, not running, through the tunnel at nighttime. Getting out of the house was easy enough, his parents were drinkers, and both had passed out on the couch by the time the evening was truly dark.

By the time Jenrick had reached the opening to the dark passage he was soaked with rain and his feet were drenched through his sneakers, yet here he was, and he was going to go through with fulfilling his dare. He switched his 'phone on to camera and video mode, with its torchlight giving of just enough luminescence to show the way just in front.

The first step snapped him to attention as his foot went into a deep puddle, the water was ice cold, and the shock ran up his leg. The first thing he filmed was this incident and he imagined his friends laughing at this when they saw it.

The painting of the impaled man should have been just ahead, but when he raised his camera, he only saw an empty space where it had been, and Jenrick worried that his friends wouldn't believe it was the same tunnel. Then he saw it, bigger and more defined than before, higher up the wall, more detailed than he remembered. As his eyes adjusted to the darkness he realised to his horror, this was no painting. This was fresh and real, and the blood flowed from the pipe like a new wound.

He screamed and ran, when his face was hit by the bare bloodied feet of a hanged naked man, faeces running down the freshly strung body. Further on he could hear the groaning of someone in slow pain, and he saw the red gash in the dying lady's neck.

The next day the police found a new image, a young boy...

A Good Town to Grab a Bite

Diane Arrelle

Gregory woke weak and shaky.

He was exhausted, but snuggled under the warm blanket, he felt great about deciding he'd had his last run. He hated driving the big rigs, hated grabbing cat naps in rest stops, hated rushing just so he could get paid.

This last trip had been a gruelling twenty-eight hour run, but that order of frozen plasma filling the double trailers had a rush stamped on it. Gregory sighed and remembered how he'd pulled into town last night an hour ahead of schedule. As he backed up to the loading dock, the tiredness just rolled off him. He'd made it and got the bonus.

He saw the tavern across the street, its red neon sign flashed 'Teddy's'. He turned to the guys unloading the trailers. "Teddy's a good place to grab a bite?"

The young guy snickered. "The best!"

The older man, in his fifties, smacked his co-worker across the top of his head and answered, "Buddy, I suggest you go to the convivence store, for a sandwich and go directly to bed. This is a tough town at night."

Gregory shrugged, "Thanks, I can handle myself."

"Well, you were warned," the man said and turned away.

An hour later, after a rare steak and a couple of beers, the cute, young waitress who'd been eyeing him since he walked in, smiled, licked her lips and set up three shots, "on the house."

Gregory didn't really remember anything after that.

Now, through the dirty window in a motel room he didn't recall renting, as he noticed pre-sunrise lightening the horizon, Gregory scratched a stinging itch on his neck. His fingers came away wet and sticky. Puzzled, he turned on the lamp his gut tightened, and his heart started pounding. That sweet, young waitress, naked on the bed next to him, smiled with blood-coated fangs.

Gregory stared at her in absolute horror just as an armed police officer burst into the room.

An armed cop at the door and a vampire in my bed. Could this get any worse, Gregory thought as panic tightened his chest and made him feel like he was having a heart attack.

The uniformed cop snarled at Gregory, his fangs glinting in the lamplight. He barked, "Mister, you just fucked my fifteen-year-old daughter!"

"Jailbait!" Gregory moaned, Cold, clammy, sweat suddenly covered his body and he began shivering. *Yep, it got worse*!

The cop continued, "Should arrest you, but, well now, we like to handle things differently here. Let's just skip the legal paperwork."

Horror clawed at his gut, and yet, Gregory felt a flash of hope *Maybe the cop would take a bribe.*

He watched the man level his gaze at his daughter and growl, "Gloria, how many times do we have to punish you?"

Then officer sighed, glanced at Gregory, looked back at his daughter and snapped, "Gloria, you finish drinking him off right now! Then consider yourself grounded . . . again."

Turn Up the Volume

Julia Rajagopalan

"Computer, play classical music," Stephanie said. A clear, piercing slice of violin music slipped out of the little speaker on her end table. An open bottle of Malbec sat on the coffee table with two glasses. Stephanie poured herself a glass.

The clanging started again, a metal tink-tink-tink from below, that made her want to shatter her wineglass against the fireplace. Instead, she set it on the table.

"Computer, turn up the volume." The string instruments grew louder, and she stood. Stephanie wasn't the type of person to put things off or bury them in the basement. She was proactive. She faced her problems.

In the kitchen, the door to the basement was closed, but she could still hear the metal tink-tink-tink. With a huff, she grabbed the brass knob and turned.

"Steph? Is that you?" His voice called from the darkness. She stepped slowly down the narrow stairs, not looking up until she reached the bottom. Finally, she pulled on the string next to the overhead bulb, and with a snap, light flooded the small, cement-block room.

He sat on the floor in his boxers, arms bound behind him to a pole with the handcuffs he had bought her for her birthday. To spice things up, he had said. Stephanie was feeling pretty spicy now.

"Please, let me go," he begged. "You know I'm an idiot. Remember spring break? But you always forgive me." He had been so easy to trap, so trusting, even after he had betrayed her trust so thoroughly. Then again, she had never given him any reason for doubt.

"You wanted this, right?" she asked. "You wanted exciting. That's why you cheated?"

"I'm an asshole," he said. "I know, but it's been hours."

"I hear you and I see your perspective," she said, in the same tone the couple's therapist had used. She walked around the post to his back. The acrid smell of bleach stung her nostrils as she neared the laundry area.

"Oh my god, thank you," he said. "I'm so sorry. I really am. We can start over, I swear."

Stephanie ignored him and lifted a cloth covering the workbench next to the dryer. From the variety of precisely laid-out weapons, she picked up a large sushi knife. Then, she turned and knelt behind him, the cold cement biting her knees through her yoga pants.

Slitting his throat was easier than she had anticipated. The sharp blade slipped through his skin like it was cutting raw tuna, and blood flowed hot and thick out of the neck she had once kissed so tenderly.

She went to the worktable and picked up his phone, unlocking it with his dead face. There were several unread messages.

How's it going? How'd she take it?

Where are you?

You'd better not be hooking up with her one last time.

A violin wailed upstairs as she typed up the text.

Just finishing up here. Be over in a bit

The Plague Church

CJ Hooper

The church bells were heard clearly ringing out over the treetops. For years the local farmers had talked about this, but Mark and Mary thought it just an endearingly whimsical folk tale. A fantasy for the few visitors that occasionally, and mostly accidentally, came by. Tonight, however, as they walked across the causeway and up the winding road to the church beyond, the peals were definite and real. Both of them shivered, but neither mentioned the uncommon cold on that summer night. Mark not wishing to admit that he felt it and Mary not seeking to disappoint her new husband.

They had researched the history of the building together, having discovered its deconsecration over a hundred years ago, and that the diocese had recently put the near ruin up for sale. As entrepreneurs they had the money, and, as a result of this, the time to take on this little project. To buy their own little church and convert it into a home.

The church of St Claire was not attached to any particular parish but to the former town of Helmsford, a plague town. A tale of despair as, in 1665 AD, the population of this once thriving village had been almost entirely wiped out by the bubonic plague, except for the few who had to bury the many corpses. Helmsford was no more, only the church ruins remained. The rural rumour was, however, that the church bells could still be heard ringing on a windy evening. The catch for any who were interested was that, despite the sound, there were no bells left in the tower.

The church revealed itself as a dark shadow set against the light shade of the trees in the early evening. From the approach it was a forbidden void against the tenebral sky. The bells rang still. Echoing among the trees and tombstones. Not to be put off Mark and Mary laughed at the warnings of the old farmer, Jennerkin, and resolved that the bells must remain in the tower, the sound was too real and definite. Mark angled his mag light up at the slated windows on high, and could clearly see movement between the shades, the shape of great swinging bells. Together they laughed at this revelation and considered themselves cute to have not fallen for the whimsies of the locals.

Mary pushed open the church door, allowing Mark to squeeze past her with his torch on a wide beam. Only now did they begin to fear, for there was no strong wind tonight yet the pealing of the bells was louder in here and the sound bounced off the walls.

There was movement in the tower. Great shadows shifted up and down against the darkness above. In the torchlight Mark and Mary saw them clearly. Corpses clad in rags, their skin pock marked with buboes, wrapped in the bell-ropes. Hanged by the neck, but damned as suicides. The unlucky few who had remained to bury the town.

The Unboxing

(May's Winner)

Khala Grace

One

Streetlights shine through the fog like fireflies. A light drizzle taps the ground. A person appears on the scene and that person is... **You**. During your late stroll, a strange sight comes into view. A small table equipped with an umbrella for cover. As you approach the table you find a box. Indeed, the box is small but lacks a lock. As your fingers hover over the lid... You stop to think. *Should I?* Your mind is conflicted. If **Yes**, continue to the next paragraph. If **No**, skip to the third.

Two

Your curiosity grows as your heart palpitates with anticipation. *Wait... How can I be* ***that*** *excited?* The thought crosses your mind. You proceed to slide the latch. Once the box opens, you notice the streetlamps flickering like static on a broken television screen. You turn to find a tall man standing with a pale face and a charcoal smile. What do you do? Should you be bold enough to **confront** the man, then head to paragraph four. Perhaps, you prefer what lies in the fifth paragraph-- raising a brow and **turning away**.

Three

A brisk breeze blows from behind. Raindrops dampen your shirt. The cold sensation sends shivers to your fingertips. *I rather not.*

You deny curiosity's grasp. You turn to leave. Yet, who is that man standing there in a bowler's hat? His face is pale and has black diamonds painted over both eyes. Before you can ask, the man holds up a sign:

Are you sure?

Well, do you refrain from the box's temptation, or do you reconsider? When keeping the lid closed, you may read paragraph five. Otherwise, scan for the sixth paragraph.

Four

The man in front of you takes a slight bow. He introduces himself in sign language:

A-R-T-H-U-R H-O-L-M-E-S.

You stand in the rain with a confused gleam. *That name doesn't ring a bell.* You can't help but to feel a bit frustrated from the strange affair. Your eyes dart from the man to the box. As they slide back the man, he holds up a sign:

Are you going to peek?

That's been the question the whole time! Does your frustration win, and you leave the stranger and his stupid box? If so, read the next paragraph. Does the curiosity's grip return, and you want answers? Then finish with paragraph six.

Five

You find yourself in a precarious situation. Still, without batting an eye, you simply walk away. Once several feet apart from the stranger, you can't resist a glance behind. He stands with a sign reading:

Such a pity!

You set your gaze ahead. Even so, as you head home, you cannot help but to wonder...
What was inside that little box...

Six

You open the box to reveal a decorative card. While turning around, you see that the man is no longer there! Another glance at the card provides the reading:

Greetings, Curious Mind!
You are cordially invited to the party hosted by yours truly,

Arthur Holmes.

Reflections

(Reader's Choice)

Dr. Kerry B

In the quaint town of Elmwood, nestled between towering pines and whispering winds, stood an ancient manor. It was an architectural marvel, with its gothic spires and creeping ivy, yet it remained shrouded in mystery. The townsfolk spoke in hushed tones about the manor's most peculiar artifact: a large, ornate mirror, said to be haunted by a family of ghosts.

The mirror hung prominently in the grand hallway; its gilded frame tarnished with age. Legend had it that the mirror was a portal, a window into the spectral realm where the spirit family resided. It all began with the tragic story of the Langley family, who lived in the manor more than a century ago. The family met their untimely end under mysterious circumstances, and their souls were trapped within the reflective depths of the mirror.

The Langley's were a loving family—Henry, the wise patriarch; Margaret, the nurturing matriarch; and their two children, Edward and Anne. Together, they lingered in the mirror's realm, eternally bound to the manor they once called home. On moonlit nights, their spectral forms would press against the glass, their anguished faces visible to those brave enough to look.

One autumn evening, a curious young woman named Lily inherited the manor. Fascinated by its history, she moved in, unaware of the mirror's dark secret. Lily had always been drawn to the supernatural, and the manor's eerie ambiance intrigued her.

The first night, as the grandfather clock struck midnight, Lily found herself inexplicably drawn to the mirror. She stood before it, her reflection wavering as though submerged in water. As she gazed deeper, the air grew cold, and the room seemed to darken. From the glass, the shadowy figures of the Langley family emerged, their eyes filled with longing.

"Help us," whispered Anne, her voice a haunting melody. "Release us from this prison."

Lily, though startled, felt a deep sympathy for the trapped souls. She spent the following days researching the family's history, determined to free them. Her investigation led her to discover an old diary hidden within the manor's library. The diary, penned by Margaret Langley, revealed a chilling detail: the family had been cursed by a jealous relative, their souls bound to the mirror until a selfless act of love broke the spell.

Armed with this knowledge, Lily devised a plan. On the night of the full moon, she stood before the mirror once more, clutching Margaret's diary. With heartfelt sincerity, she read aloud a passage of love and forgiveness. The mirror trembled, its glass shimmering with ethereal light.

As Lily spoke the final words, the Langley's began to fade. Their faces softened; their expressions of torment replaced by peace. One by one, they vanished, their spirits finally free. The mirror, now just a mirror, reflected only Lily's smiling face.

The manor, lifted from its curse, felt lighter, as if the very walls sighed with relief. Lily knew she had done a good deed, bringing closure to the family and ending the haunting legacy of the mirror. She stayed in the manor, her heart warmed by the knowledge that she had given the Langley's the release they had long yearned for.

Faces

(Reader's Choice)

Sandra Petrinovic

So many faces. So many screaming faces.
So many faces leering back at me. So many faces, which one am I?
I feel so isolated, so alone, so scared. No one to hold my hand.
Holding my head between my hands. I must shake out those faces.
Screw up my eyes so I can't see those faces. I know they are still there. Those grotesque faces refuse to leave.

I shout, "Leave me alone. Go away."

Grey walls all around me, or is it a dirty white? Does it matter?

Walls cracking, plaster flaking, bricks falling. Walls are closing in all around me. I can't take it anymore.

Where is this place? I can't think straight.

People gawking at me through a window in a door. Why?

My mind is broken. Who will fix me?

I am screaming 'help, help', but no one hears me. Is this in my head?

The only sound out of my mouth is a wail.

I'm not strong anymore. What's killing me, making me weak? Oh! So pale.

Doctors administering life-giving blood, but I snatch the bag away and slash it open.

Blood everywhere. Blood running down the walls.

Orderlies holding my arms and legs down. I am moaning, "No, No."

My arms and legs were strapped down, and I couldn't move to get away.

This time… a mirror is placed on the ceiling. They tell me to try again. Look into your soul, find where you have gone.

Torture 101.

I close my eyes. Water is poured on my face, forcing me to open my eyes and see. I cough and splutter. I don't want to see. I can't see, the hellish demons won't let me see. Those gruesome demons want to take charge.

I am too weak to resist. My body and mind are imprisoned in this jail of torment.

They won't let me rest. A jab to my arm, finally, a sedative.

I wake up sitting up straight, bound in a straitjacket. I am rocking back and forth, back and forth. I am slowly losing my mind.

The doctors say this is because of my drug and alcohol abuse. I will not pull through.

The demons in my head are all talking at once. When will they stop?

When will the pain end?

One last look in the mirror—so much weight loss.

I am losing my eyesight, no, my eyes are slowly closing, closing, closing.

No more pain and suffering.

Gone.

Endless Ladder

(Reader's Choice)

John Weagly

Why do I look so tired?

"Rung by rung
Climbin' that ladder to your caress,
Rung by rung
Our love will always be endless"

You remember that boy band from the late-80's? Jayden, Jordan, Jason, Jackson and Albert. You remember them, right?

Yep – Fresh Teens On The Turf.

"Your eyes drive me crazy,
Like love is insane,
Life gets all hazy,
Climb to Heaven and back again."

They did that concert in '89, remember? At Alcatraz. The prison. Some kind of fundraiser for Anti-Animosity or Arts In Our Hearts or Save The Singing Centipede or something. After the concert, their plane crashed on the way to North Dakota. Turned out one of the teens had a pet tarantula. It got in the cockpit and bit the pilot. Allergic reaction. Eight-Hundred feet above the ground. They never stood a chance.

"Baby, don't you understand?
Do I have to shout it from a bandstand?
Life without you, nothing could be worse,
Our love is like a beautiful curse."

The weirdest thing about that tragedy was that a three-foot-by-three-foot mirror survived the crash. Not a crack. Not a scratch. Not a single blemish. It was like that looking glass was touched by otherworldly influence.

The mirror went to a relative of one of the teens. Then it got sold at an auction. Then it got stolen or something, it just disappeared. And now, well, now I've got it. How? I'm getting to it. I went to this traveling fair and bought it from a one-eyed hunchback. Really! The mirror's frame was peeling and the glass looked like it hadn't been cleaned since George was King, but it was otherwise in pretty good shape, and I needed a mirror. I won't go into deeper detail about the misshapen merchant that sold it to me except to say he was a pleasure to deal with and smelled faintly of cinnamon.

"You and I will have a blast,
Forget the future, forget the past,
Others may call it a kind of perversity,
But we'll be together for all of eternity."

How do I know it's the Fresh Teens On The Turf mirror? Because they're in it. That's right. You heard me correctly. Jayden, Jordan, Jason, Jackson and Albert are trapped in the mirror. I guess when that plane hit the ground, their souls went into that looking glass. I look into it, and I see all five of them.

And hear them.

"Rung by rung
Climbin' that ladder to your caress,
Rung by rung
Our love will always be endless"

They sing. I hear them. Mouths open in yawning wails. I hear them. The same song over and over and over again. I can't not hear them.

"Rung by rung
Climbin' that ladder to your caress,
Rung by rung
Endless, endless, endless"

So, why do I look so tired? I'm not getting any sleep. I'm living a waking nightmare. An awful, annoying, loud nightmare.

Honestly, I wasn't a fan even when they were alive.

The Rat in the Mirror

(Reader's Choice)

JB Wocoski

They say the dead recall how they died, but I could not even recollect how I got into this abandoned rundown room. I stood there in the centre facing grey, peeling mildew-covered wallpaper. Glancing around at the four walls, they were all the same. A quick glance upward confirmed the ceiling had the same mildew pattern, but no wallpaper on it. Am I imprisoned?

Standing there, I stood inside the middle of the largest Rorschach inkblot test pattern ever conceived. This is when I noticed no door to get out of the room.

Nor any light on the floor, wall, or ceiling to illuminate the room, yet the room was still illuminated. How could I see the dead rat on the floor? I picked it up by its long hairless tail between my thumb and forefinger. Behind me in the middle of the wall was a mirror. A rapid glance over my shoulder confirmed it was a mirror. As I stood in front of the mirror, my reflection did not stare back at me. Instead, the rat floated alone upside down in midair without my reflection standing there. I shook the rat and observed it shimmer and shake upside down in the mirror. Flipping it over my shoulder, it sailed across the room. It bounced off the back wall without me anywhere to be seen. Once more, I glanced over my shoulder, and the rat lay on the floor matching its reflection to perfection.

I turned back towards the mirror. Startled! I caught my breath, there were five cobweb-covered bruised faces in the mirror, all with bloodshot eyes staring back at me. I sneered, extended my hand and waved ever so slowly at them. They followed my hand. I laughed at them; they did not laugh back with me.

Pressing my cheek and both palms against the mirrored surface, I pushed harder on its reflective surface, as hard as I could. Ripples like a pond formed about my wrist as it gave way a little bit. My stronger left hand and arm began to slip through the puddled looking glass surface; my head followed both hands through the rippling mirrored surface into the other realm.

Halfway through the looking glass, I reached out for the five, now, froze in fear. Within seconds, almost all of me was out of that room into this other realm. I grabbed on to them, knocking them over, down on to a grey stone floor. Their weight jerked the last of me free away from the mirrored surface.

I feasted on their blood before any could escape my fangs. Refreshed at last. I remembered how I came to be trapped alone inside that one room tomb. Once again, I'm free at last to feed on their kind.

The Real Nightmares

CJ Hooper

Mack slumped in the chair staring forwards at the stain. That east wall, plain but for the growing marks of damp upon it, was as oppressive as the looming shadow of the building's exterior, and yet he continued to stare, unable to move his eyes from the blank space before him. He hadn't forgotten the crazed vision of the fiery hell-scape from last night, or the nightmare of drowning in his sleep on the first evening here.

It was getting late on the Friday night when he found himself drowsing in that same place, his tired eyes unable to focus upon the book in front of him, and so he ditched it on the floor beside the increasing pile of empty cans. As he drifted in the penumbra of sleep a small breeze flickered the pages of the fallen book, then blew past him and around lifting his greying hair, but he was too sleepy to react. Though in his darkening mind he realised it was happening again, this was another nightmare enacting itself before him. Trying to keep his eyes open Mack could just make out a growing shadow on the wall opposite, a swirling hole from that stain of damp, darker than the night outside but with cloudy tendrils slowly reaching out and towards him. The growing wind was building up around his room and, desperately, Mack tried to focus his vision, but it was no good. Whether this was sleep or unconsciousness he couldn't tell, and he couldn't fight this oblivion before the darkness took him. Unable to move, paralysed with fear and exhaustion, Mack could do nothing but pray he would wake up, and it would all be gone. The last thing he remembered was wispy mycelium like webs appearing around the edge of the opening and spreading across his walls, and there in the deep dark something skittered towards him.

The morning brought panic, and Mack found himself unable to move and lying on the floor. His body was bound with weblike material that held him prone and collapsed by the wall, only his fingers were free to move. The sticky fibre was across his head, his eyes also, he could just make out his room, and at least his nose was free so that he could breathe. Wrestling with his bonds didn't make any difference as the webbing just stretched and retracted with his movement. The struggle continued until he was too exhausted to move. What was certain was that he was alone, the social worker would find his body in a few weeks' time, emaciated and bound in web, whether this was wholly or with his fleshy organs dissolved by the sputum of the great spider from the darkness he didn't know, and his mind was breaking at the thought of either. He would die here, either consumed by the creature from the web, or just from starvation.

Deadly Chimes

Soter Lucio

The chimes came through in the middle of the night while the party was in full swing and the music was blasting. Yet still there were the chimes seeping through the din until it was heard by everyone. It was unrecognizable, but that did not stop the blood from oozing out of the ears of the party goers.

They were disrespecting the home of the owner of the grandfather's clock. And he being a stickler for discipline and decorum was having none of it.

Nobody noticed the oozing blood through the fancy-coloured lights. Then the owners came home from their Bingo night. They watched, opened their eyes as wide as they possibly could, then as one walked to the breaker box down the stairs and turned off the electricity. The music stopped then the chimes were heard and recognized by all and sundry.

The moonlight shining through the glass windows spotlighted the blood on everybody's neck and cascading down the walls from the light bulbs. They all stood mesmerized, in shock, at what was happening to them all. The chimes increased in volume doing something to their minds, to their brains, resulting in all of them screaming mercilessly as they slowly went blind. Moving around with arms outstretched. The two bingo ladies came up the stairs and opened wide the front doors and guided them out.

They closed back the doors and faced the apparition of the bearded old man like a light on the wall.

"We did tell them no parties Papa."

"I know. I still have three more great great granddaughters. Maybe…maybe…"

The two women faced each other.
"Nobody listens anymore."

Hamilton Hall

Bryan Kamtsios

The Herringbone pattern of dark red and black bricks are aged. Worn, rounded corners and fissures have developed over the last 216 years. The trees, which have been here much longer than the brick walkway, loom over me.

Leafless branches cast eerie shadows all around from the midday sun. A breeze makes its way through an opening in my peacoat where I missed a button as I left my house this morning. It sends a frigid chill up my spine, which only adds to my nervousness.

I look straight ahead to see the main building of Pendergast University. It, too, shows signs of age, but has been maintained far better than the walkway. To my left is Hamilton Hall. There she sits, unchanged since I was last here. The secrets of what occurred all those years ago still taunt me after all this time.

Slowly, I approach the large wooden doors. The wrought iron handle, once polished black, is now faded and worn, displaying the bare steel underneath. It's cold to the touch. A groan escapes from the hinges as I open the door. Walking into the foyer, it's still dark inside, even with the sunlight creeping its way in.

Hamilton Hall has been closed ever since the accident. But aside from the dust that had built up over the years, it looked just as I had remembered it.

Standing at the staircase, various coloured shapes cast themselves dimly across the floor at my feet. I didn’t need to look up to know it was coming from the stain glass window of the Pendergast Peacock. The hairs on the back of my neck stand up at the sight of it.

I can't do this! I need to leave. I turn to go, and as I do, the large wooden door slams shut. A thunderous boom follows, ear-splitting. It echoes throughout the foyer and endless hallways.

An uneasy feeling permeates my body. I knew I shouldn't have come back here. I try to pull on the door handle. It doesn’t budge. Beads of sweat make their way down my face. A lump forms in my throat. My heart rate turns chaotic.

Tears flow from my eyes uncontrollably as everything around me transforms back into its former glory. Panic latches onto my spine.

I feel a hand on my shoulder. I turn to see my classmate, Jimmy. His appearance is unchanged since the last time I saw him, twenty-three years ago. How can that be? My mind can't process what it sees, and while it tries to catch up with what my body already knows, my knees weaken. My arms are heavy. Each breath escapes in an audible rasp.

Jimmy looks at me, and the faintest smile spreads across his face. My vision blurs and members of my old baseball team crowd around me. “We’ve been waiting a long time for your return,” Jimmy says. “Welcome home, Bernard.

The Bees and All Their Honey

Willow Nichols

I slowly turned into my sister's driveway, ready to lay on the horn once I reached the top. Sara was always late, so of course I had to plan accordingly. My headlights illuminated her front lawn as I pulled closer. A figure in the road caused me to slam on my breaks. I stopped abruptly, the force throwing my body forward into the steering wheel.

She was standing in the middle of the driveway, her hands wrapped gingerly around the base of her neck. Her throat swelled, the skin crimson and slick with a golden substance that dripped in long spindles reaching towards the asphalt.

She looked not at me, but past me. Her eyes were milky, and her pupils no longer existed. A sea of clouds swam through her vision. She smiled painfully wide, her gummy grin not matching the vacant expression that plagued the rest of her.

A soft buzzing arose from her, a swell of hums that began to vibrate in her swollen throat. I gagged at the distorted sight of my sister as she ambled forward. She placed her hands on the hood of my car, and I stared over the wheel. Her fingers were covered in infected lumps, stings that turned fetid.

The absence of pressure on her throat made the congealed fluid drip aggressively, fighting its way through the pin holes that speckled her skin. The silence was sickening, the only sound heard was the buzzing in Sara and the cicadas hidden in the grass.

Sara looked to the sky and opened her maw. At first, nothing. And then, everything. The anger of the earth manifested in her, the buzzing becoming a cacophony. The first insects crawled their way out, climbing over her teeth and tongue.

She gagged on the swarm as it fought its way out. Her fingers curled on the hood, her nails scraping a line of paint away. She screamed as the swarm caressed her, the buzzing now deafening. The insects covered her skin; some bore into her body once again. The bees had made her their hive. Honey flowed from her eyes and mouth before she dropped from my sight.

Her body lay crumpled on the ground, unmoving. The Queen bee circled her mouth and slowly fought her way back into the hive.

Cheese Sweats

CJ Hooper

They say that cheese before bedtimes gives you bad dreams, it doesn't, it just gives you indigestion. Lying flat allows the congealed fat of the coagulated and treated milk to lie hard in your stomach almost refusing to digest and pass along to the bowel, where it changes momentum and runs through you faster than soup. This is why many people drink coffee with the cheese course; it helps the process of breaking down the gluttonous guests' guzzling's. This in turn leaves them awake and in discomfort too.

This was exactly what I had intended to happen. No one had noticed that I avoided the blue veined cheese, and artisan product made specially for tonight. Made by me. It was called 'Emberton Blue', named for the village where I grew up. The pretentious dinner party attendee's "ooh'd" and "aah'd" as I unwrapped it from its grease proof paper and unveiled it before them. Naturally I gave them all the first cut of the wedge, as any good host should, leaving only the merest sliver for myself. Being canny I knew to save myself a slice without any of the veins of mould in it. It was unusual, I'd thought, that mould was considered essential for a strong blue cheese. Anywhere else in the world it was considered abhorrent, except for the production of aspirin I supposed. But even that could be deadly. It was often the way with such things though that a little of something may be good, whereas too much would kill you. Like fly agaric, and other fungi. It was the mycelium of such growths that I had mixed into the churn for making my new cheese. It had taken the harmless appearance of near turquoise veins as the cheese matured and became the glorious final product.

I watched my piggish guests snaffling down the cheese and crackers, leaving crumbs down their over gorged fronts and across the table. Their fat faces spraying sputum and nubs of the Emberton Blue as they each tried to talk over each other. Each of them personally selected for this meal because of their vociferous opinions, their desire to control the conversation both in the town and on the local group Facebook page. For too long I had listened to them talk, watched them spill their bile online, about people they never had met but hated people in boats who had no impact on their lives but filled the pages of their tawdry rags that passed for newspapers.

This night I shall endure their groans and bellyaches once more, both literally and figuratively, and, in time, they shall succumb to the growing pains in their gut, the hallucinations they suffer, and the long painful death over the course of the night. Should I be arrested or put away for my troubles I would care not. I had hosted these parasites, but they would entertain me as I watch them die of their own avarice.

When Something Grave Crossed my Path

JB Wocoski

This is about what happened to me last Friday night, on Jensen Beach in an uncanny Florida fog. It was a dreadful night that gave me the fright of my life as I made the mistake of hiking home alone from the cottage of my love across the low tide shoreline.

I thought a fog so thick wrapped around my hands, arms, waist, and throat would not harm me, just chill me to my bones, but never suck the living meat away from my unbleached bones. A fog so thick, I could not see the footprints my leather boots left behind. My footprints pressed deep within the sea-dampened sand along the shore of the ebb tide beach. The lapping of the waves ebbed away to be heard no more during that night. I made my way over the damp sand back home again.

Crossing that fogged-in beach, I sensed something grave blocking my way. So, I halted my slow pace, trying to sense what or who was ahead of me. Behind my ears, a thump slapped down, shaking my feet within my boots as the sand particles reverberated where I stood in the wet sand.

Without thinking, I spun around too many times, losing track of the correct direction leading away from this beach, back to my home. Taking in a lungful of air to give a shout for help, I heard sand scrape from the beach behind me as a sour seaweed stench engulfed me. I'm not sure what unseen, hungry, monstrous creature reached out for me.

To make a run for it, I turned away from where I perceived the sea and that creature or thing on the beach now lay. Each footfall I stepped upon the sea damp packed sand moved me up higher to softer, less-firm sandy ground until the dune grass brushed my boot laces and pant cuffs.

I breathed easier. My stomach turned when the ground closest to me shook. I dove towards where I assumed behind the dune to safety would take me. I laid there the rest of the night in the high grass, awaiting my doom. That thumping reverberation shook the dune I hid behind, within. I dared not cross any open sand while those thumping, smacking, dragging noises continued reaching around this dune. Something crashed onto the tall grass, flattening it atop me. I shivered, not from the cold. Of all things to happen, exhausted, somehow, I fell asleep where I had fallen.

A breeze brushed the tall dune grass against my forehead and cheeks, awakening me to a fogless world about me. Standing up. Unsure of where I was, the welcome sunshine cracked the sky beyond the eastern horizon. With every step in the sand, I approached the incoming tide as waves slapped the firm damp sand, erasing the giant round suction marks atop my footprints from where I stepped earlier during ebb tide time.

Baby Teeth

CJ Hooper

The first thing that she saw was the broken glass by the back door. Moonlight reflected on the broken shards caught her eye, which was fortunate as, barefoot, Emily would have cut herself on the shards. The window had been broken from the outside, the glazing bars bent out of place to allow the intruder to reach the door handle and the lock. Someone was in the house. Emily's bungalow was small and there were few places that one could hide, but being deaf, she would not have heard the glass breaking or the door opening. It had been the draught of cold air from the garden that had awoken her.

Her phone was back in her bedroom, and she ran to collect it, almost colliding with the door frame as she did. On her bedsheet was the small rectangle impression of where her phone had been. For someone to have taken that without getting past her meant that the intruder had managed to secrete themselves somewhere in her room before she had woken. They must have known that there was a chance that Emily would have not heard the intrusion, and therefore they knew that she was unable to hear.

Emily span to turn her back to the room and crouched to reach the stick by her bed. To all accounts this would have looked like a broom handle, but this was her jo staff. The Japanese oak stave had lain discretely by her bed should such a situation occur. Now Emily gripped it close, but it provided no comfort. She pressed her back to the wall and began to manoeuvre herself towards the door. When it came within a metre's reach she ran for it, then slammed it closed behind her just in time to see a shadow pass by the gap of light between the door and jamb. There was no way that Emily could hold it closed with only one hand, so she had to choose between the door or the stave.

With a shove she pushed the door open against the person on the other side, and they sprawled across the floor. They were wearing black and had their head covered with a balaclava but in the bright light of the bedroom Emily could see their teeth. The intruder had fangs, like a cartoon vampire, and Emily almost laughed half expecting this be a prank, but the figure leapt at her. She brought down the oaken stave upon its head with a solid crack and it fell against the wooden floor again. Now she could run.

Her bedroom door was now filled with a darker shadow; it loomed high and over her as she turned towards it. There was a pale face with baleful eyes in that moving shadow, then it spoke,

"Clumsy, my apprentice, you will need to do better next time, for now though she is yours."

From behind her she felt a body press against hers, and teeth bit.

The Ware-Wolf

Matt Adcock

Mike loved being a journalist, peddling stories of the fantastic which held very little 'factual content' but sold online subscriptions...

His latest assignment was the Hertfordshire town of Ware.

Officially, he was there to write fluff: *The Ware-Wolf: A Hairy Tale from England's Haunted Heartland.* Unofficially? He just wanted to get paid and maybe expense a pint.

But the town was... seriously wrong.

Wolfsbane everywhere. Purple blossoms sprouting like nature's warning sirens, from gutters, gravestones, the ovens of Greggs. Something ungodly was happening at pace.

Mike looked up and there was Ava, standing in the mounds of weird flowers.

A girl, maybe ten. Barefoot. Gold eyes. The sort of look that makes small dogs whimper and old priests reach for holy water.

He followed her. Because curiosity is stronger than common sense, and he sensed a story.

She slipped into the local cinema like a whisper.

The Howling was playing.

Mike couldn't help himself; he ran in too.

He burst through the door just as she changed.

A spectacle only ever witnessed onscreen was happening with the film still playing, its grainy werewolf mid-transformation, while Ava's real one outdid it in surround sound and 4D arterial spray.

Bones snapped. Skin shredded. Fur exploded as muscles sprang into form. Her jaw stretched open with a sound you could *feel* in your spine.

Everybody screamed.

She moved so fast, it was like someone had pressed fast-forward on a slaughter TikTok.

A man in the front row tried to run. She caved his skull in with a swipe that sent his teeth flying like wet popcorn.

Another tripped, got up, then got cut in half. One half made it to the fire exit. The other? Not so much.

Ava climbed the walls. She howled in harmony with the movie. The on-screen werewolf bared its teeth as Ava tore someone's throat out, revelling in the bloody fountain.

Mike vomited into his cup holder.

And then gunfire...

Black-clad tactical troopers stormed in. Firing silver bullets, shouting, the works.

They managed to hit her. A few times.

She hit back harder.

One went down with his intestines wrapped around his neck like a slippery scarf. Another got thrown through the projector glass.

But *finally*, someone got close enough with a huge syringe filled with enough sedative to down an angry rhino on cocaine.

Ava dropped. Shrinking. Bones cracking back into place.

The man with the needle slapped silver cuffs on her and turned to Mike.

"You saw nothing."

Mike nodded. Hard to argue when your trousers are wet and none of its rain.

Days later.

The news said, "leopard attack." A freak, exotic accident.

Mike drank. Deleted his footage. Tried to sleep.

Then came the knock.

Three short raps.

He opened the door.
Ava stood there. Human again. Gold eyes glowing.
“Hello, Mr. Brookes,” she said. “Can I come in?”
Mike let her.
Behind her, the wolfsbane was blooming again.

Post-mortem Resilience

Marcelo Medone

Irina had always been extremely beautiful. At eighteen, she was the loveliest being on earth, the sum of the most delicate and splendid at the same time. To make matters worse, Irina was a virgin.

Then it happened that one night, returning home from the liquor shop where she worked, Irina was ambushed by an infamous bloodthirsty horde. She was savagely attacked. She fought back tooth and nail. At one point, struggling with a giant one-eyed man with stitched eyelids, she managed to snatch his revolver and knock him down, blowing out his healthy eye. The giant collapsed with a hideous hole in his head. Irina was an innocent girl, but she knew how to defend herself.

However, she was vastly outnumbered by her attackers. Her fight was in vain. The rest of the pack, enraged by the death of their leader, viciously subdued her until death took pity on her.

She ended up in a morgue, on a stainless-steel gurney, barely covered by a cheap white sheet.

In the middle of the night, in the gloom of a dim lamp hanging from the ceiling, Irina felt the vital energy returning to her lifeless body. She opened her lacerated eyelid eyes, took a deep breath and gave a shriek of joy. She rolled over and threw off the sheet, which landed on the concrete floor.

She looked around and noticed that she was in a huge, cold room, surrounded by a multitude of corpses on gurneys like hers.

She looked at her mutilated hands, with fingers turned into shapeless shreds, and began to run them over her naked body.

She caressed her breasts and felt a shudder of pleasure. She felt her fractured ribs. She rummaged disgustedly through her exposed guts. Her pale fingers ran through her pubic hair and lodged in her wet vulva, searching for her secret pleasure spots. She resumed her long-perfected routine of self-satisfaction.

Suddenly, she heard a moaning bellowing all around her, like a hellish choir. Her fingers froze in terror, as the bestial moans continued to add and increase in intensity.

Before she could react, she found herself surrounded by once-human beings, monstrously disfigured, naked and mutilated corpses like herself, lusting after her.

The largest of these ghouls, wielding a huge, sore, pustulous phallus, pinned her at the knees, spread her thighs and viciously penetrated her, inoculating her with his sticky, putrid fluids while uttering demonic screams.

Irina struggled futilely against the beast. In the heat of her struggle, she recognized it by its one-eyed eye with its eyelids stitched shut and the other pierced by a bullet.

The rest of the infamous pack clapped their stumps and drooled, in a bestial frenzy.

Welcome to the zombie world, thought Irina, as she relearned how to enjoy.

Khala Grace

Leaves fall from the trees
An eerie whisper crosses the breeze
Our village is small and quaint
Never needing a shaman or saint
Until that fateful and horrific night!

The Mimic came to show its might!
Missing persons have been claimed
The Mimic's victims were found brutally maimed
As a young farmhand, I was at a lost
Unable to tend to the harvest at fear's cost!

Yet, after weeks of unrivalled terror
An old woman appears with a smile so clever
She stands afront the monster in offense
Oh, how I cowered behind the fence!

The Mimic laughed at her with an open maw,
Amazed at the absurdity it saw
The creature rushes for an attack
The old woman stood without taking a step back

She pulls out a talisman within a flash,
Activating her spell with cigarette ash
As the parchment lands on the Mimic's snout,
The creature's life drains completely out

I watch as the mysterious woman walks away
My voice calls out: "Wait! Take a moment to stay!"
She turns and looks at me with a curious gaze
I couldn't help but to add: "Teach me your ways!"

Oh, how I expected her to laugh at such a request,
Yet, she replies: "Only, if you can handle the test-
Travel beyond the gate until you reach main road,
As the sun meets the water you'll find my abode."

My thoughts are caught in the middle
Confusion swirls while I try to note her riddle
Then I realized out loud: "What's your name?
She laughs: "Once you find me, I'll ask the same."

Oh, how much excitement swelled in my chest
As she left, I gathered my things for the quest
I knew that our village was lucky for her presence
So, that I wanted to be the next line of defense

That my dear Duri is how I found life anew,
When Yeong-Gi, the farmhand finally grew
No longer could I escape the urge
Of becoming an apprentice to the Thaumaturge!

The Man in The Mirror

CJ Hooper

At first, I was the only one, I could see him staring at me in disbelief, unable to comprehend my appearance, as I stared back at him. Each night he would be there on the other side of the glass, stricken with terror, and to me it felt good that he was experiencing this. I hoped that the cold sliver of discovery went down his spine and back up to his brain, via his iced over heart. Then after weeks of this passed his thin-lipped rictus face became a smile. Perhaps he had realised that I could do nothing from where I was, unable to reach beyond the bounds of my prison, ineffectual against his madness.

This changed again one night when I realised that I was no longer alone, there was a terrible groan beside me as shadow covered me and then shifted to allow me to see clearly. My companion was a tall man with a mop of black hair, and eyes bound up tight as if trying to hide the sight before him. Then he tried to shriek again but the deep cut in its neck prevented anything intelligible from coming out except for that hoarse gurgle of dry skin and viscous fluid from the wound.

The man on the other side of the glass stared back at us, his face now a picture of morbid fascination. His eyes widened with glee as both of us tried to yell and scream at him in our rage, but whatever separated us beyond the glass it was evident that sound could not pass it.

Next it was twins, they held each other and wept before acknowledging that they were not alone, and yet still they could not talk. The same tell-tale wound, the deep cut across the vocal cords that prevented any communication. Last was a thick set man, strong in the arms and shoulders but silenced in the same modus operandi as we had all been victim too.

The killer returned every night after that, with his rictus grin, mocking us as we sought to break the glass, and sound our fury across that ethereal threshold. Every death increased our numbers, and every new face increased the savage joy of the man in the mirror, revelling in his collection of trapped spectres, desperately awaiting the night that we could get free and exact our revenge.

The End

The Descent Continues

You've Reached the End. But the Descent Doesn't Stop Here.

Thank you for reading *Dark Descent: Whispers from Beyond.* This collection marks just one year in an ongoing archive of horror — a living, breathing body of micro fiction that continues to grow each month.

If these stories stayed with you… if something in the shadows whispered your name… there's more waiting.

Dark Descent is a monthly horror webzine featuring original micro fiction that unsettles, disturbs, and resonates. For just £2.99/month, you'll get access to new tales each month — sharp, strange, and beautifully haunting.

Your first 7 days are free. Cancel anytime. No strings. Just stories.

☞ www.darkholmepublishing.uk/ddportal

We hope you'll keep descending with us.

— *Dark Holme Publishing*

Made in United States
Troutdale, OR
07/09/2025

32755896R10184